PRAISE FOR THE NOVELS OF

Maya Banks

"A must-read author . . . her [stories] are always full of emotional situations, lovable characters and kick-butt story lines."
—*Romance Junkies*

"Heated . . . romantic suspense . . . Intense, transfixing."
—*Midwest Book Review*

"Definitely a recommended read . . . filled with friendship, passion, and most of all, a love that grows beyond just being friends."
Fallen Angel Reviews

"Grabbed me from page one and refused to let go until I read the last word . . . When a book still affects me hours after reading it, I can't help but Joyfully Recommend it!" —*Joyfully Reviewed*

"I guarantee I will reread this book many times over, and will derive as much pleasure as I did in the first reading each and every subsequent time." —*Novelspot*

"An excellent read that I simply did not put down . . . A fantastic adventure . . . covers all the emotional range."
—*The Road to Romance*

"Searingly sexy and highly believable." —*Romantic Times*

sweet possession

MAYA BANKS

Heat / New York

THE BERKLEY PUBLISHING GROUP
Published by the Penguin Group
Penguin Group (USA) Inc.
375 Hudson Street, New York, New York 10014, USA
Penguin Group (Canada), 90 Eglinton Avenue East, Suite 700, Toronto, Ontario M4P 2Y3, Canada
(a division of Pearson Penguin Canada Inc.)
Penguin Books Ltd., 80 Strand, London WC2R 0RL, England
Penguin Group Ireland, 25 St. Stephen's Green, Dublin 2, Ireland (a division of Penguin Books Ltd.)
Penguin Group (Australia), 250 Camberwell Road, Camberwell, Victoria 3124, Australia
(a division of Pearson Australia Group Pty. Ltd.)
Penguin Books India Pvt. Ltd., 11 Community Centre, Panchsheel Park, New Delhi—110 017, India
Penguin Group (NZ), 67 Apollo Drive, Rosedale, North Shore 0632, New Zealand
(a division of Pearson New Zealand Ltd.)
Penguin Books (South Africa) (Pty.) Ltd., 24 Sturdee Avenue, Rosebank, Johannesburg 2196,
South Africa

Penguin Books Ltd., Registered Offices: 80 Strand, London WC2R 0RL, England

This book is an original publication of The Berkley Publishing Group.

PRINTING HISTORY
Heat trade paperback edition / April 2011

Library of Congress Cataloging-in-Publication Data

Banks, Maya.
    Sweet possession / Maya Banks.—Heat trade paperback ed.
        p.   cm.
    ISBN 978-0-425-23907-0 (trade pbk.)
    I. Title.
    PS3602.A643S833   2011
    813'.6—dc22

                                                    2010049778

PRINTED IN THE UNITED STATES OF AMERICA

10 9 8 7 6 5 4 3 2 1

sweet possession

Chapter 1

"You're out of your goddamn mind!"

Pop Malone scowled at his son, Connor. "Watch your mouth. I can still wipe the floor with your scrawny ass."

Connor wiped his hand over his short hair and clamped down on the top in an effort to pull it out. Nathan Tucker had the right idea by shaving his head. It was something Connor was going to have to look into if he kept getting bombs dropped on him.

"Pop," Connor said in exasperation. "We install security systems. Sophisticated, state-of-the-art computer monitoring equipment. We do consulting. We evaluate security for other people. We are not a god-damn bodyguard service."

Pop huffed, crossed his arms over his chest and leaned back against his adopted daughter's desk. Faith stared wide-eyed at her father and brother but didn't say a word. She was too glued to the conversation.

"If you'd stop your yammering for two seconds, I'd explain why you're perfect for this job."

"Oh boy," Connor muttered. "I can't wait to hear this. I'd better sit down for it."

He flopped into one of the chairs in front of Faith's desk and waited for his father's latest harebrained scheme. Not that his father wasn't a smart man. He was one of the most intelligent and cunning men Connor knew. It was the cunning part that bothered the hell out of him right now. He wasn't sure how, but he knew he was fucked. And it looked like he was about to find out.

"Phillip Armstrong is a longtime friend. We go way back. Served together in the marines. He's a big-shot record executive now and he has a big-name artist on his label."

"What's the name?" Faith piped in.

"Lyric Jones."

Faith frowned.

"What's the frown for?" Connor demanded. "What do you know?"

"You've never heard of her?" Faith asked.

"Does she sing country music?"

Faith chuckled and shook her head.

"Then I rest my case. So why the frown?"

"She's a bit of a . . ."

"She's difficult," Pop said with no preamble. "But you've dealt with difficult before. She won't be a problem for you."

"Why is she my problem at all?"

"Because most of her security detail was fired. What was left quit. She has two bodyguards that are as useless as tits on a boar hog."

"And I'm supposed to fix this?"

"Phillip is scrambling to hire a replacement firm. One better than the last since they sucked ass. His words, not mine. She only has one more show and then she's going to be sort of on vacation here in Houston."

Faith lifted an eyebrow. "Why the hell would she willingly vacation in Houston? I mean, a girl with that kind of money ought to go to Paris. Or Italy. Maybe a beach house in the Caribbean."

"I said *sort of* because she's doing a show at the Houston Livestock and Rodeo but she'll be here a total of two weeks. She also has some signing and fan meet-and-greet at one of the downtown music stores."

"Oh, I get it," Connor said as he pushed himself forward in his seat. "What they want is a babysitter. They want someone to sit on her so she'll be good for two weeks."

Pop had the grace to look abashed. "Well, yes and no."

Connor made a rude noise. "Why the hell are you asking me? There are three other guys in this office all capable of doing this job."

Faith made a show of blowing on her nails and whistled softly.

"Because everyone is either married or getting goddamned married and you're the only single guy left. If I try to send one of the other guys to spend twenty-four/seven with a gorgeous pop star, I'll have three pissed-off women on my ass. No, thanks. No offense, Connor, but you have nothing on the girls. I'll take my chances with you."

Faith smiled sweetly in her brother's direction.

"Don't think I won't get you for this," Connor muttered at Faith.

"Look, at least fly out to L.A., catch her last show, introduce yourself, see how it goes. What can it hurt? I think you'll find it's not as bad as you think. You'll spend two weeks with her here keeping her out of trouble and keeping her safe."

"Just how unsafe is she?"

"Oh, the usual celebrity shit, I'm sure. Everyone wants a piece of her. Without adequate security, it could get dangerous. Phillip is going to get a local firm to do the peripheral security but he wants someone he can trust next to her until he can go through and interview larger firms that will handle her security on the road. He's worried, and Phillip doesn't worry about much."

"Why the hell don't they just cancel the rodeo appearance, stash her somewhere private for two weeks and get their shit together for when she goes back on the road?"

"You're asking me?" Pop said in irritation. "When has show business ever made any goddamn sense? These people don't think with their brains. They think with their checkbooks and use dollar signs as their guides. It's your job to be their brains for two weeks."

Connor groaned. "Difficult and brainless. I can hardly wait."

The door to Faith's office opened and Angelina Moyano poked her head through. When she saw the two men, she hesitated. "Am I interrupting anything?"

Connor grinned and motioned her in. "Of course not. How are you, sweetie?"

Angelina walked in, graceful and petite despite her bulging abdomen. Most women her size would be down to a waddle by now, but she still moved with ease.

She smiled at Connor. "I'm good. How are you?" She bent down to hug him tight and he put his hand on her belly.

"Is Miss Priss moving around today?"

"Stop calling her that," Angelina said in exasperation. "Her name is Nia. Hi, Pop," she said as she brushed a kiss over the older man's jaw.

"Hey yourself, Angel. Where's Micah? Shouldn't he be working? For that matter, where the hell is Nathan? And Gray? Are we the only people working?"

Connor and Faith exchanged eye rolls. Pop was on his way to working himself into a dither.

"I came by to get Faith. Julie offered me a pregnancy massage and Faith is going to go hold my hand."

"More like get her own massage," Connor muttered. "You girls don't fool me one bit. I'll go hold your damn hand and then maybe Julie will massage me too."

"Find your own woman's hand to hold," Micah Hudson growled from the doorway.

Pop looked up and scowled. "It's about time you decided to show up. What is this, come to work late day?"

Micah ignored Pop. All his attention was on the curvy Latina woman heavily pregnant with his child. It amused Connor to no end to see Micah so gobsmacked over a woman. Not that he didn't love women as a rule, but there was nothing casual or flirty about Micah's relationship with Angelina. The poor boy was whipped and it was pretty pathetic to watch.

"How sure is Julie that a pregnancy massage is good for the baby?" Micah asked.

Angelina paused and turned with one hand on her hip. "I think the point is that it's good for the mother."

"But will it hurt the baby?"

Angelina smiled. "You worry too much, Micah. Go do some work so Faith and I can go have some girly time. We're going to be late, and Damon expects Serena to be home by noon."

"Or what?" Connor murmured. He always wondered what the hell went on in Damon and Serena's marriage. Of all the people who worked for Pop, Connor was the furthest out of the loop when it came to Damon Roche. From what he'd gleaned the man was a control freak and he kept Serena under his thumb.

Faith grinned, and he should have known by the devilish glint in her eye that she was going to say something outlandish.

"I'm pretty sure if she's late, she gets a crop to her ass."

"Something Gray needs to think about for you," Connor said pointedly.

"Who says he doesn't?" she teased as she grasped Angelina's arm and the two headed for the door.

Was the whole damn world crazy around him? He'd heard enough to know that his sex life had to be the only normal one in his group of friends. He didn't even want to know what kind of shit Micah put Angelina through. It would probably only piss him off. And Faith. God. His sister, for Pete's sake.

He shook his head. No, he didn't want to know the depravities that his friends indulged in. He was perfectly happy to be the boring vanilla one in the bunch.

He turned to eyeball Micah after the girls had gone. "Any luck getting her to the altar?"

Micah snorted. "I'm trying. Believe me. I'm a persistent man. It'll happen soon."

Pop grunted. "The problem with men today is they're too busy being politically correct. You ought to just snatch her up and haul her to a priest. Or to Vegas like Gray did with Faith. If you wait around for a woman to make up her mind, you'll be old and impotent by the time your wedding night gets here."

Connor cracked up. "This might explain why you've now embraced bachelorhood indefinitely."

Pop shook his finger at Connor and Micah. "Mark my words. I'm right. Look at what happened when Nathan stopped pussyfooting around Julie. He went over to where she was and hauled her out over his shoulder. Then he told her how it was going to be and voilà. Now they're married. He's happy. She's happy. End of story. Not like Micah over here who mopes around like a friggin' kicked puppy because he can't convince the woman he loves that he really loves her and really wants to marry her. Jesus has to be crying up there somewhere. Or laughing hysterically. I can't figure out which one."

Micah's lips curled into a snarl. "Enough already, Pop. You know I fucked up with her. I can't just run over her and make her do what I want."

"No, but you could damn well put your foot down and make her believe how you feel."

"I've tried!"

"Then try harder," Pop grumbled. "It's getting to be like some couples' retreat around here. It's damn nauseating."

Connor knew when a good time to escape was. Right now, when Pop was busy bitching about something else. Maybe by the time he remembered what he wanted Connor to do, the record company would have given up and hired someone else.

He was almost to the door. One more step and he would have made it home free.

"Your airline ticket is on your desk," Pop called. "You fly out tomorrow morning. Now go home and pack a suitcase."

Fuck a goddamn duck.

CHAPTER 2

*T*he arena reverberated with frantic music and a rainbow of cascading lights. Connor stood at the top of the stands, staring over the railing at the stage below. His ears were going to explode at any second, and he felt so dizzy from the rapid staccato of flashing lasers that he gripped the cool metal bar in front of him to steady himself.

With his free hand, he reached back and massaged a kink out of his neck. He'd been tense ever since this circus had started. How in the hell could anyone stand this cacophony on a regular basis? This wasn't his type of music. How could it be anyone's? How the hell did anyone even understand the screeching, if they could even hear it over the band? He'd much rather throw down with some Montgomery Gentry or Jason Aldean if he was going to subject himself to a concert.

Finally, the screeching stopped. There was a god.

Connor glanced back at the stage to see Lyric Jones saunter back out after her last hasty departure. Costume change, though why she bothered with this one, he wasn't sure. He didn't even have to be close to the stage to know she was barely wearing anything at all.

He glanced to the side where the record executives from Cosmic Records were taking in the show with him. They'd met his plane and drove him out to the arena in a limo. The whole thing was ridiculous, and he was still cursing the fact that he'd gotten saddled with flying out to talk to the parties involved.

As the music assaulted his ears again, he turned his attention back to the stage, just in time to see another scantily clad woman stroll toward Lyric. Best he could make out, the words to the song sounded something like "Girl Love." He snorted.

The two women faced each other as Lyric sang. They were a study in contrast, probably well coordinated. Lyric was small and black-haired, if you didn't count the god-awful pink streak in it. The other woman was tall, luscious and blond, with a set of tits that had to be bought and paid for. He didn't need binoculars to see that.

Then they moved closer, undulating their bodies in a suggestive manner. The crowd went nuts as the women pressed against each other. Lyric held the mic to her chest as she swayed in the other woman's arms. As the song continued, Lyric turned and nestled her ass right into the blond woman's crotch. The two continued their little bump and grind as the crowd roared their approval.

Why couldn't Micah have taken this job? This would be right up his alley. Watching two women go at it? Micah would be drooling like a rabid pit bull. Of course, Angelina might kick some serious ass over it, but still. All Connor wanted was a good stiff drink and a bottle of ibuprofen.

By the time the song was winding down, the two women were meshed tighter than a snag in a fishing line. When the music died, Lyric let the mic fall and got into a lip-lock with the blonde that a fire hose wouldn't have separated.

There was no way he could do this. Everything about the woman got on his last nerve, and he hadn't even met her yet. He didn't have to. It was all there for everyone to see. The record executives would be pissed, and Pop probably wouldn't be too happy, but if he wanted the gig so bad, he could either do it himself or make Nathan or Micah do it. Their women would just have to get over it. Connor would take good care of the girls while Nathan and Micah were gone. That image made him grin.

He was ready to turn around and walk out when a softer, melodious tone poured into the arena. It made him pause for a brief second and look back at the stage. Lyric stood in the middle, a single spotlight focused on her. The rest of the stage was blacked out.

Her eyes were closed, and he got the crazy image in his head that she looked vulnerable. Then she opened her mouth, and for the first time that night, he could clearly hear her voice. It poured out of her like smooth, sweet honey. It crawled right over his skin and sent a shiver down his spine.

He stared, entranced by the image of her alone, her haunting, *beautiful* voice filling every nook and cranny of the packed house. He was struck by the sadness he felt radiating from her. More than sadness, it was pain.

His hands gripped the railing as he moved closer, his attention focused entirely on the woman singing. It wasn't one of those insipid, self-reflection songs. It was about going home. He could feel the ache in her voice. It made *him* ache. Hell, it made him want to go home.

Across the arena, cigarette lighters flared and bobbed as hands shot into the air holding them. They waved in time as she stood, so still, face turned to the ceiling. He imagined her eyes were closed as the last of the words spilled from her lips.

The music faded, and for a moment, silence descended on the crowd. Then shrill whistles rent the air, followed by raucous cheers.

Lyric stepped back and waved to the crowd. She bowed once and hurried off the stage.

The record executives shifted beside him, and Connor looked over to see them staring at him.

"You ready to go meet our girl?" Phillip Armstrong asked.

Connor nodded, forgetting for a moment that all he really wanted to do was get the hell out while the getting was good. With a resigned sigh, he followed the suits to the backstage area.

Security, if you could call it that, was minimal. Fans swarmed the corridor, pushing, shoving and screaming. When a beefed-up, muscle-bound security guard standing outside the backstage door looked up and saw them coming, he snapped to attention and started shoving rabid fans to the side so they could pass.

When the door opened, Connor was pushed forward as the fans tried to rush past him. He stumbled inside, a string of obscenities dying to blow past his lips. He managed to keep his cool. Barely.

Phillip and his sidekick, Barry, smoothed their suits and looked questioningly at Connor. Connor's lips thinned but he gritted his teeth and kept his expression neutral.

They motioned him toward a slightly less congested area and the two men accepted a drink from a gangly boy who couldn't be more than a teenager. When they offered Connor a glass, he shook his head. Not that the idea of a pint of vodka wasn't vastly appealing, but at this point, if he started drinking, he wasn't going to stop.

He peered around the room, which, after more consideration, was much larger than he'd first thought. It was just crowded. He stuffed his hands in his pockets and tried not to look as bored and as uncomfortable as he felt.

A few seconds later, the door burst open and Lyric stumbled in, a wide grin on her face. Two men he could only assume were her bodyguards flanked her. He arched one eyebrow as the bodyguards proceeded to get very up close and personal as they staggered in Connor's direction.

As one hand closed around her breast, she swatted playfully, then smiled up at the bodyguard with a "not now, later" look.

Another man stepped in front of Lyric, halting her progress toward the record execs. She frowned and her eyes narrowed but just as quickly her expression became neutral as she stared up at the guy.

"You looked and sounded like shit out there, Lyric. What the hell is your problem?"

Connor's brows drew together and he found himself frowning at the blatant disrespect in the other man's tone. Whoever the guy was, he wasn't worried about the repercussions of his outburst. Connor glanced over at Lyric, fully expecting her to tear the guy a new asshole, but he couldn't read a thing on her face or in her eyes. It was like she wasn't even there anymore.

"You need to use this time off to get your act together," the guy continued. "Get a massage. Get laid. Whatever it takes, but don't show up in Houston sounding like a screechy has-been."

Whoa. This was starting to get entertaining.

"Who's the guy?" Connor asked Phillip casually.

"Her manager, Paul."

Connor couldn't read any disapproval in Phillip's tone. Maybe Paul was saying what everyone else was thinking. But then Connor caught the look in Phillip's eyes. He looked murderous.

"He always talk to her like that?"

Phillip gave a short nod. "Yeah. Look, you're going to have to deal with him. There's nothing I can do about that. But you work for me. Not that little prick. Remember that."

The men went silent as Lyric finally pushed by her manager and then she came up short when she laid eyes on Connor. Connor took his time acknowledging her presence. The problem was, the woman was clearly used to having people come to attention when she entered a room. Hell would freeze over before he'd be one of them.

When he finally lifted his gaze to meet hers, he saw crystal blue eyes staring back at him with the same disinterest he knew had to be reflected in his gaze. She adopted a bored look as her two minions continued pawing at her.

His gaze moved purposefully to her hair. Jet-black strands shot in different directions and a neon pink streak of color ran from the top of her scalp down the side of her head on the left side.

"Nice hair," he said.

Amusement glimmered for a moment in her eyes before she looked pointedly at Phillip and Barry.

Phillip stepped forward, a broad, indulgent smile on his face, and why should he be anything else when this chick was likely making him millions?

"Lyric, I'd like you to meet Connor Malone. He's here from Malone and Sons Security. We're talking to him about your upcoming stop in Houston."

She flashed a challenging stare and didn't extend her hand, but then, neither did he.

Finally she broke and looked over at Phillip. "You know my feelings on this. Why is he here?"

Connor almost smiled. Apparently she wasn't any happier about the whole thing than he was. She crossed her arms over her chest, which only served to plump her small breasts upward. The swells peeked over the top of her corset and the pale skin glowed in the harsh light. Soft. A direct contrast to her demeanor.

Barry frowned and stepped forward. "Now, Lyric, we've discussed this. Malone and Sons comes highly recommended. You don't have nearly enough security, and after the last few months, you of all people should see that you need more."

She reached up to shove one of the bodyguards, who was nuzzling at her neck. Instead of being rebuffed, he settled back, a lazy smile on his face that suggested he'd be satisfied later.

If these were the morons charged with her safety, it was no wonder her record label was screaming for more. Their only concern seemed to be how quickly they could get into her pants.

Her gaze found his again, and her eyes narrowed. He looked calmly back at her, refusing to be the one who backed down. He didn't much care if she could read his disgust. It was doubtful he could hide it anyway. No one was that good an actor.

His skin started prickling in peculiar awareness. The back of his neck itched something fierce, but he wouldn't give an inch in this silent tug-of-war.

"I don't like you," she finally said.

To his utter horror, he went hard.

He smiled then. A lazy, "I don't give a fuck" grin. It was either that or groan at his growing discomfort, and he'd eat nails before allowing her to know how affected he was by her. "The feeling, Ms. Jones, is entirely mutual."

She frowned, then slipped an arm around one of the giants at her side, who immediately leaned down to kiss her cheek. The other huddled in close on her other side and she slanted a sly grin up at him.

She may as well have worn a sign that said "I'm fucking both of them" for all the discretion she exercised.

"I'd invite you to join us, Mr. Malone, but somehow you seem too uptight."

He chuckled and prayed she couldn't see his erection, because . . . damn. "I'm afraid I'm a bit choosier than you are when it comes to my bed partners."

Color tinged her cheeks and then she turned away, both guards immediately surrounding her as she walked to the door.

Phillip cleared his throat next to Connor. Connor glanced up.

"Lyric is, uhm, shall we say a little difficult?" Phillip began.

Connor was beginning to think it was her standard description. He held up his hand. "Save it. You don't have enough money to make me take this job. I'd have to be fucking insane."

He was already goddamn insane because from the moment she said she didn't like him, his cock had roared to life and said, *Come get me.*

The very last thing he wanted was a bratty pop star around him twenty-four/seven, one who gave him a hard-on every time she argued with him.

He'd be nothing but a walking erection.

Lyric walked into her suite and fended off Trent when he went for her top. Surprise flashed in his eyes when she instead headed for the minibar to pour herself a glass of water.

R.J. sidled over to her and put an arm around her shoulders. "Something wrong, Lyric?"

She shrugged him off, unable to explain why she could suddenly not bear for either of them to touch her.

"Just not in the mood," she said darkly.

Trent chuckled. "But, sugar, you're always in the mood."

"Not tonight," she said sharply. "I just want to be . . . alone. Okay?"

The two men looked at each other in shock, then stared back at her as if she'd lost her mind. And maybe she had. Alone? What was she thinking? She didn't do alone. Ever. The only thing worse than being alone was being one-on-one with someone. She didn't like either option and surrounded herself with people even in sleep.

But tonight? Yeah, she could do alone. Connor Malone's disapproving stare had rattled her. Way more than she'd ever admit aloud.

She got plenty of that on a regular basis. Thrived on it, even. She didn't give a rat's ass what people thought of her and had made it her mission in life to give the public as much ammunition as possible. So why did one condescending asshole get under her skin so badly?

She shook her head but couldn't get his sneer out of her mind. He made her uncomfortable. As if he could see right past her shields, all her secrets and all her fears. It was as if he'd seen her naked and vulnerable and hadn't been at all impressed. But then, why should he be?

"Lyric, are you all right?" R.J. interrupted. She could hear the worry in his voice, but at the moment she didn't care and didn't have the mental energy necessary to reassure him.

She waved dismissively at them and turned away. It was a clear signal for them to leave, and they'd be fools to ignore it. They might be intimate with her, but sex was all they offered. They weren't her friends. Weren't her confidants. She didn't have those.

When she heard the door open and close, she turned back to survey the empty suite. Cold panic clawed at her throat and she took several long, steadying breaths. Sweat that had nothing to do with her exhaustive performance beaded on her forehead, and she could feel nausea well in her throat.

She gazed around, absorbing the loneliness that surrounded her like fog. It seeped into her skin. Wrapped around her bones until she was paralyzed by its grip.

She crossed her arms over her chest. Gripped her arms with her fingers and then rubbed up and down to assuage the coldness that emanated from the inside out.

Connor Malone had looked inside her. He'd looked past the flashy, brassy veneer and stared coldly at her. Disapproving. She'd felt stripped bare before him and it pissed her off. He was nobody to her. Just some flunky that her record label wanted to hire to babysit her. Fuck that.

They wanted someone to rein her in, and that cold bastard would probably delight in doing just that. Over her dead body.

She grabbed on to the anger, harnessed it like someone desperate to ride the wind. The alternative was fear.

A knock sounded at her door and she flew to open it, relief rocketing through her system. She yanked it open to see Phillip and Barry standing there in their smarmy executive clothing, but in that moment, she was so relieved to see them, she didn't care.

"Lyric, are we disturbing you?" Phillip asked.

She shook her head and opened the door wider. "Come in. Can I get you a drink?"

They walked inside and looked around, surprised, she knew, to find her alone. Phillip shrugged out of his expensive coat and tossed it over the back of the couch. "We need to talk, Lyric."

She bristled at his tone and donned her best belligerent sneer. "You can talk. I don't have to listen."

Barry, who didn't do confrontation very well, looked as though he wanted to be anywhere but here. Which was fine because she wasn't too crazy about here either.

"You need Connor Malone—"

"I don't need anybody," she said icily.

"You need him," Phillip said firmly. "I've let things go on as long as I'm going to. You're in breach of contract and I've let it go. Until now. Connor Malone basically told me to fuck off and headed back to Houston. You're going to go there and do whatever it takes to make him reconsider."

Her mouth fell open. "Excuse me?"

"You heard me," he said grimly. "I'm not giving you a choice, Lyric. You'll do this or you'll be out on your ass, and trust me, even as big as you are, I don't see another record label lining up to pick you up with all the shit you've pulled."

Her eyes narrowed. "Don't threaten me, Phillip."

His expression softened just a bit, but determination still glinted in his eyes. "Things can't go on as they are, Lyric. You've been lucky, but sooner or later, your luck is going to run out. We need Connor Malone to buy us some time to hire more security whether you like it or not. He's not any happier over the arrangement than you are. I've put in a call to his boss, who's going to lean on him. I want your ass in Houston to reinforce the issue. You'll be nice. You'll be accommodating. You'll do what it takes to make him agree to the job. And then," he said, putting up a finger, "you're going to behave yourself."

She set her jaw until her teeth ached. She opened her mouth to argue but he shut her down with one swift shake of his head.

"Don't speak. You'll fly out after the show this weekend. That'll give him *and* you a few days to cool off."

He snapped his fingers at Barry and the two of them walked out of her room, closing the door with a sharp bang. She sank onto the couch like a deflated balloon.

She ran agitated fingers through her hair, pulling on the ends in repetition. Connor Malone was an arrogant ass. But more than that, he frightened her. And that pissed her off.

He was smug and too damn good-looking. Her brow wrinkled in irritation. Good-looking? Yeah, he was. It might get her goat to admit it, but he was exactly the sort of man she was attracted to. Tall. Strong and silent. And blond. Muddy blond with different tones and shades, like he spent a lot of time out in the sun. He wasn't pretty blond, but rugged, yummy blond. She had a weakness for blonds. She didn't normally go for the good guy, military-type cut, but on him it looked good. It looked damn good. Just added to his badass appearance.

He had those piercing green eyes that saw way too much. He cut through the layers at supersonic speed. Maybe he was some goddamn superhero. She laughed. Maybe he was supposed to be *her* goddamn superhero.

Yeah, she could have taken him back to her room if not for the fact they loathed each other on sight. She couldn't even say she'd had an instant reaction to him. Her dislike had been in self-defense. More of an "I hate him because he hates me" response.

And now Phillip wanted her to fly to Houston and grovel? Jesus. She didn't grovel. Ever. The mere thought nearly choked her.

Why did she need Connor fucking Malone? She didn't need goddamn anyone, and that was the way she liked it. Connor could take his self-righteous prig self and take a long walk off a short pier.

She leaned farther back on the couch and propped her feet on the coffee table. She shouldn't have sent Trent and R.J. away. They could be having hot, sweaty sex right now and she could slip into oblivion. Instead she was mad as hell because if she wanted to stay employed, she was going to have to go play nice with some good old boy without a sense of humor.

For a moment she was tempted to call Trent and R.J. back. They'd be more than happy to climb into bed with her, and then she wouldn't feel so terribly alone. But try as she might, she couldn't make the disapproving look on Connor Malone's face dissolve from her memory. And it pissed her off even more that it had mattered.

CHAPTER 3

*C*onnor stalked into Malone's with the beginnings of a headache already wracking his brain. His flight from L.A. had been delayed. He'd spent six hours in Dallas, and just when he was ready to say fuck it and hire a damn car and drive the five hours to Houston, his flight had boarded.

Then, when he'd landed, he had six voice mails, three of them from Pop and another three from Micah, who'd delighted in giving him hell about his meeting with the pop diva. Asshole.

"Hey, you're back," Faith called from her office as he passed.

His frown eased into a smile, and he backed up to Faith's doorway. "Yeah, I'm back. Finally. You're a sight for sore eyes."

"Heard it didn't go too well," she said, her green eyes bright with sympathy.

He gave up the idea of sneaking to his office to blow off some steam and sauntered into Faith's office, where he slouched in a seat in front of her desk.

"Let me guess. Micah has been regaling you with tales of my torture."

Mirth glistened in her eyes as she tried to stifle her laughter. "Well, uhm, yes. I'm afraid he has."

"Jackass," Connor muttered.

"Was it that bad?"

Connor sighed. He loved his sister dearly, and he had no intention of bitching at her for the better part of an hour. So he ignored the question. "Where's Gray and Nathan?"

She accepted the change in subject with her usual good nature, but her eyes gleamed speculatively as if to say she'd get the dirt later. Yeah, she was sweet, but she could also be downright evil.

"They're out on a job. Pop should be in shortly, and, to be honest, I have no idea where Micah is."

"Damn."

"Avoiding Pop?" she asked, her lips quivering with another smile.

"It's pointless. The old coot would just show up at my apartment."

Faith did laugh then. "Yes, he would. He's been muttering under his breath about insubordination and hardheaded employees ever since the record execs called to tell him you'd walked."

Connor rolled his eyes. "If he wants the job so damn bad, he can send Micah. He'd totally dig the chick."

"And you don't."

"She's . . . she's . . . I don't have words."

"Wow, Connor Malone speechless. And over a woman. Never thought I'd see it."

He glared at her. "It's not what you think. She's . . ." He couldn't even finish. Faith burst into laughter, her long blond hair shaking over her shoulders. She reached up to wipe tears from the corners of her eyes and kept on laughing.

He rolled his eyes heavenward and wondered if asking for a sudden lightning bolt would be asking for too much.

"There you are."

Connor flinched when Pop's raspy voice filled the room. "Here I am," he muttered, not turning around in his chair.

Pop ambled up and smiled at Faith. "Your husband said to tell you that he's going to be running late and for you not to wait on him."

Her cheeks pinkened, and a soft smile spread over her features. "Guess I'll head out, then."

Traitor, Connor mouthed at her.

She winked, then collected her purse and headed for the door.

Pop turned his hard stare on Connor. "Now. You."

Connor held up his hand. "I don't want to hear it, Pop."

Pop grunted. "Well, you're going to hear it." He leaned against Faith's desk and crossed his arms over his chest. "I don't care what happened in L.A. This job is a personal favor to a friend. I told him we'd do it, and I can't spare one of the others to do it. You're it."

Connor set his teeth together. "Just because they all had the poor sense to get all fucked-up over a woman and think they need to all be married does not mean that I get every shitty job that crosses your desk now."

Pop snorted. "No sense getting your panties in a wad. You're acting as bad as that pop star you don't want to babysit."

Connor scowled but Pop held up his hand. "I'm asking as a favor."

Connor groaned.

"She's flying in this Friday. You're meeting her for dinner Friday night and then she's coming in to the office on Saturday for a meeting with you and me."

"Why am I meeting her for dinner?" Connor demanded.

"Because the two of you are obviously off on the wrong foot, and you need to kiss and make up if we have a hope of making this work."

"Goddamn it, Pop. You go out to dinner with her. I'll make the Saturday meeting, but I have no desire to spend five minutes with her alone, much less an entire dinner."

Pop stared at him for a long moment. "Are you refusing the job?"

Connor swore long and hard. "No, I'm damn well not turning down the job. You've made it personal by asking a favor and you know damn well I'm not going to tell you no. But I don't have to like it."

Pop grinned. Cagey old bastard. "Phillip Armstrong will be e-mailing all the pertinent information as well as what they want from us as far as security. Tomorrow afternoon I want you to sit in on the conference call that he and Barry Kennedy will be heading up. Then you and I will hash out a game plan so that when she arrives on Friday, you two can discuss what will be done during her time in Houston. I left a detailed file on her on your desk. It will give you a very good idea of what this job will entail."

"Fine," Connor muttered.

Pop straightened and started for the door. Grudgingly, Connor stood and turned around to follow. Pop paused in the doorway and faced Connor. The old coot was working to keep a straight face. "Think of it this way. You've been bitching about wanting to take vacation for a long time now. Now you get two whole weeks."

"Fuck you," Connor growled.

Connor sat at the bar in Cattleman's, sipping a cold beer as he waited for Lyric Jones to make an appearance. He checked his watch again, irritated that she was fifteen minutes late.

Pop was disgruntled that he hadn't picked a classier spot, but then, from what he'd seen, Lyric wasn't the epitome of class, and if he was going to be forced to endure this meeting, then she could damn well come to him on his turf.

He'd spent the better part of yesterday reading the notes that Pop had compiled. Micah had even made an appearance, only too happy to shove the latest tabloid under Connor's nose with a smug, shit-eating grin. How one woman could cause so much trouble and garner so much press was beyond him.

His trip to the grocery store to get a steak and a six-pack of beer had been soured when he noticed that every single magazine at the checkout had some tale of her latest antics or publicity stunt plastered over the covers.

It would seem that nothing the woman did was shielded from the world, and worse, she seemed perfectly okay with that.

He downed the last of his brew and shoved the empty bottle across the bar. As he glanced sideways, he saw her come in. To his surprise, she wasn't accompanied by her bodyguards. Not very smart.

She was dressed in tight-fitting jeans and a regular white T-shirt. There wasn't a hint of pink in her hair and not a spot of makeup dotted her face. She looked remarkably clean-cut and wholesome. Good grief.

Her fingers were shoved into her jeans pockets, and she looked around warily. Unease billowed off her body in a cloud. She looked uncertain, and again he was struck by the odd vulnerability he had glimpsed during her last number at the concert. Clearly he was losing his mind.

Finally her gaze locked on to his and he lifted his hand in greeting. Her eyes glazed over, and it was as if she locked the attitude in place. The cockiness was back in spades.

She twisted her lips and sauntered over, throwing her bag over the bar stool as she slid up to the bar beside him.

"Nice place," she drawled.

"I think so." He held up a finger and motioned to the barkeep. "Drink?" he asked her when the bartender walked over.

"Just water."

"Beer and a water," Connor ordered.

She leaned forward and rested her elbows on the scarred wood of the bar. As she wiggled her body to move closer so she could lean, he caught a whiff of her perfume. To his surprise it smelled soft, nice even. He would have expected something strong and overpowering. Like her.

"So," she said as she made a V with her fingers and pressed them to her lips. "Here we are."

Connor nodded.

She sighed and turned sideways to look at him. "Look, let's at least be honest. I don't like you. You don't like me. Neither of us wants to be here and you don't want to babysit me any more than I want a god-damn nanny."

Despite himself, he chuckled. He couldn't help it.

"Not bothering to deny it, are you?" she said dryly.

He shook his head. "Nope. Don't see the point in blowing smoke up your ass."

She sighed again. "I'm guessing you weren't given any more choice than I was."

"Nope."

"Not a man of many words, are you?"

He shrugged. "You pretty much said it all."

"Well, it's obvious that we aren't going to be best friends forever, so why don't we sit here for a few minutes, you can have a beer or two, and then we can leave and pretend we played nice?"

Connor smiled and, though it pained him, he found himself not quite hating the thought of spending a few more minutes with her.

"I can play nice for a few minutes," he conceded.

She snorted. "You mean if we ignore each other."

His smile widened. He glanced over her again, noting the absent flash and glitz. "You look . . . different."

She cast him a baleful stare. "Just in case you think that the pink hair and flashy clothes are just part of the stage show and that underneath I'm this really nice, boring girl, let me dissuade you of that notion. I just didn't want to get my ass kicked by coming into a place like this in anything but good-ole-boy gear."

Connor was fascinated by the snarl on her lips. It almost looked cute. Then he shook his head. She had as much personality as a pit bull and the pit bull was probably friendlier.

She spread her hands and turned up her palms in a supreme "I don't give a fuck" gesture. "What you see is what you get."

"Who are you trying to convince? Me or yourself?"

Anger flashed over her face and her eyes narrowed. He could get off on pissing her off. She rose to the bait so easily.

"Just tell me what it is you're supposed to do for me so we can get this over with," she muttered.

Connor studied her for a moment, her stiff posture, her obvious discomfort being here with him. She shouldn't have come alone, especially not in light of the details he'd gotten from Phillip.

"How bad has it been?" he asked bluntly.

She looked up, her blue eyes flashing in surprise. Then she shrugged. "You've talked to Phillip and Barry, I'm sure."

"They haven't been with you," Connor pointed out. "A few visits on the road and phone calls from their office don't count. Not with me. If I'm going to be responsible for your safety, then I need to know exactly what I'm dealing with."

For a moment it seemed her shell cracked, and he could see the lines of fatigue grooved around her eyes.

"It's not as bad as they make it out to be. I bring a lot of it on myself." She lifted one small shoulder in a gesture of indifference. "I never wanted to surround myself so tightly with security that the public couldn't get in. But now . . ."

"It's too much," Connor guessed.

"It's exhausting. There have been a few threats."

"And Phillip wants to crack down, not make you so accessible."

Lyric nodded.

"So tell me. How hard is my job going to be?"

A small smile curved the corners of her mouth upward. "I won't lie to you. I'm used to doing things my way."

"We don't have to get along for this to work, but you do have to listen to what I tell you. Every word. And you have to follow directions."

She made a rude noise under her breath. "Just stay out of my way as much as possible."

"Deal."

She glanced sideways and appraised him with a seeking stare. "I think I like that you're not kissing my ass."

"It's not your ass I want to kiss."

The statement stunned both of them. Holy fuck, had he just said that? She blinked in surprise and then visibly retreated. The cocky, self-assured veneer was back, but for a moment, he'd seen something in her gaze that spoke to him. Longing.

With a smirk, she leaned forward and planted her lips solidly on his. Heat scorched a path from his mouth straight to his dick and flayed open every nerve ending along the way. She licked over his lips as if challenging him to open to her, but before he could, she pulled away and slid off the bar stool.

"Guess I'll see you tomorrow, then." She gave him a flip wave and strode out of the bar.

CHAPTER 4

After an early morning jog, Connor showered and headed into Malone's, hoping for some time to go over the file on Lyric Jones before everyone else showed up for this farce of a meeting. He should have known that Pop would already be in.

When Connor let himself into the office, he heard voices from the conference room and frowned. Pop wasn't the only one in way ahead of time.

He went to the doorway to peer in and saw Phillip Armstrong having coffee with Pop. Pop looked up and motioned Connor in.

"Glad you came in early, son. Phillip has something he wants to discuss with you before Lyric arrives."

Barely able to control his sigh, Connor pulled out one of the chairs and took a seat across from the two men.

"I really appreciate you rethinking this," Phillip said. "William tells me you're well suited for this job, and the truth is, I need someone I can trust."

Connor shot Pop a glare. Well suited? What qualified him to be a babysitter slash bodyguard? His years in the army didn't exactly prepare him to hover over a spoiled diva.

Pop glared back and Connor refocused his attention on Phillip.

"The danger to Lyric is more specific," Phillip admitted.

And Connor hadn't thought this could get worse. "Care to explain what you mean by that?"

"We've received what we believe to be credible threats. I pay a team a hell of a lot of money to discern whether a threat is merely someone mouthing off and wanting attention or whether it's something we need to pursue.

"Mostly it's the former and we nip it in the bud. People aren't terribly smart and the trail back to them is usually easy to follow."

"You're getting threats you can't trace back to an identifiable source."

Phillip nodded. "Exactly. What concerns me is that whoever is doing them is delivering them in person. It started five shows ago and he's followed her from city to city."

Connor raised an eyebrow. "He?"

"We assume it's a he."

"An obsessed fan?"

Phillip frowned. "I'm not sure. Typically when you have some fan who's obsessed or fancies themselves in love with a star, there's a courting stage and then anger because their feelings aren't acknowledged or reciprocated. This . . . this is just plain weird and unsettling."

"Tell me."

"He always leaves a note. Where varies. Once, it was taped to the bus. Once, it was on her guitar case. Another time it was in her dressing room."

"No wonder you fired her security," Connor muttered. "No one should be getting that close to her."

Phillip nodded. "One of the many reasons. I also couldn't be certain it wasn't one of them. I got rid of everyone I had the power to fire. Unfortunately, Pete and Repete, her two pet bodyguards, are hers. She hired them. But I want you to keep an eye on them. I don't trust them."

"Lyric didn't mention any of this when we met last night," Connor said. "She mentioned that it had gotten harder to keep a distance from the fans and that she'd made a mistake in making herself too available."

Phillip shifted uncomfortably in his chair and glanced over at Pop. Pop grunted. "You may as well tell him. You should have told us all this from the beginning. Last thing he needs is to go in blind."

Jesus. What now?

"Lyric doesn't know," Phillip said. "I've kept a tight lid on it."

"You want to say that again?" Connor asked.

"She doesn't know."

Connor shook his head in disbelief. Pop was right about one thing. People in show business had no common sense.

"What could you possibly hope to gain by keeping this from her? She has to be careful, which means she has to be aware of the potential threat to her. She can't do that if no one tells her that some creep is stalking her. I don't understand why you haven't canceled her show or at least her appearance at the music store. Are you just trying to get her killed?"

Phillip's lips pressed together. Connor hadn't come out and said, *You're a dumbass*, but his tone certainly implied it. Phillip didn't look happy, but if the shoe fit . . .

"Lyric is her own worst enemy at times," Phillip said. "If she knew some weirdo was leaving notes for her, there's no telling what she'd do. She's not the type to be cautious and play it safe. And we can't go around canceling events every time some whack job starts threatening her. If we did that, we'd be out of business."

"It seems to me, whether there's a threat or not, she does whatever the hell she wants and damn the consequences."

"Yeah," Phillip said wearily. "Something like that."

"So if she's doing it either way, it makes no sense not to tell her what's going on. At least then she might adopt a little self-preservation. Especially if you aren't going to cancel a public appearance that most definitely puts her at risk."

Phillip's eyes narrowed. "Look, you don't know Lyric—"

Connor held up his hand. "You're right. I don't know her. I don't have a desire to get to know her. But if I'm going to take this job, I'm not coddling her, which means I'm going to be straight with her from the start. She's going to be briefed on everything. And then she's going to do what I tell her, when I tell her, or I walk. It's as simple as that."

"She's never going to go for such heavy-handed treatment."

Connor shrugged. "It seems to me you need me a hell of a lot more than I need you. I'd love nothing more than for her to fire me."

"You work for me," Phillip was quick to say. "She doesn't have a choice."

"Then I guess she better get used to a heavy hand. She's too used to having her ass kissed."

Phillip surprised Connor by laughing. "I suppose to you that's the way it looks. When someone makes your label as much money as she has, you do whatever's necessary to keep her happy. That's business."

"It's not my job to make her happy," Connor said evenly. "It's my job to keep her safe."

Phillip smiled broadly. "You know what, son? I think I'm sorry I'm going back to L.A. It might be worth being a fly on the wall for the next two weeks. I'm not sure Lyric's ever met someone she couldn't steamroll in two seconds flat."

"Well, now she has."

*   *   *

Lyric tapped her finger on the steering wheel of the BMW and glanced over at the GPS guidance system. She was just a block away from the place she was supposed to meet Connor Malone. It was tempting to show up late, just because, but to be honest, she wanted to get the whole thing over with as soon as possible.

She could have showed up in a limo and made an entrance, but Connor would probably be expecting that—he did seem to expect the worst—and while she'd normally enjoy feeding it to him with a silver spoon, she preferred to be perverse and surprise him.

How pathetic did it make her that she'd actually spent an inordinate amount of time analyzing what he would expect and therefore go the opposite direction?

She glanced at her manicured nails as she turned into the parking lot, relieved that she'd gone an entire day without breaking one—a new record.

Her outfit was hot, again, in a totally-not-what-he'd-be-expecting way. She didn't really care for the slutty pop rocker look except on-stage because, well, it worked there. She loved expensive clothes, or, more important, clothes that looked expensive. She liked they way they felt on her. The way they looked.

She'd come a long way from Bum Fuck, Mississippi, and it would be a cold day in hell before she'd ever go back. She wouldn't even do shows there. Not that there were many places to put on a concert the size of hers.

Hell, she wouldn't even drive through the godforsaken state. She was sure her road crew thought she was nuts because she made them detour around the state when they'd driven from New Orleans to Atlanta.

She got out of her car and straightened her suede miniskirt. She had on a killer pair of heels. They were total fuck-me shoes and gave her a much-needed three inches in height. She liked looking good. It gave her confidence, especially in situations where she felt at a disadvantage. Not that she'd ever admit such a thing to anyone. Only a moron admitted weakness to her enemies.

She slipped her shades down over her nose like a shield and entered the building.

"Ms. Jones?"

Lyric turned in the direction of the feminine voice to see a blond woman standing in the doorway to the front office.

"I'm Lyric Jones," she acknowledged.

The woman smiled and walked forward, her hand stuck out. "Faith Montgomery. I'm Connor's sister. They're waiting for you in the conference room. I'll show you back."

Lyric shook her hand and felt distinctly uncomfortable. Faith struck her as one of those genuine, disgustingly nice people, and Lyric was never sure how to act around them. Nobody was genuine in her world.

Silently she followed Faith down the hallway. Faith walked through the open door and the room went quiet. All eyes fell on Lyric when she came in behind Faith. Lyric surveyed the room with a frown, noticing quite a few faces she didn't recognize.

"Please have a seat," Faith said. "Can I get you some coffee?"

Lyric shook her head but managed a smile since Faith was being so . . . nice.

"Lyric, glad you made it," Phillip said as he stood.

There was surprise in his voice. He'd expected her to be late. A quick glance at Connor told her nothing about what he thought or didn't think. She wasn't going to admit that she was disappointed. She'd wanted a reaction of some type. Even if it wasn't a good one. This seeming indifference he showed toward her irritated her.

The older man who'd been sitting next to Phillip also stood, and he made his way to where Lyric stood.

"I'm Pop Malone, Connor's father," he said. "It's nice to meet you, Ms. Jones."

"It's nice to meet you too, Mr. Malone," she said smoothly as she extended her hand.

"I want you to meet the rest of my staff," Pop said as he turned in the direction of the seated men. "You've already met my daughter, Faith. That's her husband, Gray Montgomery. Next to him is Nathan Tucker and sitting by Connor is Micah Hudson."

"Are they going to be my security team?" she asked sweetly.

"Their women would chew you up and spit you out," Connor said dryly as he stood.

She raised an eyebrow. "Then why are they all here?"

"To see me suffer."

Color rose in her cheeks. She couldn't think of a single comeback for that one. She was used to being a veritable circus act. It shouldn't surprise her that Connor's coworkers had come to see the train wreck.

She took a seat at the very end of the table so she'd be as far from the others as possible. To her surprise, Connor moved to the chair next to her.

He was way too close and she fidgeted nervously in her seat. He glanced her way once and lifted a brow. Damn, but the man was sexy in a disdainful, you-annoy-me kind of way. She had to be a masochist. It was the only explanation for her bizarre attraction to him. Rejection wasn't her thing. Neither was hooking up with someone who looked at her like he would dirt on his shoe.

But the truth was, she'd thought a lot about that kiss. It had kept her up the previous night—that and the fact that she was alone, and she hated being alone.

There was some serious chemistry between her and Connor

Malone, and it was a pity, because they could barely stand the sight of each other. He was probably the only man on earth who'd turn her down flat anyway.

"Would you care to offer your opinion, Ms. Jones?" Connor asked dryly.

She blinked and realized that the entire table was looking at her, obviously waiting for her response. She faked a yawn, adopted a bored look and studied her nails.

"Sorry, I didn't get much sleep last night."

Connor's eyes narrowed and she gazed at him with wide eyes, a look she knew to be successful on most men. But then, Connor wasn't most men. He didn't look impressed even if the other men at the table looked a little gobsmacked.

"If you're through wasting our time," Connor began.

"I'm paying for your time, so it's mine to do with what I want," she drawled.

Connor stood and looked down the table at the others. "Would you all excuse us? I believe Ms. Jones and I have things we need to discuss. Privately."

"The hell—"

The look he gave her stopped the protest before it could be fully launched. For the first time, she felt herself backing down. The man made her nervous, and that pissed her off. Didn't just piss her off. It made her furious.

When everyone had left, Connor turned and planted his palms on the table in front of her. "Let me get something straight. You didn't hire me. You can't fire me. You have nothing I want or need. I don't give a shit if you like me. I don't particularly like you. It's my job to keep you safe, and I'm going to do just that. Which means you're going to listen to everything I tell you."

How utterly ridiculous that she flinched when he'd baldly said he didn't like her. Like that should come as a surprise? Nobody liked her. People tolerated her. They used her. But they didn't like her. Why should Connor Malone be any different? Why did she want him to be?

"What your idiot of a record label executive hasn't told you is that they've been monitoring threats over your last five shows. Some ass-hole is leaving you notes in places he shouldn't have access to."

Lyric curled her fingers into fists and stared up at Connor. "What are you talking about?"

"Just what I said. They've found notes on your bus, in your dressing room, on your guitar case. Whoever's doing it is getting way too close to you."

She forced her hands to relax and then wiped her palms down the soft suede of her skirt. "Why didn't they tell me?"

"They didn't trust you not to do something stupid."

She blew out her breath in frustration. "Nice."

He arched an eyebrow. "Do they have reason to believe any other way?"

"Whether or not they thought they knew how I'd react, I had a right to know."

Connor nodded. "On that point we agree, which is why I'm telling you now. Maybe now you'll see that this isn't some fucking game. This is your life, and it's my job to make sure you stay alive. Now, are you going to help me or are you going to do everything you can to make my job harder?"

Slowly she shook her head.

"Which is it?"

"I'll . . ." She swallowed and then turned her gaze up to meet his once more. "I'll cooperate. I'll try."

He folded his arms over his chest and leaned against the edge of the table. "You'll do more than try."

She held her hands up in surrender. "Whatever. You're the boss."

He smiled and it made him look so arrogant she was tempted to haul him down and kiss him senseless again.

"Glad you recognize that fact. We'll get along just fine as long as you remember that little tidbit."

Slowly she got to her feet. "Are we finished now?"

He nodded.

She reached into her bag for her keys and walked toward the door, unsure of what the hell had just happened. She was a little shell-shocked and off balance. She needed a little time to process the storm that was Connor Malone.

Connor fell into step behind her but she paid him little attention. She walked into the reception area where the others were all standing around talking. She didn't miss the way conversation stopped or the way they all stared at her as she went by.

"Bye, Ms. Jones. It was nice meeting you," Faith called.

Lyric looked up and smiled, because really, not smiling at the really nice blond woman was like kicking a puppy. You just didn't do it. And the truth was, there was something about Faith that just made a person a little warm on the inside.

Clearly Lyric needed a drink to get over that little burst of poetry. She could get drunk and write a song about sunshine and dedicate it to Faith.

She bit her lip to call back the laughter and offered a wave to everyone as she left the building.

Ah, freedom. Not that she liked being alone, but somehow, right now it was preferable to being cooped up in a room full of people who made her feel vastly inferior. She was the famous superstar, and yet a group of good ole boys and Miss Sunshine made her feel not good enough.

It wasn't until she reached her car that she realized Connor had followed her out. She frowned as she unlocked her doors. He was taking his job a little too seriously for her liking.

Determined to ignore him, she slid into the driver's seat just as he opened the passenger door and got in beside her.

She paused after she put the key in the ignition and looked questioningly at him. "What are you doing?"

He looked at her like she was a moron for asking the obvious. "I believe we've been over this. You're in danger. I've been hired to keep you safe. Therefore, for the next two weeks, where you go, I go."

Her mouth gaped open. "Are you serious?"

He gazed coolly at her. "Does it look like I'm joking?"

"But I'm just going back to my hotel."

"Hope you have a double, because I'm not sleeping on the floor."

CHAPTER 5

*L*yric flexed her hands as she navigated the busy streets back to her downtown hotel. Connor rode in silence next to her, his gaze fixed out of his window as if he found her company tedious.

She frowned. She did not want him in her hotel room. He wouldn't fit! He was too big. Too overbearing. Maybe she could inquire about an adjoining room and he'd be satisfied with having access. Then if she forgot and locked the door, she could say *oops* and he wouldn't be invading her space.

She hadn't reserved a suite. Too much empty space with no people to fill it up and make her feel less lonely and . . . panicked. She'd taken a ridiculously small room and then filled it with all the stuff she'd brought with her because it had made her feel like she wasn't alone.

No way she wanted Connor Malone intruding. The mere idea had her breaking out in a cold sweat. She embraced a crowd. But being one-on-one? Especially with someone like Connor?

God.

She drove up to the front entrance and the valet opened her door for her. She dropped the keys into his hand and strode around to the revolving doors that led into the lobby.

Connor was waiting and walked in practically attached to her hip. The man was tall and muscled and he took over her space to the point that with every inhale, his scent was permanently imprinted on her.

He frowned when she resisted him herding her to the elevator and headed to the front desk instead.

"What are you doing?"

"Seeing if they have another room for you," Lyric muttered. She put on her widest smile when the desk clerk asked if her if he could help.

Connor put his hand over hers and squeezed. A warning. "There'll be no separate room."

The clerk raised his eyebrows and glanced between Connor and Lyric with undisguised interest.

Lyric tried to wrest her hand from his grip but he tightened his fingers over hers.

"There isn't room for you," she hissed. "Not even on the floor! I have a single. It's barely a shoe box."

"Since you're only spending tonight here, we can deal."

"But my reservations are for two weeks!"

Connor turned to the clerk and smiled. "She's had a change in itinerary. We'll be checking out in the morning."

Before she could utter another word, Connor took her elbow and propelled her toward the elevator. She had to hoof it to keep up with his pace, and the heels she wore weren't conducive to a footrace. It was hard to look sexy and elegant when she was worried about tripping over her own feet.

"Damn it, Malone," she huffed when the elevator doors closed. "I don't care what you were hired to do. You aren't staying in my room."

"The name is Connor. Use it. And get over it. We're going to be up close and personal for the next two weeks. My advice is to quit bitching and resign yourself to the inevitable."

She closed her eyes and bumped her head against the back of the elevator. She knew she sounded petulant and unreasonable, but the idea of him being in her personal space was seriously freaking her out.

Her breath huffed out in jerky little spurts until her vision blurred and she grew light-headed. She was dimly aware of Connor's frown and a muttered curse, but then, that shouldn't surprise her. It seemed it was all he did around her.

The elevator doors opened but that didn't relieve the tightness in her chest. She stood helpless against the wall, unable to make her legs cooperate.

Black spots danced in front of her eyes and the world seemed to get smaller and dimmer with each passing second.

Connor yanked her from the elevator and she found herself plopped onto one of the leather couches in the small sitting area on her floor.

"Breathe, Lyric. Look at me."

When she didn't immediately do as he'd demanded, he coaxed her chin upward with gentle fingers. "Look at me," he said again. "That's it. Focus. Now breathe with me. Just like this."

She watched as he inhaled deeply and then exhaled in one smooth motion.

"Think about what you're doing. Watch me. Do what I do. I won't let anything hurt you. You can trust me."

If she could manage the breath, she'd laugh. Trust him? He had no idea what he was asking. Trust was as foreign to her as the things most people took for granted. Love. Friendship. Companionship.

His fingers stroked soothingly over her cheek and it was all she could do not to lean into his touch and rub like a cat. It shocked her how good it felt to be comforted, to be touched by someone who didn't want something from her she wasn't willing to give.

She sighed and closed her eyes as some of the awful pressure in her chest eased. She could literally feel her lungs open up and shudder with relief as fresh air rushed in.

Her hands shook and her knees were so wobbly she'd never make it down the hall to her room. How humiliating to fall apart all because she was faced with the prospect of sharing her space with Connor Malone. Wouldn't the tabloids have a field day with this? Superstar suffers panic attack and passes out in hotel elevator.

"Where's your room key?" Connor asked quietly.

Her fingers trembled so much she nearly dumped her clutch on her feet.

He took the purse, and, after a moment of digging, he flashed the room card. He handed her back the bag. "We need to get you to your room. Can you make it if I help you?"

She nodded, furious with herself for allowing this to happen. Embarrassed. Gutted for making such an idiot of herself.

Gritting her teeth, she clutched at his arm as she rose from the couch.

"What room number?"

"All the way to the end," she whispered. "Last one on the left."

"Okay, take it nice and slow. Hold on to my arm and don't get in a hurry."

With each step, she regained more of her strength and some of the panic abated. By the time they reached her room, her knees had stopped shaking. Connor slid the card into the slot and opened her door. A rush of cool air blasted her in the face and gave her a much-needed shock.

"Christ, it's like a meat locker in here," Connor said as he ushered her inside.

"I like sleeping in the cold," she mumbled. "With the covers up to my ears."

Connor sat her on the edge of the bed. "Do you have anything to drink in here?"

"There's water in the fridge."

"You need something a little stronger than water."

"I don't drink," she said defensively. "No matter what you might read about me."

"I wasn't suggesting alcohol," he said dryly. "If anyone will be drinking, it'll be me. I was thinking more along the lines of something with caffeine in it for you."

"Caffeine makes me jittery and I don't sleep well."

He went over to the fridge and returned with a bottle of cold water. He opened it and shoved it toward her. "Drink."

She sipped at the refreshing liquid and took in several steadying breaths. "I'm fine now. Really. I'm sorry. I feel like an idiot for losing it like that."

He sat beside her on the bed and was silent for a long moment. He seemed to be studying her—or the issue—she wasn't sure which. The idea of him analyzing her made her twitch. Enough shrinks had done that to last her a lifetime.

"Why *did* you lose it, Lyric?"

She frowned. She hadn't expected him to be so . . . blunt. Most people danced around her. The few times she'd ever had a panic attack in front of someone else, they'd pretended it didn't happen, and she was more than happy to do the same.

He cocked his head sideways, and she could feel his gaze boring into her. Lifting and peeling back layers that she was helpless to defend against.

"Does my being in your room scare you that badly?" he asked softly.

Her nostrils flared and it was on the tip of her tongue to deny that anything scared her. But that would be pretty stupid, and Connor Malone wasn't stupid.

"I'll deal," she said. "I won't like it. I doubt you'll like it. But I get it. My record label thinks I'm in danger and they hired you to babysit me. I'm not the idiot you think I am. I have no desire to die at the hands of some lunatic. Or be kidnapped and forced to live in a basement somewhere as a sex slave."

Connor let out a chuckle. "You have a vivid imagination. That's good. The more hideous a fate you can imagine if this guy gets his hands on you, the easier you'll make my job because you'll stick like glue to me."

She turned so that their gazes met. "I thought you were supposed to stick to me like glue."

"That too. If we stick to each other, then we won't have to worry, now, will we?"

Coming from him, in his sexier-than-sin voice, the innocent words sounded like seduction. She'd never been wooed and seduced in her life and damn if he didn't make her want to be.

She'd be willing to bet he was one of those rare males who took his time with his lover. Coaxing, pleasuring. Unselfish. She'd bet money he'd give a woman complete and total satisfaction.

Chill bumps danced down her arms, raising the tiny hairs on her skin. She could feel the heat radiating off him and it made her want to burrow against his broad chest and absorb him.

What would it be like to lie in his arms? To have him hold her. Nothing else. Just . . . be.

It was a ridiculous fantasy given the fact she didn't want to be that close to anyone. The only thing worse than being alone was being one-on-one. Allowing someone to see inside her. To see the truth.

Connor stood, shaking her from her reverie. "You were right about this room. It's barely bigger than a closet. I wouldn't have thought you'd be caught dead in anything smaller than a suite. You have so much stuff stacked up in here that you can barely take a piss in the toilet."

She smiled faintly. "I was supposed to be here for two weeks. I need my stuff. I didn't bring my tour bus and I don't have anywhere else to put everything. I gave my crew time off. I'm doing the show with a skeleton band. It's just a few songs. The rodeo isn't a full concert and they do the stage."

"It's going to be a bitch to move all this stuff," Connor muttered.

She looked up sharply. "Why are we moving it? Why did you tell the clerk I was checking out tomorrow?"

"Because you are."

She raised her hands in exasperation. "But why? Where am I going?"

"Someplace safe. No one but Phillip will know and the only reason he will is because he's making the arrangements."

She frowned. "But that's ridiculous. I can't just fall off the face of the earth. I have things to do."

He leaned against a stack of luggage and eyed her. "Like?"

"I don't know. Yet. But I'll need Trent and R.J. You'll need them too. They've been my personal bodyguards since I began touring."

"Bodyguards or fuck-buddies?"

She flushed and looked away, and then it infuriated her that she allowed him to shame her.

"If they're fucking me, then someone else can hardly hurt me," she taunted.

"If they're fucking you, they aren't doing their job," he said through tight lips. "Their first and only priority is your safety. If they're focused on you and the next time they can get in your pants, they aren't watching what's going on around them."

She didn't want to acknowledge that he had a point. Trent and R.J. weren't around for their security skills. She didn't even know if they had any prior experience before coming to work for her. They were glorified male prostitutes and the truth of it hit her like a punch to the face.

She paid them. They slept with her—or at least they used to. She wasn't about to admit to Connor that she hadn't had sex with them for the last few shows because it would seem too much like she wanted his approval.

Oh, it wasn't as if she'd hired them for the purpose of sex, but it had dissolved into that and nothing more, so really what were they if not prostitutes?

Nausea swirled in her stomach. When had her life become such a sad mess? When had she become so desperate not to be alone that she paid people to surround her? And then anyone who got too close was quickly shoved as far away from her as possible.

"I can't fire them. They have a contract," she said in a low voice.

"They can have their duties reassigned," Connor said with a shrug. "I don't give a shit whether you pay them or not. But they aren't going to be trusted with your safety."

She closed her eyes, aware of the headache that was intensifying rapidly. She was tired. She hadn't lied when she'd said she hadn't slept the night before, and it wasn't for the reason she'd led Connor to believe.

She'd lain awake in this very room, like she did so many other nights, afraid of monsters from her past, afraid to turn out the lights because she was alone.

Giving her crew vacation time had been a necessity. They were as burned out as she was. But right now, she'd sell her soul to have them with her, surrounding her, to lose herself in the noise and chaos of so many people.

But no, she'd sworn to herself that the next two weeks were going to be a test of her mettle. She was going to step out and face her fears. Even if it killed her.

Only now, if Connor was telling her the truth, someone might do the job for her.

"I'm really just supposed to step back and let you take over."

It wasn't a question and she didn't phrase it as such. It was more of a resigned statement that she already knew the answer to.

"That's exactly what you're going to do," he said. He didn't even attempt to soothe her and offer platitudes. But then, that would have shocked her, and strangely, it would have disappointed her.

She swept out her hand to the piles of luggage and boxes. "Where do you propose to sleep tonight?"

He studied her for a long moment. "That depends. If it won't frighten you, we can sleep on the bed. You under the covers. Me on top of the covers. We can put pillows between us. If that idea scares you, I'll make do on the floor."

She managed a smile although her heart started thudding painfully as adrenaline spiked through her veins. "I thought you didn't do floors."

"For you I'll make an exception."

She cocked her head. "You don't worry about boundaries much, do you? I mean, most people would never dare to push like you have. I can't decide if you're really stupid or just plain ballsy."

He shrugged. "It doesn't really matter as long as I do my job."

She glanced at the bed, judging how much of it Connor would take up. It was a king bed stuffed into a really small room and Connor was a really big man. He'd need at least half the bed, and then the pillows would take up a fourth, which left her with the remaining fourth.

Or she could just make him sleep on the floor.

All she had to do was say the word, but she couldn't bring herself to tell him she was afraid.

"You can sleep on the bed," she said before she changed her mind.

"Lyric."

She looked back up at him and saw something other than scorn or irritation in his eyes.

"I won't hurt you."

She nodded and a hundred butterflies were released into her belly.

He surveyed the room again with a grimace. "I had planned to hole up in your room for the afternoon, but I think we'll both go crazy if we have to spend too much time here. It's probably not your speed, but I thought I'd take you over to see some friends. I don't want you out in public. You're going to keep an extremely low profile for the next little while."

"Not my speed?" she murmured.

He shrugged. "We get together, have some beer and shoot the shit. You met them all today—or most of them."

It actually sounded fun and she felt a twist of jealousy that he had friends—good friends—that he kicked back with.

"I'll go."

He raised an eyebrow. "You're going to behave. Micah, Gray and

Nathan are all very attached. To women I care a lot about. I don't want you upsetting them."

She swallowed the hurt and bit back a scathing remark. Every time she thought Connor might be different, he said something to make her remember that to him she was a spoiled, bratty diva who went through men like most people went through toilet paper.

She was a job. A job that he obviously didn't want but for whatever reason had agreed to. She needed to remind herself of that before she did something stupid like care what he thought about her.

CHAPTER 6

Lyric didn't argue when Connor walked her to the passenger side as the valet brought the car around. After she was in, she laid her head back on the rest and closed her eyes.

The car rocked when Connor got in and shut his door.

"Head still hurt?" Connor asked as they drove away from the hotel.

She cracked one eye open to look at him. "How did you know?"

"It doesn't take a rocket scientist to figure it out. You've been sensitive to light and sound all afternoon. Have you taken anything for it?"

She shook her head.

He made a sound of exasperation. "Why not? Are you a masochist?"

"I don't like to take anything unless it's necessary," she defended.

"I'd say a headache deserves an Excedrin or two. I'll stop by a drugstore on the way and get you something."

Dumbfounded, she watched as he pulled into a CVS and parked at the front entrance. He glanced over with a regretful expression. "You probably don't want to get out, but where I go, you go, so you'll have to come in." He switched off the engine. "Sit tight. I'll come around."

She was used to a certain amount of deference. People tended to fawn over her and kiss her ass. She didn't have any illusions it was anything personal to her. You could be a complete asshole and be famous and people would still line up to bow and scrape. She wouldn't lie and say she didn't enjoy it. Who wouldn't like being treated like a rock star?

But Connor's consideration meant something, and she couldn't even say why. Maybe it was because he wasn't the type to give a damn about her fame. It was obvious he wasn't impressed with her as a person. And yet he did things he didn't have to do, and it gave her more pleasure than she would have guessed.

He opened her door and extended his hand. She slid her fingers into his, enjoying the warmth and strength of his grip. He helped her from the car and held her elbow so she was flush against his body as they walked inside the pharmacy.

They fit, which was stupid of her to notice or to dwell on. But they fit perfectly. His body shielded hers like it was made to do so.

Never once did he actually look at her, which was fascinating because she was used to people staring at her and watching her every move. No, Connor looked at everyone else. He sized them up, assessed the potential threat and hurried Lyric toward the back of the store.

Not that anyone would recognize her. Out of deference to Connor—and because she was too tired for a fight—she'd dressed in jeans and a T-shirt. Her hair was pulled back into a ponytail and she wore no makeup. With a pair of sunglasses to shield her eyes from the sun that made her head pound, she could be anyone and no one.

Connor stopped in front of the array of pain relievers. "Do you have any drug allergies?"

She couldn't even believe he thought to ask. Was there anything he didn't think of? She shook her head in response.

Nodding, he selected the box marked "tension headache," then touched her arm and herded her toward the checkout.

"I can't figure you out," she said a few minutes later when they'd gotten back into the car.

He opened the box, shook out two pills, then handed her a bottle of water he'd also bought at the checkout. "What can't you figure out? I'm a pretty straightforward guy. We aren't hard to learn. Women, on the other hand . . ."

"Oh no, you're anything but simple. One minute you act like I'm below pond scum, and the next minute you're nice to me."

"I didn't think you wanted me to like you."

Okay, he had her there. Or so she thought. Did she want him to like her? It was obvious she did from the ridiculous way she acted around him. She hadn't been this aware of her actions and how they were perceived by others in years. Not since her last stint as a ward of the state where she finally learned that she was just another case number in an unending stack of paperwork.

Not giving a damn was freeing. If it didn't matter whom you hurt or whom you offended, then you never felt bad when you did so.

"I didn't say I wanted you to like me," she said carefully. "Just that you do and then you don't. Thank you for the headache medicine. It was thoughtful of you."

Connor shrugged. "It was obvious you were hurting and you didn't have to be. You need to learn to take better care of yourself."

She frowned at that assertion but let it go. "So where is it we're going exactly?"

"To my sister and brother-in-law's house. They're having everyone over for beer and barbecue. It's practically the law down here that you have at least one a week."

"Life in the South, huh."

She couldn't help the disdain or the way her lip curled. She tried to hold it back. Really, she did.

He lifted a brow as they stopped for a light. "You have a bit of a drawl. Bet you were born south of the Mason-Dixon."

She looked at him, aghast. No one had ever commented on an accent. She'd worked damn hard to remove any instance of it in her speech.

"I do not have a drawl!"

He nodded. "Yeah, you do. It's subtle, but it's there. More of a lazy lilt to your words than a distinct accent. You definitely have the flavor of the South, though."

She was utterly appalled. Her stomach churned and her head throbbed painfully. "Where do you think I'm from?" she croaked.

"Oh, I dunno. Like I said, it's just a hint. You don't have to look quite so disgusted. We're not all backwoods hicks, you know."

She could still hear the drawn-out, slow drawl in her nightmares. Whispered in her ear. It made her physically ill. For some people, a Southern drawl was like brown sugar. For her it was like nails on a chalkboard.

"Hey, no reason to get uptight. It was just an observation. I'm wrong once or twice a year."

She tried to smile at his joke but her face felt too tight. She decided a change in subject was the best course before she did or said something to make an even bigger ass of herself.

"So all your friends are married?"

"Micah's not. Not for lack of trying. Angelina is pregnant, and he'd like to get her to the altar before she pops the kid out."

"Good for her," Lyric said. "Just because a guy gets you pregnant doesn't mean he's the right guy to marry."

"Apparently he was right to sleep with," Connor said dryly. "And it's not like a guy gets a girl pregnant by himself. There's definitely some cooperation on the egg's part."

"Oh huh-uh. The boy sperm chases down the girl egg and throws himself on her."

"More like the girl egg crooks her finger and then when the poor unsuspecting sperm comes near, she sucks him in."

Lyric wrinkled her nose. "I think this is perhaps the most unromantic reproduction talk I've ever had."

Connor chuckled. "Micah loves Angelina, and she loves him. They'll get married. She just wants to make sure it's what he wants."

They pulled into a neighborhood that had all the hallmarks of middle-class suburbia. The entrance was manicured and mowed, trimmed to the nth degree. All the lawns looked like showcases.

The houses were cute cookie-cutters and it was like a scene from Currier and Ives with children playing in an idyllic setting. She'd never been to a scarier place in her life.

"Good God, it's a Stepford neighborhood," she muttered.

Connor snorted and pulled into a driveway at the end of a cul-de-sac. Lyric's brow went up as she viewed the Welcome sign just off the walkway to the front door. She burst out laughing and got out.

"Your sister and brother-in-law can't be all bad," Lyric said as Connor motioned her to go in front of him.

There in the middle of a neighborhood filled with houses without so much as a grass blade out of place was a house with a sign that read: Beer served here daily.

"I'm impressed. The grass looks like it's gone a week without cutting," Lyric said with a grin.

Connor rang the doorbell and laughed. "Yeah, it's Gray's way of rebelling against the Homeowners' Association. It pisses him off that they presume to tell him what to do with his house and lawn, so he waits until he says the neighborhood watchdog starts twitching and foaming at the mouth before he mows the lawn."

"I think I'm going to like your friends," she said just as the door opened.

"Well, I hope so," Gray Montgomery said. He gestured at Connor. "You can't judge us by this knucklehead."

Again Lyric was struck by how out of her element she felt. And how intimidated she was by these people. Average, everyday, normal people. It didn't compute. She should have all these good ole boys kissing her ass just like the rest of the country.

She winced even as the belligerent thought crossed her mind. It was a natural reaction, one she had to fight with increasing regularity. *When threatened, lash out. Cover up. Never let them see you at a disadvantage.*

"Would you like to come in?" Gray asked.

It was then she realized Connor had already stepped inside the house and she was still on the doorstep gawking like a moron.

"Yeah, thanks," she said lamely.

She followed the men inside the house and heard distant laughter. Her palms went damp and she rubbed them down her jeans when they entered the living room.

She recognized Faith, and she remembered Nathan Tucker and Micah Hudson from her meeting at Malone's. Sitting on Micah's lap with Micah's hand splayed possessively across her swollen belly had to be Angelina.

Micah was more her usual speed with his floppy hair that hung to his shoulders and the earring glinting in his ear. Nathan Tucker was just downright yummy, though, with his bald head, earring and total badass body. If the woman sitting next to him didn't look like she could kick Lyric's and Connor's asses both, she'd allow herself to drool over the man.

"Hi, Lyric!" Faith called out. "I'm so glad you came."

The blond woman walked over and took Lyric's hand before Lyric could draw away. She tugged Lyric forward until she stood in front of the other two women.

"Guys, this is Lyric Jones. Superstar pop singer Lyric Jones, just in case you've been living on another planet."

Lyric had certainly been introduced in more glowing terms than that, but for some reason the implied praise in Faith's voice discomfited her.

"Lyric, these are two of my best friends, Julie Tucker and Angelina Moyano. I'm just sorry Serena isn't here to meet you. She and her husband, Damon, are fans. They caught one of your shows in Vegas."

Lyric smiled and fidgeted under the other women's scrutiny.

"Nice to meet you," she offered.

"Hi, Lyric," Angelina said with a sweet smile. "I'd get up but it would require a forklift."

Julie snorted and rose from her perch beside Nathan, though Nathan's hand lingered on her hip. She stuck out her hand. "I'm Julie. It's nice to meet you, Lyric."

Lyric shook her hand and smiled again. Now came the awkward part where either uncomfortable silence fell or they made inane small talk about nothing. She hated both options.

To her surprise, Connor came to her rescue. He touched her arm and motioned her back toward Faith while Julie took her seat next to her husband.

"Connor said you haven't eaten today, Lyric," Faith said. Her brow creased with concern. "He also said you have a headache. I wanted to ask you what you'd like to eat. Connor wasn't sure you liked barbecue. Are you a vegetarian? I can make you a salad."

Lyric threw a puzzled look in Connor's direction. It was really nice that he'd noticed the fact she hadn't eaten and that he'd spoken to his sister about her potential likes or dislikes, but where had she gotten the idea that Lyric was a vegetarian?

"No, I'm not a vegetarian. And barbecue is fine. Really."

"Faith, you dork," Julie said. "Just because she's a celebrity doesn't mean she eats tofu and bean sprouts."

Faith's cheeks reddened but guilt flashed in her eyes. Lyric laughed. She couldn't help it. Of all the assumptions made about her, this was by far the tamest one yet. She wanted to hug Faith.

"You're very sweet to think of me," Lyric said sincerely. "But to be honest, I'm a huge carnivore. I don't eat vegetables. I think I'm still rebelling against my childhood when I was told to eat my veggies or go to bed without eating. More often than not, I snuck crackers and cheese after everyone went to bed."

Julie grinned. "My kind of woman."

Faith hooked her arm through Lyric's and pulled her toward the kitchen. "Then how about a little snack before dinner? Gray just fired up the grill before you and Connor got here, so it'll be a while yet before the meat is done."

"Snack?" Lyric asked hopefully. "It's not carrots or celery sticks, is it?"

Faith's eyes twinkled and her smile broadened. "No, I made cupcakes."

Lyric decided she was really a lesbian and immediately plotted to steal Faith away from Gray. She loved anyone who offered her a cupcake.

"I'd love one," Lyric said with a little too much excitement.

The two women entered the spacious kitchen and Lyric caught her breath. It sounded silly, but this was the first time she'd been in an actual home in a long time. The kitchen was cheerful and warm and it reminded Lyric of long-ago moments with her own mother.

"I have strawberry with cream cheese frosting, or vanilla with chocolate frosting," Faith said.

Lyric hesitated and stared at the perfectly iced cupcakes on the platter in the center of the island.

"Or you could have one of each," Faith offered.

"Sold!"

Faith laughed and handed over two of the cupcakes.

Lyric bit into the strawberry cupcake first and sighed. It had been a long time since something so simple as a cupcake made her happy, but at the moment she couldn't imagine anything better.

"Would you like something for your headache? I have ibuprofen and Tylenol."

Lyric licked frosting from her lip and shook her head. "Connor took good care of me. He bought some Excedrin."

"I'm glad," Faith said softly, "that he's taking good care of you. Connor . . . He can be difficult."

Lyric cracked up. She couldn't help it. Faith gave her a bewildered look and Lyric set the chocolate cupcake down on the island.

"Most people would say I'm the difficult one. You know, spoiled pop star diva? I'm sure it's all been said more than once."

Faith frowned. "We women have to stick together. Never admit you're more trouble than a man even if it's the truth. It's better if they get it in their heads early that they are the source of all angst in this world."

Lyric smudged her finger over the top of the cupcake and sucked the frosting from the tip. "I think you are a very wise woman, Faith. I had you pegged as a total Susie Sunshine, and when I saw your neighborhood I figured you for a Stepford wife. I'm relieved that I was wrong on all counts."

"Hmmm. Susie Sunshine. That's a new one. I'll have to remember it for when Gray starts complaining that I'm mean."

Lyric grinned.

"I want one of those cupcakes!"

Lyric turned to see Angelina enter the kitchen, her gaze fixed on the cupcake in Lyric's hand like she was about to attack.

"You can't have it," Faith said in exasperation. "Micah would kill me."

"He doesn't have to know," Angelina said pointedly.

"Don't you give her one," Faith said when Lyric started to hand a cupcake to Angelina. "She has to watch her blood sugar. She failed her first glucose tolerance test and they want to do a repeat. Until they get the results, she has to watch her sugar intake."

"Wow, I take back what I said about you being nice," Lyric said. "That's pretty ruthless. Withholding sugar from a pregnant woman."

"I'll take that," Julie said as she walked by and lifted the cupcake from Lyric's hand.

Lyric shot her a dark look. "I've killed people for less."

Julie's eyebrow shot up. "And you people call me vicious. If she keeps that up, I'll have to tell Connor to collar her."

"Only if you want it wrapped around your mouth," Lyric drawled.

"Did you all desert the guys?" Faith asked as she frowned at Julie.

"Oh, they're out bonding over charcoal," Angelina said with a wave of her hand. "You know what happens when you mix men, lighter fluid, a grill and beer."

"Sit," Faith directed Angelina. "I swear I don't know how you stand. You're all belly. It seems like you'd teeter over."

Angelina scowled at Faith but hoisted herself up onto a bar stool. Julie took a seat across the bar from Angelina and arched an eyebrow in her direction.

"Okay, so give us the scoop, Angelina. When are you going to put Micah out of his misery?"

Faith shook her head. "It's like déjà vu. We had this same conversation with Serena before she married Damon."

Lyric shifted from one foot to the other. As if sensing Lyric's discomfort, Faith turned to explain.

"Serena is our other best friend and she made Damon wait before she agreed to marry him."

"Yes, but she waited because *she* wasn't sure," Angelina softly interjected. "That's not the case here. I'd marry Micah tomorrow, but I have to be sure this is what *he* wants. I won't be second best. I won't have him marry me because he feels it's the right thing to do."

Faith moved beside Angelina and wrapped an arm around her. "He loves you, honey. He loves you and Nia so much. You're all he talks about at work. The guys avoid him because he drives them crazy asking them baby stuff they don't have a clue about."

"That's sweet," Lyric murmured.

Angelina sighed. "He's great. Really, he is. He's been so wonderful with me and the baby. I'm crazy about him and I don't want to be without him."

"Then why are you driving yourself crazy?" Faith asked gently.

Angelina chewed on her lip, her dark eyes shadowed by worry. "I have this fear that he'll wake up one day and think to himself that I'm not the one he wanted. That he's trapped. That I pressured him into a relationship he didn't want. You have to admit, I pursued him relentlessly."

Lyric raised an eyebrow. Her opinion of the other woman just went up by several notches. She liked a woman who knew her mind and didn't sit around waiting for what she wanted.

"It's all about taking a chance," Julie said. "I've thought the same thing about Nathan more times than I care to admit. I used to worry that he'd get tired of me and move on. But he convinced me to give him a chance, and really, there aren't any guarantees. Men do stupid shit all the time. There's a trigger when they hit middle age that they want dumber, younger and prettier."

"Oh Jesus, Julie." Faith groaned. "You're not helping here."

Julie shrugged. "Just telling the truth. The point is, you have to take a chance and you have to not only love your guy but you have to trust that he loves you just as much. What else can you do?"

"When you put it like that," Angelina said ruefully.

Faith squeezed Angelina again. "You almost make me want to give you a cupcake."

Lyric laughed at the disgusted look on Angelina's face.

"I hope we haven't bored you, Lyric," Faith said anxiously. "I'm sure you're used to a livelier party."

Lyric held up her hand. "Don't, please. This is great. Really. It was really nice of you to have me. I know you weren't expecting us."

Faith reached over and impulsively squeezed Lyric's hand. "I'm so glad you came. It's so interesting to see the woman behind all the gossip and realize you're nothing like everyone says you are."

Horror crawled across Faith's face as soon as the words were out. She clapped a hand over her mouth. "Oh, that was stupid. I didn't mean . . ."

"It's all right," Lyric said lightly. "Don't apologize. Half of what they say is likely true and the other half is probably a variation of the truth."

Julie's eyebrows went up. "So you really had an orgy on your tour bus?"

Lyric hadn't heard that one. "Sure, why not. I'm sure it's written in the rule book somewhere that all rock stars have at least one on the bus per tour."

She kept the hurt from her voice and wondered what demon possessed her to perpetuate the rumors. She figured if people were dumb enough to believe that crap, they didn't deserve the truth. They probably wouldn't believe it anyway.

"I totally made that up," Julie said darkly.

Lyric shrugged. "You aren't the first."

Faith frowned. "That must be an awful way to live, Lyric. How do you stand it?"

What to say to that? She could leave her life at any time, but it wasn't like a new life awaited her. Maybe one day she'd figure out what to do beyond her singing career, but the thing was, she loved to sing. She even liked the fame, the hoopla, the fans and the crowds. She wouldn't apologize for that as many celebrities felt compelled to do. She'd worked damn hard to get to where she was and she wasn't about to piss it away over false guilt.

"I like it. It pays well," Lyric cracked.

She hated the sympathy shining in all their eyes. It was like they looked at her and thought, *Oh, you poor thing.* Whatever. There were millions of people who had it far worse than she did. What were a few rumors and a bad reputation next to starving in some shithole in Mississippi?

The people she grew up with were probably still there, dirt-poor in the same pissant town, married to the same shitty people and raising the same shitty kids.

"Julie, would you go out and ask the menfolk how much longer on the meat? I need to make the salad and bread," Faith said, breaking the silence.

"I'll go. I can't sit in one spot for too long. Makes me crazy," Angelina muttered. "My back is killing me."

As soon as Angelina had left the kitchen, Julie leaned forward with a wicked grin and whispered, "I keep telling her she's really having twins and that they missed one of the babies when they did the sonogram."

Faith shook her head and laughed. "You are so evil, Julie."

CHAPTER 7

$\mathcal{M}$ ale voices drifted through the screen as Angelina approached the door leading into the backyard. She paused for a moment to rub at her aching back. Micah was so sweet and attentive. If he knew her back was giving her problems, he'd be rubbing it. She was tempted to drop a hint because right now she'd give anything to have his hands soothing away the discomfort.

She was just about to go out when she heard her name. Then she smiled when she heard the guys give Micah a hard time about impending fatherhood. No matter what she may have thought in the beginning, Micah had embraced the idea of being a father with both hands.

He fussed endlessly over her. He went to every doctor's appointment and drove her crazy with innocuous pregnancy trivia, some of which she was convinced he made up.

She went still when she heard Micah's determined voice rise above the sounds of the neighborhood and distant lawn mowers.

"I want her to marry me, but I'm at a loss as to how to convince her that I'm not doing it out of obligation. I know she worries that she's somehow trapping me into a relationship I don't want, and it's making me crazy."

"Maybe you're putting too much stock into marriage," Connor said. "Angelina's a great girl. If she loves you and stays with you, does it really matter if it's official or not?"

Angelina could visualize Micah's scowl perfectly.

"It's not the marriage thing. It's that she still has doubt. Not that I blame her, but I don't like to think of her worrying that I'm not dedicated to her and Nia. They're my life."

"Maybe you should back off for a while," Nathan said carefully. "She's pregnant and vulnerable. From what I hear, their emotions are a mess when they're pregnant. Maybe she feels pressured."

Micah sighed. "Maybe you're right. I don't know. I'm pissed at myself for not seeing it sooner. I don't deserve her after the way I acted. I love her, and more than that I don't want her to ever think I don't, that she's not the most important thing in my life."

"You can't force trust," Gray said. "It'll come. The more she sees that you're in it for the long haul, the more she'll trust in the truth of your relationship."

Angelina lifted trembling fingers to her mouth. Trust? Trust had never been an issue for her with Micah. She trusted him implicitly. There was no way she could cede absolute and total control in their relationship to him if she didn't trust him.

The idea that she'd hurt him by making him think she didn't trust him was painful. She loved Micah and it was for him that she'd hesitated in accepting his marriage proposal.

Now she wondered if she wasn't doing more damage to the future of their relationship by holding back. If he ever doubted her love, it would kill her. It was the one thing she'd always given him unreservedly.

Micah was her future. She knew it without a doubt. She rubbed her hand over her protruding belly. Micah loved her. He loved their daughter. He wanted them to be a family. Micah had always wanted a family. Right now *she* was the one standing in the way of his happiness.

How stupid and shortsighted she'd been. She didn't regret not relenting right away. She and Micah had desperately needed time to work out their issues and to find their way amid the tumultuous beginning to their relationship.

But for the last few months, Micah had done and said all the right things. He'd once told her that when she knew without a doubt that he loved her more than life and when she trusted him fully to cherish her gift of love, that was when he wanted her to marry him.

"Oh God," she whispered. How must her continued resistance look to him? Like she didn't trust him. That she didn't believe he loved her.

None of that was true.

Suddenly she wanted to nothing more than to go home and spend the evening in Micah's arms. His hand on her belly and them talking about Nia and their future. Tears stung her eyes. Micah had said when that day came. It was here and she didn't want to wait any longer.

"I think Angelina must have gotten lost," Faith said with a sigh.

"Either that or she made another trip to the bathroom," Julie said. "Another reason I have no desire to get knocked up in this millennium. I can't imagine spending that much time in the bathroom."

Lyric raised her brow. It was nice to know she wasn't the only one with no desire to pop out a kid anytime soon. Or ever.

"I'll go see what's keeping her," Lyric said.

Faith nodded. "Thanks, Lyric. I'm going to start on the salad and pop the bread into the oven."

Lyric was relieved to escape the kitchen. It wasn't that she found the other women annoying, but she was ill at ease around the warm friendship between them. Lyric had no experience with closeness. She'd never allowed herself to have that sort of relationship with anyone. Physical, yes. Emotional, no. And she had plenty of business relationships. Nothing that qualified as an actual friendship.

When she entered the living room, she saw Angelina standing near the door to the backyard, a peculiar expression on her face. Both hands were palmed over her belly and she looked like . . . She looked like she was upset over something.

It was tempting to turn back and pretend she hadn't seen the other woman. Lyric had zero experience with emotional, pregnant women. What did you say to one?

It wouldn't kill her to be sympathetic. Everyone had been nice to her. Other than Julie's snottiness—which, she was realizing, was part of the woman's natural charm—they'd all treated her like she was normal. To her surprise, she liked it. She liked it a lot. Not that she wanted to start leading a normal life, but it was a nice change.

She took a few steps forward and delicately cleared her throat. Angelina's head whipped up and she didn't look thrilled that Lyric had found her. That made two of them.

"Are you okay?" Lyric asked gently. "Do you want me to get Micah?"

Angelina's lips quivered and she inhaled sharply, like she was tightly controlling her emotions. Then she let out a soft laugh, and her lips turned up into a rueful smile.

"Have you ever come to the realization that you're an idiot and that what you thought was the right thing was completely wrong?"

Lyric snorted. She couldn't help it. "Honey, you're talking to the queen of fuckups. If there's a way to screw something up, I've mastered it."

Angelina cocked her head. "You seem so well put together. I've watched you, you know. The few TV specials you've had and I saw a recording of one of your concerts. You seem so confident and sexy and smart."

Lyric blinked. "Wow. Thanks, I think. But wow. You couldn't be more wrong. Not that I want to go into all the ways you're wrong, but I'm glad it at least looks like I have my shit together."

"I'm an idiot," Angelina said again. "A pregnant, hormonal moron. I've spent so much time worrying that Micah would want to walk that it's a wonder I haven't made him do just that."

"Nothing wrong with being sure," Lyric said with a shrug. "I admire you for that. A lot of women don't look before they leap."

The door opened and Angelina whirled around, a guilty look on her face. Relief lightened her eyes when Connor walked in.

"Hey, sweetie," Connor said as he pulled Angelina into a hug.

Sweetie? Lyric cocked her eyebrow at the endearment and the obvious affection in Connor's voice. He was such a grumpy hard-ass, it was difficult to imagine him being so cutesy with another woman. Her eyes narrowed. A pregnant woman who was involved with another man.

When Angelina pulled away, Connor frowned as he stared down at her. "You okay? You look upset." He glanced over at Lyric and her eyes widened at the accusation in his. Did he honestly think she was responsible for Angelina's crying jag?

Angelina smiled. "I'm fine. You can stop fussing over me. Lyric made me feel much better. I think I'm going to go out and let Micah take over."

Connor glanced up, fleeting apology in his gaze, but Lyric shot daggers back at him with hers. As Angelina walked out the door, Lyric shook her head and turned on her heel to stalk back to the kitchen.

Connor caught her wrist before she took two steps and pulled her back around to face him.

"Let me go," she hissed.

"I'm sorry."

It was a sincere apology, but hurt still crowded her chest. "I don't even know why you brought me, Connor. It's obvious you think I'll be an asshole to your precious friends. They seem to like me, which is more than I can say for you. They've also been nice to me, which again—"

He pulled her against his chest and sealed his lips over hers, effectively halting her angry tirade. "Shut up. Just shut up," he growled.

She went stock-still against him as he plundered her mouth. There was nothing gentle or tentative about his kiss. His lips scorched over hers, stealing her breath and returning it as his tongue probed and explored the inside of her mouth.

It should piss her off. She should be shoving him on his ass. She should be doing a lot of things, but what she did was kiss him back. She was tentative, and the truth was she wasn't entirely sure what to do, but his taste intoxicated her and made her dizzy.

A whisper of charcoal danced through her nostrils and it blended with his natural masculine scent until she wanted to lick him to see if his skin tasted as good as he smelled.

She'd been kissed before many times but never like this. Most men were intimidated by her and it showed in how they touched her. Connor took charge and it was clear he had plenty of self-confidence.

He cupped her face, his fingers splaying over the sides of her neck. They pressed possessively into her flesh, branding her.

Shivers danced along her spine as his tongue rubbed sensuously over hers, stroking and coaxing until she responded in kind. Her response was automatic. She didn't have to think about whether she wanted to kiss him or whether she wanted him to continue kissing her. It wasn't like she had a choice. She was a helpless prisoner to his overwhelming power.

When he finally let her go, she staggered back, her lips swollen. She raised a shaky hand to her tingling mouth and stared wordlessly at him, unable to comprehend that he'd just kissed the daylights out of her. He hated her!

He closed the distance again, regret in his eyes. He touched her shoulder, a light gesture meant to reassure her.

"I'm sorry. I was an ass."

She shook her head to rid herself of the lingering effects of his wicked mouth.

"Not for kissing you," he amended. "I'm sorry for being an asshole, but not for kissing you."

"Why did you?" she asked faintly. "You don't even like me."

"You drive me insane. I look at you and you make me instantly crazy."

Her eyes narrowed and some of the euphoria evaporated. "The feeling is quite mutual."

His grin was cocky and arrogant and it was so damn sexy she wanted to march back over there and finish what they'd started.

"Every time you get all pissy and mean, I get a hard-on from hell. I wonder if you have any idea how sexy you are when you turn that nose up and start throwing attitude."

Her mouth fell open. It closed and then opened again like a fish out of water. Then she glared. "You're full of shit. You're just saying that so I'll be nice to you from now on."

His laughter rang out. "Well, I suppose that's one way to get you to stop being a bitch."

She crossed her arms, prepared to give him the look of death when she realized what the result would be. Instead she threw up her hands and stomped back toward the kitchen.

"That goes double for tantrums," he called after her.

CHAPTER 8

"*I* wonder if any of you are free tomorrow morning. I need someone to look out for Lyric while I meet with the security firm her record
label has hired," Connor said over the dinner table.

In the process of raising her fork to her mouth, Lyric dropped it
onto her plate with a clatter, and she stared mortified across the table
at Connor.

"What was all that about where you go, I go, and vice versa?" she
demanded. "For God's sake, I don't need babysitters."

"The team providing peripheral security and I will be deciding
what needs to be done to ensure your safety," Connor said evenly.
"You'll just interfere and argue. We can get it done a lot quicker if you
aren't there."

She stared at him in disbelief. She'd been accommodating so far.
She'd conceded on goddamn everything. What else did he want from
her? A note signed in blood avowing her compliance?

She itched to bolt from her chair and get the hell out of there, but he'd expect that. He watched her even now as if waiting for her to throw a fit.

She decided to ignore him instead.

She lowered her gaze and stabbed at the meat with her fork. She tuned out what the others were saying. She didn't give a shit about these people. Or Connor fucking Malone. Every time she thought it wouldn't be so bad to be tethered to him for the next two weeks, he had to remind her what a huge asshole he was.

To her absolute mortification, tears stung her eyelids. Hell would freeze over before she'd ever let him see her cry.

Damn it, she'd tried her best to work with him. She knew she could be difficult and usually she didn't give a flying fuck, but she'd honestly tried with him and his friends. She'd done everything humanly possible to tone it down because secretly she'd wanted his approval.

Fuck that and him. She didn't need anyone's goddamn approval. Only her own.

"You are such an asshole, Connor."

For a moment Lyric thought she'd totally lost control of her tongue and aired her thoughts. But when she looked up, she saw Faith glaring holes in her brother.

Connor raised an eyebrow at his sister.

Even "sweetie" looked at Connor like he'd lost his mind.

"It's not like you to be such a jerk," Faith continued. "Lyric doesn't deserve that from you."

"Maybe we don't have the full story," Gray said in a diplomatic voice.

Faith glared at her husband. Then she turned to Lyric, who had her teeth sunk firmly into her bottom lip so she didn't humiliate herself further by showing how affected she was by Connor's attitude.

"You'll come with me, Julie and Angelina to Serena's house tomorrow. The men can all go find something else to do."

Connor held up his hand. "Now wait a damn minute. No one's going anywhere with Lyric. What part of her being in danger don't you understand? I'm not risking any of you girls by sending you off together on some girls' day out."

"Damn right," Nathan said with a scowl.

Lyric rose as gracefully as she could under the circumstances. She smiled in Faith's direction. "Thank you for dinner and your hospitality. I had a really good time. But I should be going now. I appreciate the offer, but Connor's right. None of you should be around me. In addition to having some crazy person lurking after me, apparently I'm a toxic influence."

"Sit down, Lyric," Connor ordered.

"Fuck off, Connor."

She turned and stalked away from the table.

Connor watched her leave but didn't go after her. She couldn't get far without the car keys. She needed some time to cool off and he'd just do something stupid again. Like kiss her senseless.

"Nice," Micah drawled. "And you once accused me of being an SOB."

"She's driving me crazy," Connor muttered.

"It's not her you have to worry about right now," Gray said carefully.

Connor looked up to see three very pissed-off women glaring holes through his forehead.

"What was all that crap?" Angelina demanded. "This isn't like you, Connor. You've always been so . . . sweet. And protective."

Connor winced. She made him sound like a pussy.

"She didn't seem that bad to me," Julie said with a shrug. "And you were a jerk even if you didn't mean to sound like one."

"There's no reason she can't come to Serena's tomorrow," Faith said as she frowned at Connor. "Damon has tight security. No one is going to get onto his property without him knowing about it. And he has Sam."

"Who the hell is Sam?" Connor grumbled.

"His mountain of a driver slash bodyguard," Micah said dryly. "He has great affection for our women. He's like a mother hen with them. The one time they didn't let him go with him, Damon said he had a kitten."

Connor frowned. "You think Lyric would be safe there? This is serious. I can't just leave her anywhere, but if I take her with me, she's going to balk at the constraints we're going to put on her. I know you all think I'm being a jerk, but the truth is, I'm going to do whatever is necessary to keep her safe, whether she likes the measures or not."

"I can go with them," Micah said. "I'll call Damon tonight and let him know the situation."

Connor's frown deepened. Yeah, he needed a place to stash Lyric so he could get her security straightened out. What he hadn't mentioned was that if he didn't get a good feel for this team her record label had hired, he was going to tell them to take a hike.

"You need to go find her and apologize," Faith sniffed. "If I were her, I wouldn't go anywhere with you."

"She doesn't have a choice."

"Why are you so mean to her?" Julie asked.

Connor sighed. "I'm not mean to her, Julie. I just don't kiss her ass like everyone else in her universe does."

"I like her," Angelina said. "She's refreshingly honest."

"You like everyone, sweetie," Connor said with a grin.

"I don't like you right now," she said pointedly.

He winced. "Oh ouch. Damn. That hurt. Okay, okay, I'll ease up. I'll even apologize. The last thing I want is to fall into you girls' bad graces."

"Smart man," Nathan murmured.

"You go find her and tell her she's coming with us tomorrow," Faith said. "Damon will take care of things. He always does."

That earned her a glare from every man at the table.

"Well, he does," she said defensively.

"It's not a good idea to remind me of all he's done for you," Gray said mildly.

Faith blushed and Connor promptly tuned them out. He was pretty tired of hearing about Damon Roche himself. Him and his damn sex club or whatever the fuck he called it.

"You're not taking her to his damn club, are you?" Connor demanded.

Faith turned bright red. "Good God, no! We're going to his house. Not The House."

"I don't know," Julie said thoughtfully. "Lyric might enjoy a night at The House."

"Julie," Nathan growled. "You aren't setting foot in that place ever again."

Julie grinned cheekily.

"What are you waiting for?" Faith asked. "Go, go, go. Shoo already."

Connor sighed and got to his feet. Women were a plague. There was no doubt about it. He had his share of crazy ex-girlfriends, but they had nothing on the women currently in his life. He loved them all dearly, but he didn't envy their men one iota.

He should have known that Lyric would fit in beautifully.

He stalked through the house, annoyed that everyone had turned on him. He never wanted this pain-in-the-ass job in the first place.

She was probably out in the car pouting. He'd have to go out and be nice. She'd probably pop off at him and his dick would stand up and pay attention. Then he'd start having fantasies about kissing her again.

He really had to do something about this masochistic streak. It seemed the more she got mad at him, the more he wanted her. She was a beautiful woman, but never more than she was spitting fury at him like a pissed-off kitten.

He grinned as he opened the door and stepped out into the night. When he looked in the direction of where he'd parked the BMW, his jaw dropped.

It wasn't there.

He glanced down the street to see the taillights of the car fading as it roared through the neighborhood.

He dug into his pocket and pulled out the keys. What the fuck? She'd hot-wired the car?

He closed his eyes and shook his head. Then he trudged back into the house to face the others.

"I need a ride back to the hotel," he said before they could say anything to him.

Everyone looked up from the table, all wearing puzzled looks.

"Something wrong with the car?" Micah asked.

"Yeah," Connor muttered. "She hot-wired it and took off."

Julie burst out laughing. One by one the others followed suit until the entire room erupted in hoots.

"It was stupid," Connor growled. "She has some crazy stalker leaving her creepy notes and she takes off alone. This is why I don't want her at my meeting tomorrow. She's high-strung and unreasonable. And she doesn't have one ounce of self-preservation."

Micah stood and reached down to help Angelina to her feet. "We'll run you by. We were going to call it an early night anyway."

Connor would have liked to have called it a night, but he had a feeling he was going to be up for a long time. When he got to the hotel, he and Lyric were going to have a come-to-Jesus meeting. And he was as hard as a rock just thinking about it.

CHAPTER 9

*D*espite the fact she'd just hot-wired a car and ditched her only "security," Lyric wasn't an idiot, no matter what Connor Malone might think. She had no desire to be kidnapped or murdered by some psycho. She liked her life, thank you very much, even if she gave new meaning to the word *dysfunctional.*

Amazing, the words you learned from therapy.

She kept her eyes peeled, particularly to her rearview mirror to make sure no one was tailing her. She also kept a sharp eye out for a cop. Because what moron would try anything if she had a cop escort her to her hotel?

She uttered a triumphant "Aha!" when she saw a patrol car parked at a gas station. She whipped in and parked directly in front of him, just in case he had any ideas about driving off before she could get her story across.

He didn't look happy with her parking choice and before she

could get out of her car, he was already out of his and walking her way, a frown on his face.

What was it with men and being so damn grumpy?

She got out of her car as he approached.

"Is there a problem, ma'am?"

"Yes. You see, I have this crazy person stalking me and I had to hot-wire my BMW because the guy who's supposed to be my security was being a dick and he has the keys, but I don't want to be driving around by myself or go back to my hotel room in case the crazy stalker is waiting to kidnap me or make me his sex slave or whatever it is that crazy stalkers do. So I'd really appreciate it if you could follow me back to my hotel."

His brows drew together and she could swear he muttered "Why me?" under his breath. Then he sighed and started to reach for his radio. He had that look that suggested he thought *she* was the crazy one.

"How much have you had to drink tonight, ma'am?" he asked politely.

This time she frowned. "I don't drink."

"Have you taken any drugs I should know about?"

"I'm not a crackhead."

"Who does the vehicle belong to?"

"It belongs to me! Oh wait— Well, it sort of belongs to me. I rented it because I flew here. I mean, I have one just like it but I didn't want to drive it all the way from California when I'm just doing one show here."

"Uh-huh."

He nodded and raised the mic on his radio and proceeded to tell someone that he had a 10-96 and he was requesting backup.

She crossed her arms over her chest. "Look, all I need is someone to follow me to the hotel. And well, I'd really appreciate it if you could walk me in but I could always have hotel security do that if you're too busy."

"I have a better idea. Why don't you take a ride with me?"

She shrugged. "I'd rather not leave the BMW, but I suppose I could make Connor come get it tomorrow."

"Who's Connor?"

"He's the guy who's supposed to be protecting me but was being a dick so I ditched him."

The cop gripped her elbow and herded her toward his squad car. "Turn around," he directed. "This is for your protection as well as mine. You aren't being arrested. I'm detaining you for further questioning."

Before she realized what was going on, he had her handcuffed and was stuffing her into the backseat of his car. Damn, but the man was good.

But he'd handcuffed her! She stared at him in outrage. "What the hell did you cuff me for?"

He shut the door and then proceeded to talk on his radio. A few seconds later, he opened his door and slid into the driver's seat.

Realization hit her. "You're the crazy stalker, aren't you? You're not even a real cop. Have you been following me?"

He eyed her in the rearview mirror as he pulled away. "Lady, you came to me."

"Oh. Yeah."

Okay, so he wasn't the crazy guy. Which meant he thought *she* was crazy. She flopped her head back against the seat and stared upward. Helpless laughter escaped. Oh well, at least she was safe!

While it irritated Connor to leave immediately because he didn't want Lyric to think she had him on a leash, he was being paid to protect her, which meant he had to go chasing after her when she pulled a stupid stunt.

Hot-wiring a rental and taking off on her own qualified.

He leaned against the hood of Micah's truck and waited impatiently as Angelina was fussed over by Faith and Julie. Micah walked out ahead of Angelina and stood beside Connor.

"You realize I've waited a long time for this," Micah said casually.

Connor raised an eyebrow. "Do I even want to know what you're talking about?"

Micah chuckled. "Being able to give you shit over a woman."

Connor scowled. "You say that like this situation can be compared to yours or Nathan's. Lyric is a job."

"Uh-huh. She's a beautiful woman."

"And? That matters why?"

Micah shrugged. "Just an observation. She's beautiful and brassy. A little unconventional."

"A little?"

"I'd say she's perfect for you," Micah said with a shit-eating grin.

Connor held up his middle finger. "Just remember. I didn't want this job. I thought it would be perfect for you, but Pop threw a fit because he said Angelina wouldn't like it. Same for Nathan and Gray because their women wouldn't be happy." He snorted. "So I get stuck with a woman who drives me crazy so it doesn't interfere with your love life."

Micah's grin broadened. "I appreciate that."

Angelina hurried up. "Sorry. I didn't mean to take so long. I know you have to go, Connor."

Micah pulled her up against him and kissed the top of her head. "Yes, by all means. He's chomping at the bit to get back, so let's get on the road."

"Fuck you," Connor grumbled as he climbed into the extended cab.

It was a good bit out of the way for Micah to drive Connor to the downtown hotel, and Connor fumed the entire way. They were just a few blocks from the hotel when Connor's cell phone rang.

He fished it out of his pocket and frowned when he looked at the number. It wasn't in his contact list but the number was a local one.

"Connor Malone," he said shortly.

"Mr. Malone, this is Sergeant Willis with the Houston Police Department. I believe you know a Lyric Jones?"

Connor closed his eyes and pinched the bridge of his nose between his fingers. "What's she done?" he asked wearily.

Twenty minutes later, Connor climbed out of Micah's truck in front of the police station where Lyric was being held.

"You sure you don't want us to wait?" Micah asked.

Connor shook his head. "I'll call a cab. You and Angelina go home. This could take a while."

"Okay, man. Let me know if you need anything."

Connor waved and stalked toward the entrance. At the front desk, he asked for Sergeant Willis, and the clerk jerked a thumb over his shoulder.

Connor walked through the swinging gate to the array of desks separated by thin partitions. He stopped and stared when he caught sight of Lyric sitting on top of one of the desks holding court among a half dozen policemen.

Her legs dangled and she was talking and waving her hands in animated fashion. Her cheek dimpled with a smile and her eyes twinkled. It dawned on him that she hadn't smiled much and certainly not so unreservedly.

Micah was right. She was fucking beautiful.

Her eyes dimmed when she caught sight of him and she crossed her arms over her chest as she stared past the cops. They turned and followed her gaze to where Connor stood, and he got the impression he wasn't a very popular guy right now.

He folded his arms in an imitation of hers and cast a baleful look in her direction.

One of the cops, a guy who made Connor feel small, and Connor wasn't a small guy, headed in Connor's direction, a frown etched into his face.

"You the guy who's supposed to be looking out for Lyric?"

Connor sighed and nodded. "You Sergeant Willis?"

"Yeah, I am. Lyric said you were being a dickhead so she took off. She stopped me to ask me for an escort. Said some crazy stalker is after her."

"Well, at least she had the sense to ask for help," Connor muttered

"She shouldn't be out on her own."

Connor stared the officer down. "Try telling her that."

Sergeant Willis nodded. "We did. We sat her down after we figured out who she was. We gave her a Breathalyzer. I thought she'd been drinking."

Connor chuckled. "She's a handful."

"She's nice. Not at all uppity like some of the magazines say. She gave all the boys autographs and let them take pictures with her. She even offered us tickets to the rodeo the night she's performing."

Leave it to Lyric to make conquests and make Connor look like a first-class asshole for not falling under her spell. She could be positively charming when she wanted to be.

"Can I take her home now?" Connor asked cautiously.

Sergeant Willis hesitated. "If she wants to go."

Connor scowled. "She'll go. She's been enough trouble for one day."

He stepped around the sergeant and strode to where Lyric was still sitting on the edge of the desk.

"Are you ready to go?"

Lyric frowned. "No. I don't want to go anywhere with you. You're fired. These nice officers have offered to take me back to my hotel."

Connor sighed and resisted the urge to wrap his hands in her hair and kiss her right there on the desk. The last thing he needed was to get arrested.

"You can't fire me, Lyric. We've been through this before."

Her frown grew fiercer and she glanced toward Sergeant Willis. "He can't make me do anything, right?"

Sergeant Willis shook his head. "No, ma'am, he can't. If you want him gone, say the word. You can even get a restraining order."

"Oh, for the love of God, Lyric. Be reasonable."

Her eyes narrowed. "Me be reasonable? You're the asshole here. I've been accommodating. I've done everything you asked me to. I even wore this ridiculous outfit so I wouldn't offend any of your friends. I agreed to let you stay in my hotel room. How am I the unreasonable one here?"

He arched one eyebrow. "What the hell's wrong with your clothes?"

She gave him a look of disgust. "I'm wearing jeans and a T-shirt and no makeup what so ever." She glanced up at the officers and let her lips quiver. "He humiliated me in front of his friends."

They all turned and glared at Connor. Hell. Just what he needed. A bunch of pissed-off cops with their protective instincts riled. He glared back at Lyric, not at all fooled by her acting job. Next she'd probably turn on the tears and they'd all kick his ass.

"Are they going to be able to stay with you every hour of the next two weeks?" Connor challenged. "The threat against you is for real, Lyric. I need you to take it seriously."

"I take it very seriously," she gritted out. "If you took it so damn serious, you'd work harder not to piss me off."

Okay, so she had a point. He blew out his breath and shoved his hands into his pockets. "All right, Lyric. Truce."

She stared suspiciously at him.

"It's late. You need rest. You've had a headache all day. Let's go back to the hotel so I can give you some more medicine and get you to bed."

As he'd hoped, the other cops nodded their agreement. Score one for him.

"It's a good idea, Ms. Jones," Sergeant Willis said.

She scowled at the sergeant. "I haven't forgiven you for cuffing me yet, so you don't get a vote."

"You cuffed her?" Connor demanded.

It was the sergeant's turn to look uncomfortable. "I thought she might be a little unstable." He tapped his temple as he spoke to indicate what he meant.

Lyric's mouth popped open in outrage. "Is that what ten ninety-six means?"

Sergeant Willis gave her a sheepish look. "Yes, ma'am. We don't normally use call signs, but I thought if you understood what I was saying over the radio, you might prove more difficult."

"Men," she muttered. "All assholes. I ask you for help and you think I'm psycho."

Connor held in his laughter at her disgruntled look. "Can we go now?"

"Oh, all right. I'll go with you. But if you piss me off again, I'm going to get that restraining order Sergeant Willis said I could have done."

Every single one of the policemen fished a card from his wallet and thrust it toward Lyric. All with the assurance that if she ever needed anything, she had only to call.

Lyric smiled and took each of the cards and thanked the officers for their help. Connor had to hand it to her. She knew how to work a crowd. She had every one of the cops eating out of her hand. Hell, if she kept it up, she'd have *him* eating out of her hand.

"The BMW is still at the gas station," Lyric mumbled when she got to him. "How are we getting to the hotel?"

"I'll call a cab."

"One of us will be happy to drive you back to the gas station to pick up the car," Sergeant Willis offered. "I'm assuming you have the keys this time."

Connor pulled the keys from his pocket and then turned to Lyric. "You and I have a lot to talk about, starting with how the hell you learned to hot-wire a car."

CHAPTER 10

Angelina walked into the bedroom where Micah was already lying on the bed. Propped on his elbow, he watched as she closed the bedroom door and the glitter in his eyes told her what was to come.

Her breath hitched in her throat. She never got tired of that look. It was tender and possessive. It was dark and loving. It was all the things that made her feel cherished beyond measure.

"Undress for me," he commanded in a quiet voice. "I want to see you and our baby."

She obeyed without question, her hands sliding to the buttons of her shirt. Slowly she pulled away her clothing, letting the shirt and then her pants drift to the floor until she was clad in only her panties and bra.

Then she reached behind her to undo the clasp of her bra. The straps slid over her shoulders and the cups came away, baring her breasts to his avid gaze.

They were heavier now. She'd always been a bit small, or at least she considered them small. Micah had never complained. But now she'd gained at least a cup size, and they were tender and swollen from her pregnancy.

Micah took extra care when they made love. As demanding and as dominant as he was, he was terrified of hurting her. He was no less commanding than ever, but he was exquisitely gentle now that she carried his child. She hadn't felt the kiss of a whip in months. Hadn't felt the thrill of the rougher edge of his dominance.

In time it would return. For now they delighted in a new way to make love. It was as much a discovery as the rest of their relationship, and Angelina cherished every moment.

When her underwear whispered down her legs to coil at her feet, she heard the swift intake of Micah's breath.

"Do you have any idea how beautiful you are?" he asked in a hoarse, low voice.

She raised her gaze to meet his and drowned in the warm chocolate of his eyes. They burned with so much love and desire. Her heart swelled with love. Her love for him. He was hers. She was his. They had created a child together. They had created love.

"I feel beautiful when you look at me," she said honestly.

His eyes softened. "I want you to always see how beautiful you are when you see the way I look at you. I want you to know how loved you are."

She smiled and waited quietly for his command. She loved moments like these when she awaited his pleasure, knowing he was content to just look at her.

"Come to me," he said.

She crawled onto the bed and sank to her knees as she stared down at his muscled body. So perfect and beautiful. He was dark—nearly as dark as her own skin, though he had no Hispanic heritage. His hair was dark brown, so dark it looked black.

The same dark hair coiled at the juncture of his thighs and his cock lay to the side, semierect as if awaiting her attention.

She remained still, content to wait for Micah's command.

He ran his hand up her thigh, to the curve of her waist and then higher to cup the swell of her breast. He toyed idly with one nipple, careful as always with the highly sensitive tips.

"You look tired tonight, Angel. Is your back still hurting?"

"It was earlier. I think I stood too long. It's better now."

"Come here."

He pulled her down, arranging her so she faced away. His hand glided up and down the curves of her body. He ran it over her hip and up to palm her belly. Then he lowered his head and kissed the curve of her neck.

A delicate shiver raced down her spine, spreading goose bumps in its wake.

There was a dip in the bed as his hand left her and he repositioned his body. Then he began rubbing and kneading her back, his hands working sweet magic over her tired, aching muscles.

She moaned softly as he worked slowly down to her buttocks and then back up again to massage her nape.

"Feel good?" he murmured.

Tears pricked her eyelids. It was wonderful, but every day with him was wonderful. After surviving her attack months before, she was grateful for every moment she had with Micah. She lived as if each moment could be their last together, and it was ridiculous because she had the power to cement their lives together.

"Hey, are you okay, Angel girl?"

The worry in his voice made her heart squeeze. How could she find the words to tell him she'd never been better than right here, right now, in his arms?

She turned awkwardly, and in the end, he had to help her as she rotated to face him. Their noses were just an inch apart and she twined her legs with his, allowing his heat to seep into her body.

"Are you going to ask me to marry you again?" she whispered.

There was a brief flash in his eyes she could swear was pain. He stroked her cheek with one finger and then ran it slowly back and forth over her mouth.

"No, Angel. I've been pushing too much. I swore I wouldn't pressure you but I've been doing just that."

She put her finger to his mouth to cut off the words.

"Ask me again. Please."

A wild spark lit his eyes and the pupils dilated, turning the brown to black. There was hope and fear simultaneously, one warring with the other. She hated the insecurity and hesitancy she saw as he came to grips with what she'd asked.

To her surprise, he pushed himself up and got off the bed. For a moment she wondered if she'd royally screwed up. But he reached for her, holding out a hand.

She slid her palm over his and he helped her to the edge of the bed until she sat with her legs hanging over the side, her feet just brushing the floor.

Still holding on to her hand, he knelt on the floor so they looked each other in the eye. Nervousness bunched in her stomach and her breathing shallowed until she realized she was holding it.

Micah raised her hand to his mouth and pressed a kiss into the softness of her palm. Then he slowly pulled it away and gazed directly into her eyes.

"Will you marry me, Angel? Will you spend the rest of your life with me? Love me the way I love you? Have my children, grow a family with me, grow old with me and spend a lifetime allowing me to love you the way you deserve to be loved?"

Completely undone by the heartfelt words, she stared in wonder as tears slid silently down her cheeks. She raised her hands and cupped his face, gazing into the eyes of the man she adored—had always adored.

"You once told me that when I knew without a doubt that you loved me more than life and that when I trusted you with my heart, it was then you wanted me to marry you. I should have said yes a long time ago," she whispered. "Yes. I'll marry you. I love you. I'll always love you."

He rose up and crushed her to him. He held her tight, his entire body trembling against her. She felt every breath, every beat of his heart as it pounded wildly against her throat.

"Oh God, I love you, Angel girl. So much. So damn much. I thank God I didn't destroy your faith in me, that I didn't destroy your love. I couldn't live with myself if I had. You and Nia are my world. I love you both so much."

She pulled away and then took his hands and guided them down to mold to her belly. "We're your family, Micah. She and I. She'll love you as much as I love you."

His smile made her heart ache. There was such joy in his eyes. It wasn't until now that she noticed the shadows he'd worn for the past months. But now they lifted away and there was such relief in his face.

He lowered his head and pressed his lips to the hard bump of her belly. She threaded her fingers through his long hair and held him lovingly against the gentle patter of their daughter.

She closed her eyes and let the sweetness of the moment envelope her. They'd been through so much in such a short amount of time. But it was all worth it because here and now, she held everything she'd ever wanted in her arms and cradled in her womb.

Micah and their daughter. Her family.

She couldn't help but think her brother, David, and Hannah were smiling down on them from heaven.

Micah lifted his head, then curled his hand around her nape and pulled her until their foreheads rested against each other. Their noses brushed and she felt his erratic breaths puff out as if he was valiantly trying to maintain control of his emotions.

"Tell me again," he whispered. "Tell me you'll marry me."

She smiled. "I'll marry you, Micah."

"When?"

"Whenever you say when."

"Tomorrow," he breathed.

She laughed. "I think we'll need a little longer than that. While I don't want a huge wedding, I do want our closest friends—our family," she amended, "to be there."

"Yeah, I do too."

"Are you sure this is what you want, Micah? You'll be happy?"

He pulled away and cupped her face as she'd cupped his a moment earlier. "I've never been happier in my life than I am right at this very moment. But as overjoyed as I am right now, nothing will match the day you become officially mine in the eyes of the law."

"I've always been yours, Micah. But now you're mine. And I'm never going to let you go."

He smiled then and the last remaining shadows faded away, leaving only hope and joy. "I see I'm not the only possessive one in this relationship. I like it."

CHAPTER 11

*C*onnor pulled under the hotel awning and stopped behind two other cars waiting to valet park. He cut the engine and sat there for a long moment while they watched the valet tend to the first car in line.

She could sense his irritation, which was fine, because it wasn't like she didn't have plenty of her own.

Finally he looked over at her. "What the hell was all that about tonight?"

Her eyelids narrowed to slits as she glared over at him. "You don't think you did anything wrong in this scenario?"

"So I piss you off and you find that sufficient reason to hot-wire a car, get arrested and be hauled off to jail?"

She crossed her arms and huffed. "I was not arrested. I was specifically looking for a cop. It's not my fault he overreacted and thought I was some lunatic off her meds."

"I can't imagine *why* he'd think something like that."

"Cut the sarcasm. It makes you sound like an even bigger asshole," she muttered.

He sighed. "Do you always react this strongly about everything? I mean, most people would have just called me a dickhead and been done with it. Not many people would hot-wire a car, then flag down a cop and try to convince them you're off your fucking rocker."

She glared at him again. "I was being smart. I didn't want to be driving around alone and I damn sure didn't want to come back to the hotel by myself. I mean, what if the demented dude was waiting for me in my room?"

He looked like he wanted to beat his head against the steering wheel. Luckily the valet walked up and Connor opened his door to collect the ticket. Lyric got out and forced herself to wait for Connor. Whatever he might think, she really didn't want to go back up to her room alone. She didn't want to stay alone, for that matter, but neither did she want him in such close proximity for the entire night. She was fucked either way and she was resigned to spending another sleepless night. She would be a freaking zombie by tomorrow.

Connor put his hand to her back and herded her toward the door. All the way to her room, he was silent. His glower spoke volumes, and to be honest, she was happy he wasn't talking. He'd just gripe at her some more.

That deference thing she was used to would certainly come in handy right now. Unfortunately she imagined he'd cut his own nuts off before ever deferring to her.

He made her remain to the side in the hallway while he opened the door and took a look inside. Satisfied that no one was going to jump out of the closet at them, he motioned her in and then shut and bolted the door behind them.

She made her way to the bed and flopped indelicately onto the mattress. The message light was blinking on her phone and she frowned, wondering who even knew she was here. Phillip did. But she didn't think she'd even let her band or crew know where she was staying yet.

She leaned over, picked up the receiver and punched the button marked messages. Exhausted from the day's events and no sleep in longer than she could remember, she flopped back onto a pillow and closed her eyes as she waited for the recording to start.

"You can't hide from me, Lyric. Your pathetic little bodyguard can't protect you."

She bolted straight up, not believing what she'd heard. Her hands shaking, she punched at a series of buttons to replay the message but was so upset she botched it.

"What the hell is wrong?" Connor demanded. He snatched the phone from her hands and put it to his ear. "There's nothing here. What upset you?"

"The message," she stammered out. "Replay the message. I didn't erase it. It should still be there."

He frowned and depressed the button to cut the connection and then he punched the message button again. After a moment, his expression grew stormy and his eyes went so cold she shivered.

He replayed the message several times before finally replacing the receiver. He put his hand down to gently push her leg over so he could sit on the edge of the bed.

"Are you all right?"

She nodded but she wasn't really. She knew she had some creep sending her weird notes, but her record label had kept her in the dark and she had only Connor's word to go on. Not that she doubted him—she had no problem believing him at all. It was why she had been so determined not to go anywhere alone. But now that she'd heard the threat, it was much more real. It shocked her to her core.

"Lyric, look at me."

The command snapped her gaze to him.

"This is why I'm so pissed that you took off without me," he said, a distinct edge to his voice. "Now will you take this seriously?"

She frowned, upset and shaken by the threat but just as upset over his assumption that she didn't take this very seriously.

But she was too tired to defend herself. Too tired to argue with his ironclad opinion of her. It wasn't as if she'd change it.

She nodded wearily, too tired to say the words. There was no way she'd keep the bitterness out of her voice anyway. It was better to just shut up and take the path of least resistance. For once.

"It's been a long day. It'll be another long day tomorrow. You should get some sleep," he said. "I need to check with the hotel to see if we can get a trace."

As if that was going to happen. Still, she wouldn't mind getting comfortable and laying her head on her pillow. Without a word, she got up, rummaged around in a still-packed suitcase until she found a pair of cotton pajamas and then headed for the bathroom.

Her pajamas were her comfort item. Much like a security blanket or a special stuffed animal. They were old and probably had holes, but they were soft and comfortable and they made her feel safe.

Connor would probably laugh, and she'd be lucky if he didn't sneak photos to send to the tabloids. What a blow to her image if she were photographed in pajamas with faded smiley faces on them.

When she came out of the bathroom, she blinked in surprise to see Connor shirtless on one side of the bed. He wore a pair of sweat pants—thank goodness—because she couldn't handle seeing him in nothing but his underwear, although it did bring up the tantalizing question of whether he wore briefs or boxers.

Or . . . boxer briefs. She'd bet money he was a boxer brief kind of guy. Or maybe she just really liked the image of him in tight cotton, butt-molding briefs that hugged those muscular upper legs.

Mmmmm.

Okay, she had to stop because this was just ridiculous.

She trudged to her side of the bed, pleased to see that he'd already erected a barrier between them using cushions from the sofa. She wouldn't have to forfeit any of her pillows to the cause.

He watched her as she pulled back the covers. She could feel his gaze resting on her, but she refused to look up. She crawled onto the mattress and turned her back to him as she pulled the comforter up over her shoulders.

There was a pregnant silence and then, "Good night, Lyric," he murmured. She heard the click of the lamp and the room was plunged into darkness. Only a thin beam of light from the street squeezed through a tiny gap in the room darkening curtains.

Her heart thumped in her throat and she lay there so wound up and tense that her muscles ached. She hated this. Hated that being so close to Connor—in the same bed—made her so nervous she wanted to puke.

She forced her breathing to even out because even she could hear it stuttering past her lips. She gripped the covers protectively around her and huddled there, staring at the opposite wall.

She was never going to sleep.

"Connor?"

There was a brief pause. "Yeah?"

She gripped the covers a little tighter until her fingers went numb. "Why do you hate me so much?"

There was an uncomfortable pause. Then she felt him turn toward her on his side. She lay still, her fingers wrapped tightly around the sheet she held to her chin.

"I don't hate you, Lyric."

"You decided before you ever met me that you despised me. Nothing I do or say is going to change that."

He sighed. "You didn't exactly help your case when we met."

"You looked at me like I was scum. No one is going to react well to that kind of judgment."

"I don't hate you," he said again.

"You don't like me either," she said softly.

"I was a jerk tonight. I'll be honest. I didn't want this job. And you're right. I had my mind made up about you before we ever met. That wasn't . . . fair."

"You're wrong, you know."

"About what?"

"I do take this seriously."

Connor shifted again, and the next thing she knew, light flooded the room as he switched the lamp back on. She glanced over her shoulder to see him sit up in bed.

"Turn over so we can talk," he said quietly.

She rolled and clutched one of the cushions between them to her chest.

"You need to consider the possibility that someone close to you is involved in this."

She frowned. "But no one knows I'm here. I gave my band and my crew two weeks off. I was careful, Connor. I know you don't think I was."

"What about Paul? And your two . . . bodyguards?"

At least he hadn't called them her fuck-buddies again. She sighed. Her head hurt. She wasn't sure she'd ever gotten rid of the headache she'd had earlier.

"Lyric?"

"I think Paul knew too," she said wearily. "And Trent and R.J. too. Don't say it. I already feel like an idiot. But no one else knows. Or rather I didn't tell anyone."

"And you think the cops you introduced yourself to will keep your cover?"

She flushed and hugged the pillow a little tighter. "I was angry. You humiliated me."

"Do you always react so outrageously when someone pisses you off?"

"Do you always allow people to get under your skin so badly?"

"Touché. So we've both reacted badly. I'm more at fault than you. This is a job. I'm supposed to be a professional. No matter how much you irritate me, it's my job to keep cool and protect you."

She glanced up, watching the soft glow of the lamp slide over his muscled shoulders. He had a great chest. He was a tall man. Lean but tightly muscled. Not in a bulging Neanderthal way, nor did he look like he worked out a bazillion times a week. But his body was tight and there wasn't a spare ounce of flesh anywhere on his waist.

He had a great jaw. Firm and determined. Already he had a shadow of a beard that only made him look sexy in a scruffy, totally male way. He wasn't pretty and polished.

He had a quiet arrogance that suggested he was comfortable in his skin and didn't much give a damn what others thought. He wasn't impressed by celebrity. He thought she was a spoiled jerk. He was right, but it still bothered her.

"Do I irritate you that much?"

He cracked a grin and glanced over at her. "Yeah. You do."

The acknowledgment was more of a dry laugh at himself and the smile took the sting out of his words.

"We're going to work this out," he said. "Tomorrow I'm meeting with the firm your label hired. You'll be surrounded by security at all times and I'm going to stick to you like glue for the next two weeks. If someone wants you, they'll have to go through me."

She took great comfort from the vow. It didn't come across as a boast. There was complete and utter confidence in his voice, and his eyes sparked with determination.

She bit her lips and met his gaze again. "I know I'm not . . . easy."

"No, you're definitely not easy," he said in a lazy voice. "But I can handle difficult."

He reached over to touch her hair. It was a simple brush. He didn't even make contact with her skin, but an electric sensation snaked all the way through her body.

"You should get some rest," he said. "You're exhausted and you've had a headache all day."

She grimaced. "I won't sleep."

One of his eyebrows went up in question. "Why not?"

She looked away and clutched the covers to her chin again.

"Lyric?"

His voice gentled and there was a soothing lilt to the way he said her name.

"You make me nervous. It's not just you," she rushed to say. "It could be anyone. I don't like having someone so . . . . close."

When she peeked up to gauge his reaction, his brow was furrowed. "It's my understanding you always have people around you. That you're never alone. I'd think if that was the case, you'd be glad to have me here with you so you aren't alone."

"I don't like being alone," she admitted.

"You're making no sense."

She sighed and turned onto her back to stare at the ceiling. "If I have a choice between alone and being alone with one other person, I choose alone, no matter how uncomfortable it makes me."

She could feel his stare burning over her skin, like he was trying to peel back the layers even further and see her darkest secrets.

To her surprise he sat up and threw his legs over the edge of the bed. She watched from the corner of her eye as he reached for the hotel directory on the nightstand.

He rotated back around and began flipping through the pages.

"Well, if we're going to be up all night, I'm going to order room service. I'm starving."

She wrinkled her nose. "But you ate a huge supper. I mean, it looked like it was the entire cow. Or pig. Whatever we ate."

"I'm a growing boy. Need food."

"You're really going to stay up just because I can't sleep?"

He glanced over at her. "Yeah, sure." He held up the menu. "You want something?"

She slowly sat up and arranged one of the cushions behind her so she was propped against the headboard. Then she smiled. "Yeah. I could eat."

CHAPTER 12

"Hey," Connor said softly.

His voice was a tickle in her ear and she scrunched up her nose in her sleep and batted at the offending sensation.

A husky chuckle blew a strand of her hair over her cheek.

"Wake up, Sleeping Beauty. We have things to do today and Damon Roche is sending a driver to collect you in an hour. I thought you'd want to take a shower and put on something killer before he arrives."

She cracked one eye open and stared at Connor's face just inches from her own. For a moment she was confused and then realization pushed aside the veil of sleep.

"I slept," she said in wonder.

Connor nodded. "Yeah, you did. You crashed around five."

"What time is it now?"

"Eight. I would have let you sleep longer, but I've got to get your security squared away today and then we have to move you."

"Okay."

He eased back and she struggled to push herself up, her brain clouded and fuzzy. She blinked to try to clear the cobwebs and for a moment she simply stared around the room, amazed that she'd fallen asleep with him next to her in bed.

Maybe her exhaustion had finally caught up to her and she'd simply passed out. Even more surprising was the fact that she really wanted to lie back down and sleep for several more hours.

She should be jumping at the opportunity to surround herself with people for the day. Being on her own and with Connor had been a strain, and she was starting to show signs of cracking.

She rubbed at her face and then glanced over at Connor, who was sitting at the end of the bed watching her. "Are you done in the bathroom?"

He nodded. "Yeah. I've already showered. It's all yours."

"Good. I'll need a bit to get ready."

She threw the covers aside and swung her legs over the side of the bed. Damn, but she was tired. As she trudged toward the bathroom, Connor said, "You want breakfast? I was going to order room service. I'd rather you not go down and eat. More chance of you being recognized."

She covered a yawn and nodded. "Yeah. Sounds good."

"Eggs? Bacon? Pancakes? What's your poison?"

"Yes, yes and yes."

He laughed. "Okay, I'll order everything they have. It'll look like a buffet because I'm starved."

She shook her head in amazement. "You put away a lot of food just a few hours ago. How can you possibly be starving again?"

He ignored her and picked up the phone.

Fifteen minutes later, she stepped out of the shower feeling somewhat revived, and after drying herself, she put her hair up in a towel, pulled on one of the big, fluffy robes the hotel provided and padded back into the room to figure out what to wear.

She was back in the bathroom drying her hair and fluffing it out when Connor hollered that the food had arrived. She didn't have makeup on yet, but she was tempted to go au naturel. She didn't often go without full treatment, hair, nails, outfit and makeup because she literally never knew when and where she might be photographed.

Today she just wanted to be . . . normal. Unrecognized. Anonymous—and not only because she had some lunatic freaking her out. Okay, so that was the biggest reason, but the other was simply she was looking forward to being around people she could actually be herself with.

She walked back into the hotel room to see Connor putting a dent in the array of food arranged on the serving cart. If she wanted to eat, she needed to wade in and rescue something before he ate it all.

"Do you always eat so much?" she asked once she was cross-legged on the bed, her plate in front of her.

He frowned and stopped chewing for a minute. "I haven't eaten much in the last couple of days. Been too busy with you."

Her eyes widened. If he considered what he'd eaten "not much," she'd hate to see what he considered a normal appetite.

"I bet you ran your parents ragged trying to keep you fed. You probably ate them out of house and home."

He grinned. "Pop may have complained a time or two."

Her gaze roved up and down his lean, muscled body and she shook her head. "I don't know where you put it. I think I hate you."

"I work out," he defended. "Not like all I do is sit around and eat."

She snorted. "Yeah, I bet you work out like once a week. It's obvious you're one of these people blessed with good genes."

"And what about you? You aren't exactly a delicate miss when it comes to eating and what are you, a size two?"

She nearly choked on her food. Maybe this guy didn't have as much experience with women as she thought. "I'm a twelve. Sometimes a ten. I've been as high as a fourteen. No, nothing huge but not bone-thin either. I have to work hard to keep it under a ten. When I'm on tour I keep my weight down because performing almost every night keeps me fit. But when I'm not on tour and writing songs or in the recording studio, I gain weight just looking at food. I have to have a strict exercise regimen to keep it under control."

He frowned. "I think you're pretty damn perfect as you are. You don't need to be any thinner."

Then again, maybe he had plenty experience with women, because he sure knew what to say.

"I'm straining the waists of my size twelves right now," she admitted. "I'm at the end of my tour and the shows are further apart and I've been stress-eating. Not the best habit in the world, but there you have it. I have a weakness for salty and sweet. Carbs. I love carbs."

His eyes narrowed and she could feel his gaze examining her. His frown grew fiercer as he met her eyes. "You look just fine like you are."

Warm pleasure bathed her cheeks until she was sure she glowed. In her world she was never perfect. She had fitness trainers telling her she needed to shed pounds. Her manager telling her what she could or couldn't eat. Even her stylist waded in with her opinion and clucked at Lyric whenever her outfits got too tight.

And yet Connor was positively glowering at the idea that she needed to lose weight.

She beamed at him and polished off her breakfast, then chugged down an entire glass of orange juice. She nearly groaned with pleasure.

She loved juices but had been forbidden to drink pretty much any-thing but water.

"Better?" Connor asked when she pushed her plate away.

"Yum. That was fantastic."

He checked his watch. "You have a few minutes. Micah and the driver are coming up for you. I don't want you standing around in the lobby where you're visible while you wait."

"Okay. I need to brush my teeth."

She bounced off the bed feeling better than she had in days despite the fact she hadn't caught up on her sleep. She brushed out her hair one more time and left it loose. Then she cleaned her teeth, gargled with mouthwash and checked her appearance in the mirror.

She wouldn't stop traffic but she didn't look all bad. And there was a lightness to her eyes she hadn't noticed in a long time. She smiled back at her reflection, decided she'd survive being seen without makeup again and then left the bathroom.

Connor was on the phone. He turned and held a finger up to Lyric and then said, "I'll have her right down."

She raised an eyebrow as he shoved his cell phone back into his pocket. "I thought they were coming up?"

"Sam is parked at the side employee entrance. We're going to go out that way. You won't even be outside a second."

"And you?"

"I'm going to my office to meet with the security team your label hired. I want to make damn sure they're competent enough to do the job. I'll come get you when I'm done. In the meantime, I'm having a few guys come in and clear out your hotel room, so if there's anything you need, get it now."

She scooped up her purse, looked to make sure her wallet, sun-glasses and phone were still in it and then slung it over her shoulder.

"I'm ready."

Five minutes later, Connor rushed her into the back of a Bentley and she blinked at the sumptuous leather and the obvious expense of the luxury car. She was a freaking rock star and she didn't get to ride around in vehicles like these. Any wannabe could hitch a ride in a limo, but these wheels cost some serious cash.

The driver was a broad-shouldered boulder of a man who filled the driver's seat. The steering wheel looked small in his hands, like it would break off if he turned it too hard. He flicked a glance at her in the rearview mirror but his eyes were covered with dark shades, and his bald head gleamed like he'd just shaved it that morning.

Micah Hudson slid into the backseat next to her and Connor slammed her door. The driver roared off down the side street and pulled into traffic.

"Everything all right?" Micah asked conversationally.

She eyed him warily, not comfortable with the fact that it was he and not Connor who was riding with her.

"Where is Angelina?"

Micah's eyes narrowed. "No way I'd let her come along. I don't want her anywhere near potential trouble."

Lyric shrugged. Like she wanted to be near "potential trouble" either?

A half hour later they drove through the entrance of a sprawling estate. She glanced back to see the heavy security gate swing closed behind them. To her further surprise she caught a glimpse of a big dude who looked suspiciously like he was carrying an automatic rifle. Holy hell, was she at some compound for a crazy cult?

They pulled around the circle drive and parked directly in front of the palatial house. Micah got out and the driver opened her door and hovered protectively over her as he escorted her the few steps to the entrance.

Okay, she liked safety as much as the next person, but this seemed a little . . . overdone. It wasn't as if she was rolling up to a concert and had thousands of fans all pushing to get a glimpse or a piece of her. There was . . . no one. The grounds were so quiet that she could hear birds chirping.

She was ushered inside the McMansion and the driver took her into the living room where she saw women sprawled all over the furniture.

Lyric relaxed and smiled. She recognized Faith, Julie and, of course, Angelina right away, but there was another woman, long and sleek and so freaking beautiful that she made Lyric take a step back and curse the fact she hadn't worn makeup. She was tempted to pull the shades over her eyes, not that it would hide the fact she wasn't even wearing concealer.

To cover up her nervousness, she spread her hands out, palms up, and announced, "I'm here!"

The women turned and Faith shot up from the couch and hurried over to give Lyric a hug. Which was kind of weird but at the same time gave her an honest-to-God warm fuzzy. Lyric was a little shell-shocked as Faith dragged her over to the others.

"You've met Julie and Angelina, of course, but you haven't met Serena Roche yet."

Tall and elegant, Serena rose from the couch, her long black hair swinging like silk down her back. Lyric couldn't help but stare. The woman had such an exotic beauty and startling blue eyes to contrast the midnight hair.

She extended her hand and for a moment Lyric just stared at it—and the glittering, huge-ass diamond ring that adorned her third finger.

"I'm so glad to meet you, Lyric."

"Likewise."

A tall, extremely handsome man walked into the living room, and when his gaze rested on Serena, he lit up. It didn't take a rocket scientist to figure out this was her husband, Damon Roche.

He had that rich GQ look. Polished, arrogant and extremely confident. He came up to stand beside Serena, his hand sliding up her back to tangle in her hair.

"Ms. Jones," he said smoothly. "Welcome to our home. Serena and I are happy to have you."

"Thank you. I'm sorry to be a bother."

"You're no bother. Micah tells me you've had some trouble. I can assure you that while you are here, nothing will bother you."

Strangely enough, she absolutely believed him. He didn't strike her as a man who made empty boasts. He was too damn self-assured.

"Can I offer you refreshment, Ms. Jones?" Damon asked.

Remembering just how much she'd eaten at breakfast, she shook her head.

"Come sit," Faith urged. "We have a complete girly day planned. Julie's even going to give us massages later."

"I want to know who the hell's going to give me a massage," Julie grumbled.

"Oh, hush. You know Nathan will be more than happy to give you one later," Serena said impishly.

"Not that girly fun isn't high on my list of priorities, but us menfolk are going to excuse ourselves," Damon said dryly.

He drew Serena to him and kissed her forehead. There was such a look of possession in his eyes that Lyric shivered. Did every one of these women have a man who absolutely adored her? Lyric had never wanted to stab anyone more in her life. And now she had to spend an afternoon with them, and they'd probably go on and on and on about how wonderful their husbands or significant others or whatever the hell they called them were.

Damon and Micah departed, talking among themselves, but the

driver remained conspicuously behind, taking position in the doorway to the living room.

The women retook their positions and Lyric plopped on the couch next to Angelina, who had her feet curled beneath her and was propped against a pillow.

"When are you due?" Lyric asked as she glanced down at Angelina's belly.

Angelina grimaced. "I still have three months if you can believe it. I swear I'm ready to burst now."

Lyric's eyes widened. Maybe it was because Angelina was so petite but she looked like she'd swallowed enough helium to float a hot-air balloon.

"So tell us what's going on with this freak who's stalking you, Lyric," Julie said.

Lyric sighed. "Well, since my record label didn't see fit to tell me anything and Connor just informed me day before yesterday, I don't know a whole lot. Apparently he's been sending me creepy notes and putting them in places he shouldn't have access to. Then yesterday he called and left a message on my hotel phone."

"So what is Connor going to do?" Faith asked anxiously.

Lyric shrugged. "He's meeting with whatever security firm my label hired, which is why I'm here. Makes more sense for me to be there, but I think Connor is afraid I'll throw some tantrum."

Julie eyed her with a glimmer of humor in her eyes. "Would you?"

"Maybe. Depends on what they had to say. Or how brainless they thought I was. And I don't throw tantrums. I just voice my displeasure in a loud manner."

Serena and Angelina laughed. And then Serena leaned forward. "I have to admit you look a lot different than I expected. Damon and I saw one of your shows in Vegas. You were so flashy and glamorous."

Lyric winced and Serena put her hand to her mouth. "Not that you aren't now. Oh hell. I'll shut up now."

Lyric laughed. "I don't usually go anywhere without full makeup and wardrobe, but Connor seems to think the lower profile I am, the better. I haven't even colored my hair since my last show. The first time Connor met me, I had pink hair. I don't think he was impressed."

Faith snickered and Julie rolled her eyes. "That's because Connor has a stick up his ass," Julie retorted.

"Julie, he does not," Faith defended. "You're always accusing him of being uptight."

"Pretty good assessment, I'd say," Lyric muttered.

"He's a total sweetheart," Angelina said.

Lyric rolled her eyes. "Oh sure, sweetie."

The other women burst into laughter.

"She totally has you there," Serena snickered.

"You know, I could do your hair," Julie said thoughtfully. "Ice blue would look awesome with all that black hair. If you don't want to be too noticeable, we could just do the tips."

"Really?" Lyric asked.

"She's a terrific stylist," Faith said in a proud voice. "She owns her own business. She does hair, nails, massages."

Serena nodded. "Yeah, she's our Jill—or Julie—of all trades."

"Connor would have a kitten if I left here. Maybe we could work it out one day when you're free," Lyric said.

Julie grinned. "Oh, we could send Sam out for what I need and we could do it here. One of you might have to forfeit a massage, but it could totally be done."

Lyric twirled the ends of a thick strand and pulled it up to look, imagining how it would look dyed blue. She shrugged. "Hell, I'll try anything once."

"Oh, I like her," Angelina said, her eyes sparkling with mischief.

"You would," Serena said. "She's our resident wild child," she explained to Lyric.

Lyric's brows went up. Sweet, angelic-looking Angelina? Beneath Angelina's dusky skin, color bloomed and she ducked her head.

"Boy, that was a guilty look of acknowledgment if I ever saw one," Lyric said. "I guess it's true what they say. It's the innocent-looking ones you have to watch out for."

"Oh yes," Julie chimed in. "Faith being a very close second in the heathen department."

"Julie! Hush!"

Faith had turned bright red as a flush crept all the way up her throat and into her cheeks.

"I'm starting to feel frighteningly boring and normal," Lyric said in bemusement. "I assure you that never happens. I'm usually the one people are looking at like I just lit my hair on fire."

"If we're going to do hair and whatever else we get inspiration for, I say we need wine," Serena spoke up.

"Oh, I don't drink," Lyric was quick to say.

"What?" Julie scowled. "How can you be such a famous diva and not drink? Haven't you ever gotten drunk and been arrested for indecent exposure or something?"

Lyric smirked. "Depends on which tabloid you read."

"Seriously? You don't drink?" Faith asked.

"Today you do," Serena said as she turned and motioned for the driver. "Sam, can you bring us a few bottles of wine? Ask Damon for a suggestion. He'll pick something good."

As Sam departed, Serena turned and shrugged. "I'm pretty wine stupid. I mean, I love it, but know nothing about it. Damon, on the other hand, knows what wine you're supposed to have with what food and what occasions, et cetera."

"He does serve good wine," Faith agreed.

"I'm not happy with any of you," Angelina pouted. "I can't have any wine, which means you all will have all the fun while I'm sitting here as big as a house."

"I'll make sure you get the first massage," Julie soothed.

Two hours and six wine bottles later, Lyric couldn't remember what her aversion to alcohol was. The wine was good. The world was good. The company was good. Everything was good.

And the room was spinning like a merry-go-round from hell.

She was sitting dutifully still as Julie worked on her hair.

"How much has she had to drink?" Lyric asked, gesturing over her shoulder to Julie.

Julie reached over Lyric's shoulder and plucked a half-full wineglass and drained it. She set it back down with a thump. "Not nearly enough."

"I'm watching her. She hasn't had so much that it would impair her hair-doing skills," Serena said in a solemn voice.

Faith giggled. "Hair doing?"

"Well, what else do you call it?" Serena asked in exasperation. "You look like an alien with all the aluminum foil, Lyric. Very impressive."

Lyric smothered her laughter. Of any of them, Serena had drunk the most, and the girl was flying high. Although Lyric had to be close behind her because Serena kept filling her glass. And then the wine disappeared. It was the damnedest thing.

"I'm done here," Julie announced. "Well, for the next twenty anyway. Then we'll rinse you and dry you and voila, you'll be Smurftastic."

Angelina shot Julie a baleful look. "Smurftastic?"

"Yeah, you know, the Smurfs. Little blue people? Smurfette? Get it?"

Angelina's expression was blank.

"You're too young," Julie grumbled. "And clearly your education is lacking."

"Smurfette was hot," Lyric said gravely.

Faith nodded. "Agreed. Maybe we should all get our hair blue."

"Oh, that would be fun!" Serena exclaimed. "It would be worth it to see the looks on the guys' faces. How long does the color last, Julie?"

Julie scowled. "Like I want Damon kicking my ass?"

Serena waved in Julie's direction like she was an annoying insect. "Come on. We could do it in support of Lyric. Our sister from another mother."

"Just how much have *you* had to drink, Serena?" Julie asked.

Serena paused to pour another glass and tipped it in the direction of the other women. "Not nearly enough!"

"I'll do it," Faith said slowly. "Would blue tips look good on blond?"

Julie arched an eyebrow in Faith's direction. "Are you serious?"

"Yeah. It could be fun. We could be like Lyric's fan club, and if Connor tries to give her shit, we could beat the crap out of him."

"Weren't you the good sister defending him a while ago?" Angelina asked, her eyes dancing with merriment.

"Just because I don't think he has a stick up his ass doesn't mean he can't be a typical mule-headed male. Oh, I know! We could even get tickets to go see Lyric at the rodeo. We'll be all in the know since we'd have hair just like hers."

"Her concert is sold out," Julie pointed out.

"Oh I could get you guys tickets if you really wanted to come," Lyric said and then promptly hiccupped. Then she giggled. Then everyone started laughing. Lyric hiccupped some more and the room dissolved into fits of laughter. Why hiccups were so funny, Lyric wasn't sure, but the more she hiccupped, the more she laughed.

"Okay, well, if we're going to get this done, I need to get you girls started pronto. Otherwise Damon and Micah are going to come lurking to be nosy and then we'll be busted. You in, Angelina?" Julie asked, looking over at her.

Angelina grinned. "Yeah. I think it will be fun."

CHAPTER 13

$\mathscr{C}$onnor got out of his truck and waited for Nathan and Gray to catch up to him before he went up to Damon Roche's front door. He'd asked Nathan and Gray to sit in on his meeting with Lyric's security team, and the two men had agreed to lend their services whenever Connor needed them. It made him feel better to have at least two men that he could trust.

Gray gazed up at the imposing stone and wooden home and then grinned over at Connor and Nathan. "The house is still standing, so that's a good sign."

Connor frowned. "Lyric isn't that bad."

Nathan chuckled. "He wasn't referring to Lyric. Interesting things happen when our women get together."

Gray knocked on the door and the three waited. A moment later, Sam opened the door and gave them a slightly wary look. He crossed his arms and managed to fill most of the doorway as if he was reluctant to let them past.

"The ladies are currently unavailable."

"Oh shit," Nathan muttered.

Gray wiped a hand over his face and just shook his head.

Connor eyed them all in confusion.

"Perhaps it would be best if you waited in the sitting room while I inform the ladies that you are here," Sam said.

"Hell, Sam, we're not going to beat them," Gray grumbled.

"He's way protective of the women," Nathan whispered to Connor. "He spoils them shamelessly and indulges them in their every whim."

Sam glared at Nathan. "I do not."

"Sam, what's going on?" Damon asked from behind Sam. "Why haven't you invited them in?"

Sam turned and grimaced. "Have you been in to see the ladies yet, sir?"

Damon frowned and shook his head. "Micah and I have left them to their own devices."

Sam sighed and stepped back so that Connor, Nathan and Gray could enter. "They're having fun. Remember that."

Micah muttered an expletive, and Damon's forehead creased with worry.

Connor fell into step between Micah and Damon and Nathan and Gray as they headed farther inside the house. As they drew closer, peals of laughter filled the air. Then there was quiet. And suddenly another chorus of laughter.

Damon held up a finger, motioning for the men to be quiet as they rounded the corner and stood back from the doorway to the living room.

Connor blinked as he absorbed the scene in front of him. "What the ever-loving hell?"

He stared in astonishment as all five women, each holding a wineglass with the exception of Angelina, were gathered in the middle of the room dancing. Perhaps more notably, every last one of them had blue hair! Or at least partially blue. The last two inches of their hair looked like it had been dipped in blue dye, and he supposed that was what had happened given that Julie was a stylist.

Faith and Serena each had an arm around Lyric while Angelina and Julie stood across from them, and they were all singing loudly. Or trying to. They'd get a few lines out and then dissolve into laughter.

They swayed and danced, though it was obvious copious amounts of alcohol had compromised any grace they possessed. Faith nearly went down and Lyric made a grab for her. Faith held up her wineglass— it was a miracle the floors weren't covered with wine—and the women cheered.

"It's a sin to waste good wine," Serena said solemnly. "Damon always says so."

"This wasn't exactly what I had in mind when I said that," Damon muttered beside Connor.

"I'll drink to that!" Faith said as she raised her glass.

Julie held up her glass with exaggerated solemnity. Lyric followed suit, then Serena. Connor gaped as they drained their glasses, then set them down with a bang.

Angelina shot them disgruntled looks and stuck out her bottom lip.

Julie patted her. "We'll get together after Nia is born. Micah can babysit and we'll take you out. Lyric could even fly in for the occasion. Don't all you rock stars have private jets and the like?"

Lyric held up her empty glass and peered inside it as if wondering how it got that way. "Yeah, sure. I'll tell my manager I want one. Should be a snap." She tried to snap her fingers and giggled when she couldn't get her fingers to perform right.

"Well, if not, I'll make Damon send his jet for you," Serena promised.

"I'm not letting you forget this," Angelina said.

"Well hell," Micah muttered from his position behind Connor.

Nathan snickered and Gray wiped at his wide grin.

"Boy, does this bring back memories," Gray said with a chuckle. "The last time they got this drunk, Nathan found them all on the floor of Cattleman's."

Connor sighed. Then he laughed. He couldn't help it. They were all pretty damn cute. Drunk as skunks and about as steady as an alcoholic who hadn't had a drink in twenty-four hours.

"So who's going to break this up?" Nathan asked.

"Or we could just leave them," Damon said.

Serena pulled loose from Lyric and Faith and stumbled over to the coffee table where several empty wine bottles rested. "Uh-oh. We're out of wine. Sam? Sam! Sam, we need more wine. Can you bring us some?" she called.

Connor looked at Sam with new respect. "What all have they had you bring them, anyway?"

Sam straightened his stance. "It would be disloyal of me to give any detail of their afternoon."

"Is that hair color sticking out of your pocket?" Damon asked as he stared down at Sam's pants.

Sam clamped his hand over his pocket and backed away. "I'll go see to their wine if you have no objections, sir."

Damon laughed and looked up at the other men. "Well, what do you say? We can go out on the patio and have a beer or two while we wait for them to wind down. Unless you need to go, Connor?"

"Nah. I'm having her stuff removed from her hotel right now and transferred to the house we'll be staying at. Her label has rented a place for her to stay and the team has gone ahead to take make it ready and take position."

"Then let's go have a beer. Sam will take good care of them and we can check on them later."

"I have a confession to make," Lyric said as she flopped onto the couch. She leaned forward and put her finger over her lips. "But shhhh! You can't tell anyone. If it shows up in the tabloids, I'll know you told."

"Of course we won't tell," Faith said as she slashed her fingers over her chest in a cross-my-heart gesture.

"Spill," Julie said. "I've always wanted to know the deep, dark secrets of the rich and famous."

"I can't dance," Lyric slurred out.

The other women broke into laughter.

"What do you call what we've been doing for the last hour?" Serena demanded.

Lyric held up a finger, though it waved precariously. "Performers can do just about any ridiculous move onstage and it looks cool. But really, if you really look at it, it's hysterical. I have no rhythm. I never could dance. I just sort of make up stuff as I go, but once, I got carried away and tripped onstage. For weeks the magazines reported that I'd been high while performing." She shook her head back and forth. "Nope. Never been high." She giggled. "Until now. I just can't dance."

"Assholes," Faith said solemnly. "Shitheads."

Angelina cracked up. "Are you practicing your naughty words, Faith?"

"Fucktard," Julie added.

Serena got into the spirit. "Pissant. Dickhead. Twat."

Lyric covered her ears. "You guys have to stop. I'm not used to such vulgar language."

They all stared with raised eyebrows while Lyric blinked innocently. Then they all fell back in their seats and died laughing again.

Sam appeared, looking discomfited. He held two bottles in his
hands but hadn't opened them. "If you would pardon the observation,
I can't help but think maybe you've had enough to drink today. I
wouldn't like for any of you to become ill."

"Does that mean he doesn't want us to puke?" Julie asked blearily.

"That too," Sam added.

Lyric waved him off. "Fine by me. I hate puking. Did I tell you guys
I don't drink?"

"Yeah, you did," Julie snickered. "No one resists our charm for
long. And it's not every day we get to be a bad influence on a pop
diva."

Lyric yawned widely. "I'm tired."

Faith patted the pillow at her hip. "Lie down and get comfortable."

"Not a bad idea," Serena said. "Maybe then the room would stop
spinning."

Lyric sprawled on the couch and leaned against Faith. She meant
to close her eyes for just a moment but the next thing she knew she
was being gently shaken awake.

She blinked but all she could make out was a blurry face. His
mouth moved and she could swear he sounded like Connor—if Connor were to talk to her through a really long tunnel.

She frowned and tried to shove him away, then snuggled against
Faith's hip again. Faith's hip? Lyric pushed herself up to see that Faith
was passed out, half hanging over the arm of the couch. Lyric was
sprawled over Faith and when Lyric looked down, she saw that Serena
was half lying over Lyric's legs.

Julie was sprawled in an armchair and only Angelina was awake
and alert, her eyes dancing with amusement.

Then Lyric glanced around to see that the room was full of men who were all valiantly trying to keep from laughing. She scowled at them all but it only broadened their grins.

"What in God's name did you all do to your hair?" Connor asked in exasperation as he fingered one of Lyric's blue tips.

"At least they didn't get tattoos," Gray muttered.

"Don't give them any ideas," Nathan snapped.

Serena stirred and lifted her head, her eyes so blurry that Lyric was sure she had no clue where she was.

"Who's talking?" Serena demanded. "Sam, make them shut up."

Damon chuckled and reached down to run his fingers through Serena's hair. "Does your head hurt, Serena mine? It should. You put quite a dent in my wine cellar."

She sighed and arched into his touch, and it was then that Lyric saw the intricate gold band around Serena's upper arm, bared when her sleeve rose with her movements.

Damon's hand ventured lower to stroke the band, his fingers tracing the lines. He stroked her skin and the jewelry in a possessive manner that clearly told anyone watching she belonged to him.

It made Lyric's chest tighten in a funny way she didn't understand, and she shifted to alleviate the discomfort.

"We need to be going, Lyric," Connor said.

She appreciated that he kept his voice low. She already felt overwhelmed. And while it had been fun while it was going on, she was pretty sure she never wanted to drink again.

Connor chuckled. "That's what everyone says after the high is gone."

She cracked her eye open again as she realized she'd spoken the last part aloud. Or maybe he was just a good mind reader.

"I can't get up," she said. And she couldn't. "I can't even feel my legs."

"That's because I'm lying on them," Serena volunteered.

Damon laughed and then reached down and lifted Serena from the couch.

"Faith is comfy," Lyric mumbled.

Connor carefully slid his arms underneath Lyric and she found herself lifted weightlessly into the air. It was a little disconcerting since the room immediately began spinning again.

She glanced over to see Nathan leaning over Julie in her armchair. Micah sat next to Angelina and both of them looked on with amusement. She glared at Angelina. "Don't forget you're next. And I'm damn well flying in for it."

"Say good-bye, Lyric."

Lyric held up a hand and fluttered her fingers. "Good-bye, Lyric."

"Smart-ass."

"You're such a party pooper, Connor," Faith said with a frown. "We were just starting to really have fun and now you're taking her away."

Gray snorted. "Baby, you were all passed out cold on the furniture. I'd say you already had more fun than human beings should be allowed."

Lyric laid her head on Connor's chest and sighed. "You have a really nice chest, Connor. Has anyone ever told you that?"

He grunted in response and started toward the door.

"Bye, everyone," she called back. "Love you all."

"We love you too!" the women chorused.

The men rolled their eyes and Connor continued on out of the living room. Sam appeared at the door to open it for Connor. Then he followed Connor to Lyric's BMW and opened the back door so Connor could slide her in.

"Take care of yourself, Miss Lyric," Sam said.

She smiled and blew the older man a kiss. "You rock, Sam. I'm going to steal you away from Serena."

He smiled and then retreated, closing the door behind him.

"If you ever need me, don't hesitate to call," Sam said to Connor.

Connor hesitated, wondering just what this man's background was. "Thanks. I appreciate that, and I'm sure she does as well."

Sam turned to walk back to the house and Connor slid into the driver's seat. He glanced back at Lyric in the rearview mirror to see that she was already out like a light, sprawled across the backseat.

He laughed and shook his head as he cranked the engine and drove away.

CHAPTER 14

*L*yric wouldn't meet her security team under the best of circumstances. She was still out cold in the backseat when Connor drove up to the guard station of the house that would be Lyric's temporary home.

Two members of the security team manned the gate and waved Connor through. He drove up the drive and into the garage. As soon as he stepped out, Kane Murphy, who had command of the team, met him in the garage.

"Where is the subject?" Kane asked.

Connor didn't answer him and opened the door to the backseat. He reached in and carefully pulled Lyric into his arms. She was as limp as a rag doll but when he hoisted her against his chest, she turned and cuddled into him.

Kane raised one brow. "What the hell happened?"

"She and the girls got drunk," Connor said dryly.

"Must have been one hell of a party."

Connor pushed by him and into the house. "Have her things been delivered?"

Kane shut the door. "Yeah. Master suite is arranged. Yours is the adjoining room. My men are stationed around the perimeter and we'll be rotating watches in twelve-hour shifts."

Connor nodded and carried Lyric up the stairs to her bedroom. It was a far cry from the tiny hotel room where she'd holed up. The entire house was a study in luxury without being over-the-top. Whoever had built it had ultimate comfort in mind.

He set her down on the king-sized bed, hesitated and then moved into the master bathroom. A huge overflow bathtub was the focal point and stood in the middle of the room on a raised platform. There was a dual-head shower to the far right and a separate compartment for the toilet.

A bath might sober her up, but she might drown in it too. Maybe a shower was a better option.

He walked back into the bedroom and shook his head in amusement again. "Lyric. Lyric," he said louder. "Come on, honey, wake up. Time for you to sober up."

She made a sound of irritation and turned on her side away from him. He crawled onto the bed, following her over. He touched her shoulder and pulled her until she was on her back again.

"If you don't get up and do it yourself, I'm going to strip you and put you in the shower myself."

Her eyes popped open at that.

He chuckled. "Thought that might get you moving."

"Okay, okay," she grumbled. "Get off me."

"I'm not on you. If I'm ever on you, you'll know it."

Her eyes widened and he heard the swift intake of her breath. He couldn't tell if it was panic or curiosity that invaded her gaze. If she wasn't shit-faced, he'd test the theory and kiss her. But she was, and he was a flaming hypocrite.

He bitched about her fuck-buddy bodyguards and how if they were fucking her, they weren't protecting her, and now he was thinking of little other than what it would be like to be buried balls deep in her sweet heat.

Christ. He hadn't been on this job for a week yet and he'd already lost focus.

He shoved himself off the bed and strode for the door. "I'll give you an hour before I'm back. I need to take you down and introduce you to your security team. For the next two weeks, you'll eat, breathe and sleep these guys. You go nowhere without them—or me."

Lyric sat up and dragged her hair behind her ear. "Okay. I get it. Don't get all pissy with me."

Connor nodded and then stalked out the door, needing to put as much distance between them as he could. His hands shook. Never in his life had he been so helpless in his attraction to a woman. He could control a response. He'd never lost his cool or his control, but Lyric threatened both.

The next two weeks were going to be a test of his will that he didn't think he had a snowball's chance in hell of passing.

Lyric rubbed furiously at her eyes to try to dust the cobwebs from her muddled brain. She shoved up from the bed and waited to gain her bearings before trudging toward the bathroom.

She turned on the shower and went over to check her appearance in the mirror. She grinned in delight when she saw the blue shimmer at the ends of her hair. It looked great. Julie had done a fantastic job.

Lyric wished she hadn't been quite so drunk so she remembered Connor's reaction to it.

She turned, looking for her toiletries, and to her surprise saw her bags neatly stacked on the vanity. She rummaged through one of the boxes and dug out a scrunchie to put her hair up in.

Steam poured from the shower as she stripped out of her clothes. She couldn't wait.

Hot water sluiced over her skin and she moaned in sheer delight. Some of the muck rinsed and her mind cleared as she tilted her head up and let the water run down her body.

For several long minutes, she simply stood there, vowing all the time that she'd never drink again.

About the time she was on the verge of boiling herself, she turned off the water and stepped out to dry off.

She wandered back into her room wrapped in a towel and went through the clothes that hung in her closet. If she had to meet a bunch of men charged with babysitting her, she wanted to look killer.

Connor said an hour, but she took an hour and a half. When she walked out of her bathroom, makeup and hair perfectly arranged, Connor was sitting on the edge of her bed. He made a show of looking at his watch as she sauntered over.

"Sober?" he asked.

"Maybe."

"Did you have fun with the girls?"

She smiled. "Yeah, I did. I like them. I like them a lot. I don't have many women friends. Okay, try no women friends. Or friends period. It's kind of nice to think they might fill the bill even if they're just pretending."

Connor frowned. "They wouldn't pretend. They're good girls. None better anywhere. They're genuine. And trust me, Julie doesn't pretend to like anyone."

A chuckle escaped Lyric. "Yeah, I got that impression. She's cool, though. I like her. It's hard to find honest, straightforward people in my line of work. Everyone lies. No one tells the truth."

"Your line of work sucks."

She shrugged. "Yeah, I suppose to someone like you it would. I don't expect honesty. I assume everyone is out to fuck me. At least that way I'm not disappointed and I can do my job without being an emotional wreck every time I figure out someone isn't who I think they are."

"That's no way to live. Damn it, Lyric. Don't you think you deserve a better life than that?"

Startled by the vehemence in his voice, she cocked her head to the side. "It's not a bad life, Connor. Singing's what I always wanted to do. Putting up with disingenuous people is just a part of it all. A sacrifice for getting to do what I love."

He reached out and touched her cheek, his palm sliding gently over her skin. "You deserve better."

She smiled and rubbed her cheek against his hand. For once the idea of being . . . alone . . . with him didn't bother her. She liked this. Something so simple as his touch. It was nonthreatening. He wasn't like the others and she took great comfort in that.

"Well, it looks like for the next two weeks, at least, I'm going to have better," she said huskily.

His gaze bored into her, caressing her skin as surely as if he touched her. "Count on it."

God help her, but she was actually looking forward to her confinement with Connor Malone. What started out as a giant pain in her ass had turned into a break from reality that she desperately needed—and wanted. She wanted it so bad she ached.

He reached slowly for her hand and curled his fingers around hers. "Come on. I need to introduce you to the guys who are going to make sure you're safe."

She followed him down the stairs, her hand tucked into his the whole way. Only when they got to the bottom did he let hers fall away. His demeanor changed and he became all business as soon as they entered the living room where half a dozen men were watching television.

One of them pointed the remote and turned off the TV as the rest rose and focused their attention on her.

"Ms. Jones," the one with the remote said as he stepped forward. "Kane Murphy. I'll be heading your security team for the next two weeks."

She frowned even as she took his extended hand and shook it. The man was drop-dead gorgeous. He had the look of a total badass. Muscular. Menacing. He had a "don't fuck with me" look and piercing blue eyes.

"I thought Connor was in charge." She didn't like that panic raced up her spine at the thought of Connor bailing. She looked over at him, for some sign of reassurance.

"Absolutely he is," Kane said smoothly. "I report to him. The rest of the team, however, reports to me. They're my team. We work together. Connor sticks to you. We stick to you and him."

She relaxed and even managed a smile. "It's nice to meet you then, Kane."

He nodded and then turned to the other men assembled. "This is Davidson, McElroy, Hennesey, Tatum and Markowitz. I don't expect you to remember their names. You won't be seeing much of them unless you need to. If you yell, we come running. No names are necessary."

"Thank goodness. I'm terrible with names."

"This is only half of my team."

Her eyes widened in surprise. How many people did it take to protect one person?

"The other half is posted on the perimeter of the grounds. We rotate watches. In addition to the security system that is available at this residence, my team will mount around-the-clock surveillance. No one gets in or out of the grounds without our permission. That means you. You don't go anywhere without Connor and the men I assign to your detail. You'll listen to everything we tell you, and when we give an order, do not question it. Your hesitation could mean the difference between life and death. Are we clear?"

She was tempted to come to attention and snap a salute. If she wasn't half-afraid of him, she'd do just that, but he didn't strike her as a man who had a sense of humor. And to think she thought Connor was uptight.

"Yes, sir," she said crisply, unable to ignore the demon propped on her shoulder.

Kane eyed her coolly. "I've never lost a person in the ten years I've been working personal security. I damn well won't start now. Give me any trouble whatsoever and I'll lock you in your room for the next two weeks."

Her eyes narrowed. Damn if he was going to get away with bossing her around like that. Connor was the only one who could get away with issuing her orders, and she had no explanation for why that was.

"You just try it, Mr. Murphy," she bit out.

Connor's hand smoothed over her shoulder and he gave her a warning squeeze. "Enough, Lyric."

To her irritation, she quieted and went still. Like a freaking dog coming to heel. What the hell ever.

"You keep him away from me," Lyric said to Connor.

"Behave and I'll gladly oblige," Kane offered smoothly.

Again Connor's hand tightened on her shoulder, a silent warning that she resented. Apparently she was expected to be on her best behavior and everyone else got to treat her like an idiot.

She hated how her life kept spiraling more out of control. She hated not being in control.

She turned to Connor and had to resist walking into his arms. "Are we done here?"

Connor nodded.

"I'd like to get something to eat then."

Connor let his hand slide from her shoulder. "Let's go into the kitchen. I'm sure we can rummage up something. Phillip made sure the house was completely stocked before we moved in."

"I have some calls to make tomorrow," Lyric said as she opened the fridge to take stock. She frowned as she glanced over the array of deli meats, cheeses, fruits and fresh vegetables.

What she really wanted was a cupcake.

"I've put stuff off for too long. While this is a semivacation, I still have a ton of stuff to do before my show at the rodeo. I'm supposed to be writing songs, which I haven't even begun thinking of. How am I supposed to be creative when my life has been turned upside down?"

Connor slid his hands over her shoulders and massaged as she stood staring into the fridge. "Relax, Lyric. Right now your focus is on staying safe. It's only two weeks. I'll help you in any way I can."

She sighed and shut the refrigerator. "Thanks. I appreciate it. I know I probably don't show it, but I really do."

His lips quirked up into a grin. "It's part of your charm."

She went to the pantry and shoved aside boxes and cans.

"Is there anything in particular you're looking for?" he asked. "What are you hungry for? I'm not great in the kitchen, but I can manage until the chef gets here tomorrow."

She turned around, arching her eyebrow. "Chef?"

"Yeah, Phillip hired someone to cook for you while you're here. I assumed this was something you were used to. Don't all rock stars get the royal treatment?"

She searched his tone and demeanor for sarcasm, but he didn't have a hint of snottiness in the question. Just light teasing.

"I have someone who takes care of that on the road. I hate eating out all the time. I already told you I have to watch what I eat or I gain weight too easily. But usually when I go off tour, I'm on my own. Again, which is why I gain weight when I'm not on the road."

"Well, you get a chef tomorrow afternoon. Supposed to be here before lunch. He wants to meet with you so he can plan a menu."

"Cupcakes. I just want cupcakes."

Connor laughed. "You can have all the cupcakes you want."

"No, I can't," she said mournfully.

Connor's laugh died and his expression grew serious. His eyes darkened and he gazed intently at her. "You're beautiful just as you are, Lyric."

Heat rose in her cheeks, and to her horror, she felt the sting of tears. Hell. The man was lethal to her composure. She swung back around and grabbed a box of macaroni and cheese.

"This okay?" she blurted as she shoved the box toward him.

"Love mac and cheese," he said.

Another thought occurred and she frowned. "We don't have to feed Kane and his crew, do we? Because if I have to eat with that man, I'm not going to keep an appetite."

Connor shook his head. "He's not that bad, Lyric. He's just doing his job. Believe me, you want the biggest, baddest son of a bitch on your side."

"Yeah, as long as he doesn't get pissed at me and throw me to the bad guy," Lyric muttered.

Connor chuckled. "Not going to happen, and no, he's not eating with us. They have kitchen privileges, but I got the impression they like to keep to themselves and a low profile. I doubt you'll see much of them except when you go somewhere."

"Suits me just fine."

Connor took the box and put a pot of water on the stove to boil while Lyric took a seat at the bar. After pouring the noodles into the pot, Connor turned and leaned against the counter.

"Tell me something, Lyric. Do you trust anyone at all?"

She went still, caught completely off guard by the question. It was one she didn't even know how to answer. Well, she knew how to answer, but not without it making her sound like a paranoid bitch.

Deciding to make it short and to the point, she simply said, "No."

Then she held up a hand. "If you're going to start in again on how sad and pathetic that is, save it. I'm not in the mood to be picked apart and analyzed. I already have a bad enough headache."

Connor frowned. "Why didn't you say so?"

He went over to one of the cabinets and pulled out a bottle of pills and returned a few moments later with two in his hand. After handing them to her, he went to the fridge and returned with a bottle of water.

"Take them," he said softly. "There's no reason for you to suffer."

She threw the pills to the back of her throat and then chased them down with the water. Connor returned to the stove to watch over the mac and cheese, and Lyric sat there wondering how the hell she was going to get through the next two weeks with her sanity intact.

"Can we have company here?" she asked suddenly.

He glanced sideways at her. "What kind of company?"

"I thought maybe Faith, Serena, Julie and Angelina could come for lunch or dinner, or just to visit."

She needed the company. She would go nuts in this big house alone or, worse, just her and Connor. She alternated between wanting to jump his bones and being freaked-out that he was close to her. It was exhausting being such a basket case.

Maybe Phillip was right. Maybe she was on the verge of a breakdown. Maybe when all this crap with the stalker was resolved, she'd take a long vacation somewhere.

Connor frowned. "I don't know, Lyric. I hesitate to involve them any more than we have to. Their husbands won't be thrilled with them going where there's potential danger."

Lyric sighed. "Yeah, you're right. Some freak is after me and I'm a toxic influence. They're nice girls and I'd hate for me to rub off on them."

Connor stalked over and planted his hands on the bar in front of her. He looked . . . pissed.

"Do you think they're better than you? Do you think *I* think they're better than you?"

She stared up at him for a long moment. "Yeah. Yeah, I do. Doesn't take a genius to figure that one out."

"Bullshit."

"Look, you thought it not so long ago. You weren't so gung ho to expose me to your friends."

"I was wrong," Connor said quietly.

That shut her up.

"They loved you. You were great with them. I was an asshole. We've covered that. Those girls mean a lot to me. Yeah, in the beginning I was worried that there would be friction. I don't want them over here, but that has nothing to do with you. I don't want anyone to get hurt."

Lyric smiled. "You know what, Connor Malone?"

His eyes narrowed suspiciously. "What?"

She sat back with a satisfied grin and crossed her arms over her chest. "You like me. You don't want to. You didn't want to. But you like me."

He leaned over, snaked his hand behind her nape and all but hauled her over the table as his lips melted over hers. Hot and so breathless she grew light-headed.

Man, but he could kiss.

She braced her palms on the countertop and leaned farther, hungry—so hungry—for him.

His tongue traced the line of her mouth and then delved inward. She sucked at the tip, wanting more. She licked at him, meeting his tongue in a flirty duel that had him sucking back.

She nipped at his lip, first his bottom and then the top. Oh, but she wanted to devour him.

A hissing sound from the stove had him pulling away and he glanced to where the water boiled over the rim of the pot. But before he went to rescue the macaroni, he stroked his thumb over her bottom lip and his eyes glittered with intense need.

"I think you're a very observant woman," he murmured.

CHAPTER 15

*C*onnor stood in the doorway of the room Lyric had commandeered as her studio. Her guitar and sound equipment had been delivered and set up and she'd been sequestered in solitude all morning long.

She had her guitar cradled against her chest and she strummed a series of chords as her haunting voice echoed through the room and slid over his skin like silk.

It was a far cry from the noisy, raucous show she'd put on when he'd seen her in concert. He'd be hard-pressed to even believe they were the same woman if he didn't know for sure they were.

She slapped her hand over the strings, silencing the guitar, and made a sound of frustration. Then she began again and rearranged some of the words.

If you only knew
If you could only see

If you could only come inside
And see the heart of me

She paused for a moment and then looked up and saw him standing in the door. Her hand fell away and she looked discomfited by his presence.

"It's beautiful. Is it a new song you're working on?"

She set aside her guitar and rubbed her hands down her pants. "Yeah. Something a little different. I'm going for a new sound for the next album. I haven't run the songs by my label yet, so I'm not sure they'll go for it."

Connor took a seat in the chair across from Lyric. "And if they don't?"

She shrugged. "I can either play by their rules and record the music they want or I can go out on my own, find another label or start my own."

"Phillip seems pretty damn committed to keeping you. I don't see him telling you no. I'm not sure he knows the meaning of that word when it comes to you."

She shot him a baleful look.

Connor grinned. "Oh, come on. Admit it. No one tells you no very often. I doubt you'd listen to them if they did."

"Depends on whether or not they're saying what I want to hear," she said cheekily.

He chuckled. She was pretty darn cute when she was being sassy. And not that he'd ever admit it in a million years, but he liked the blue on her. It just . . . fit.

"Connor, you need to see this," Kane said from the door.

Connor glanced up. Kane's expression said it wasn't good. He got to his feet and started to tell Lyric to stay put, but Kane pressed his lips together and then said, "Bring her. She'll need to see this too."

Lyric shot Connor a worried look and rose to stand beside him.

Not caring how it looked, Connor held out his hand to her. She slid her palm over his and he curled his fingers tight around hers. Then he tugged her toward the door and after Kane.

They traveled down the stairs and to the living room where one of the other men had the television programming paused. Kane nodded at him and then stood back, arms crossed over his chest.

It was the local newscast, but as soon as Lyric's face appeared, Connor flinched.

"Pop singer Lyric Jones is in town early for her rodeo appearance, and by all accounts, the star is never far out of trouble."

The reporter segued into footage from the police station and then of Lyric leaving the station with Connor. To make matters worse, two of the police officers who'd been involved in Lyric's detainment were interviewed. While no actual details were given, the implication was certainly clear that she'd been involved in yet another undesirable situation.

Beside him, Lyric stiffened and she stared stonily at the TV.

At the end, the reporter wrapped up by saying that her rodeo appearance was sold out.

Kane turned the television set off and turned to face Connor and Lyric. "This complicates matters."

There was little he could say. Kane was right, but he had no desire to rip into Lyric. He was as much at fault for the incident as she was.

"It changes nothing," Connor said flatly. "Our job is still the same. We protect Lyric, keep her out of compromising situations and make damn sure no one gets to her."

Kane stared at Lyric, his eyes glittering. "I need your assurance this won't happen again."

Lyric's head jerked up, and her lips twisted into a snarl. Connor stepped in front of her and faced Kane.

"The situation has already been handled. It was a simple misunderstanding. Lyric is my direct responsibility. Yours is to provide peripheral security."

Kane's lip twitched but he didn't argue.

"I need a schedule of her appearances. Any appointments. Basically if she's going to set foot off this property in the next ten days, I need to know about it so I can plan accordingly."

"We'll have you one before today is over," Connor said.

"I have work to do," Lyric said tightly.

She turned away and stalked back up the stairs, and in the distance, Connor heard the door to her studio slam.

He looked back at Kane. "Cut her some slack. I doubt you're this hard-ass with all your clients. She's not as bad as she seems. It's all a front."

Kane's eyes glimmered with amusement. "I do whatever it takes to get the job done. If it means me being an ass, then that's what happens. Your girl doesn't strike me as the type to take things seriously if you coddle her."

"She's not . . ." Hell. He blew out his breath. "Agreed. I don't think she needs coddling. I've been a few rounds with her myself. But she really is taking this whole thing seriously. I can't make up my mind about her. One minute she seems so . . ."

"Sane?" Kane interjected.

"Yeah, and then the next she seems completely . . ."

"Insane?"

Connor laughed. "Okay, yeah, maybe. But I think it's a defense mechanism with her. How belligerent she is seems to be in direct proportion to how vulnerable she feels. The greater the disadvantage, the more mouthy she becomes."

"You seem to have her all figured out," Kane drawled.

"What the hell is that supposed to mean?"

Kane blinked and studied Connor for a long moment. "I think you know what it means. Just do me a favor. If you start sleeping with her, give me a heads-up so I can adjust accordingly."

"I can do my job just fine," Connor said icily.

Kane offered a shrug. "Look, man, I don't give a shit what you do. But know this. A man never sees the enemy coming when his dick is occupied, if you know what I mean."

Connor's cell rang, and he gave Kane one last glare before he turned away and put the phone to his ear.

"Malone here."

"What the hell is going on down there?"

Phillip Armstrong's voice boomed over the line, and Connor sighed. Just what he needed right now.

"Everything is under control."

"The hell you say. I get a report that Lyric is on the local news because she was arrested. Mind telling me what the hell for? You were supposed to be on her every waking moment. How can you protect her if she's out pulling stupid stunts?"

Connor stalked out of the living room and onto the back patio. "She wasn't arrested. She went to the police for safety. She's not stupid."

"Where were you when she was doing all this? She shouldn't have had to go to the police if you were doing your job."

"If you don't like the way I'm doing my job, then fire me," Connor said bluntly. "I never wanted this gig to begin with. Lyric ditched me. I took care of the situation. It won't happen again. We've reached an understanding. She's promised to cooperate."

There was a pregnant silence. Then Phillip let out another curse. "No, I don't damn well want to fire you. Hell, no one else would take the job and definitely not on such short notice. I'm still interviewing firms to take over her full-time security while she's on the road."

"If you wouldn't treat her like a brainless idiot, I think you'd find she'd be a lot more accommodating," Connor said through his teeth.

"Look, son. You've known Lyric for a week. I've known her for several years. I know how to handle her. Just do your job. Sit on her until I find a replacement and then you can wash your hands of her."

The line went dead and Connor shoved his phone back into his pocket. Wash his hands of her. Phillip made her sound like the most undesirable job on the planet. It was little wonder she had such a cynical attitude about life if these were the kind of people she trusted with her future.

It pissed him off and made him see red at the lack of respect she commanded from people she made a shitload of money for. He wanted to tell them all to go fuck themselves.

He wanted to . . . Hell, he didn't know what he wanted. He just knew he hated the fleeting hurt in Lyric's eyes—hurt she didn't think others could see and that she tried like hell to cover up. Behind the brassy, ballsy, obnoxious facade was a vulnerable woman that intrigued him. He was dying to know what made her tick.

And yeah, he was absolutely dying to fuck her too.

It pissed him off that evidently he wore a neon sign when it came to her, because Kane had been quick to pick up on his attraction. In so many ways it didn't make sense. Lyric was the type of woman he stayed the hell away from. High-maintenance chicks weren't his thing. And Lyric definitely qualified.

She was like an expensive exotic car. You might test-drive one, but you never signed on the dotted line. And you damn sure couldn't afford the insurance.

Connor turned when he heard the patio door open. Kane stuck his head out.

"Connor, the chef is at the gate. My guy is checking him out now.

If he's on the up-and-up, he'll be waved through. Thought you might want to know so you could meet him."

"Thanks. I'll go up to get Lyric."

Connor stepped back into the house and went up the stairs to her studio. He drew up short when he saw the metal Do Not Disturb sign hanging from the doorknob.

He sighed. She'd made it clear that when the sign was out, she wasn't to be disturbed for any reason. He didn't believe for a minute she was deeply involved in her music.

As much as the belligerent Lyric had gotten under his skin, he preferred that to quiet resignation. He'd be damned if he'd let anyone beat her down. She was too vibrant. Too alive. She was like holding a stick of dynamite. You never knew when she'd go off.

And she didn't trust anyone—Connor included.

He put his palm flat on the door and rested his forehead on the wood as he heard the faint sounds of her guitar floating through the air. He remembered the words she'd sung so softly just a short time ago.

If you only knew
If you could only see
If you could only come inside
And see the heart of me.

"You're going to trust me, Lyric Jones," he murmured. "You're going to see that I'm not like everyone else in your life."

He turned and went downstairs to meet Lyric's chef. The man had cupcakes to make.

Chapter 16

Lyric put her guitar down and flexed her neck, then extended her arms above her head to stretch her tired, aching muscles. She glanced at her watch and saw that it was late.

She was hungry, but she had no desire to go down and eat. What she wanted was a hot shower and a comfortable bed, in that precise order.

She let herself out of the studio and turned the sign over so that Connor would know she was no longer working. She went straight for her bathroom and turned on the shower.

A long soak in the gorgeous bathtub would be wonderful, but she was too impatient and edgy to enjoy it. She opted instead for a quick shower, careful to keep her hair from getting wet.

When she was done, she wrapped herself in a towel and shook out her hair from the clip she'd shoved into it to hold it up. She spent another five minutes removing what makeup hadn't washed off in the shower and applying moisturizer.

Eager to crawl into bed, she walked out of her bathroom only to find Connor propped against the wall in her bedroom.

She clutched the towel although the ends were securely tucked at her breasts, covering most of her from his view.

"Don't you think you've been hiding up here long enough?" Connor asked as he pushed off the wall.

She frowned. "I was busy. I have work to do. I told you that."

His eyes narrowed. "You let Kane get to you. Kane and the newscast. I saw you, Lyric. You can't hide from me."

Her nostrils flared and she turned away. "You don't get it, Connor."

"What don't I get, Lyric? Why don't you explain it to me?"

She kept her back to him, her arms folded protectively over her breasts. "The whole thing was my fault. I was a complete idiot."

"I believe we've established that I had responsibility in that fiasco."

She curled her lips in disgust. "No, Connor. I let *you* hurt me. I'm a study in don't-give-a-damn, but I let you get to me. That's why I left. That's why I took off the way I did. I didn't want to let you see how much you hurt me."

His hands closed over her shoulders and he gently turned her to face him. "I'm sorry."

She pushed away from his grasp and had to clutch at the towel to keep it from falling. "I don't want you to be sorry. I don't want you to . . . be anything."

"I don't believe you," he said quietly.

Her gaze flew to his and something remarkably like panic skittered up her spine and wrapped around her neck. He had a look in his eyes that she didn't like. It untied her like a knot and peeled back her skin, leaving her naked and vulnerable. She *hated* that feeling.

She opened her mouth but couldn't for the life of her think of what to say to that. How could he know? How could he possibly know that she had the craziest thoughts about him? She was absolutely stupid when it came to him and she was helpless to control it.

He took a step forward, closing the gap she'd opened between them. She retreated, bumping against the bed in her haste. He followed, not giving her so much as an inch.

"I think you want me to be a lot of things," he murmured. "I think right now you want me to be your lover. I think you want me to show you how different I am from everyone else in your life. You're *afraid* that I'm different from everyone else."

She stared at him in helpless fury, appalled at how well he could see into her soul. She blinked back angry tears just as his hands cupped her face and he lowered his mouth to hers.

It was like being caught in the middle of a lightning storm. Awareness sparked and sizzled, so hot that she gasped from the sensation.

He kissed her like he owned her, like she was his, like he was the only person to have ever kissed her. His tongue explored her mouth, leaving no part untouched.

Her body was not her own. Her breasts throbbed, and deep down at her very core, an ache began and spread through her groin until her clit pulsed and her pussy tightened with anticipation.

All from a kiss. Just the touch of his mouth, and desire swept over her like a tidal wave.

She loved his hands. How they touched her and held her. How possessive they felt on her skin. He wasn't tentative and she really loved that. This was a man confident in his ability to make love to a woman.

She closed her eyes and trembled violently against him. She was in turns terrified of her reaction to him and more turned on than she'd ever been in her life.

"I won't hurt you, Lyric," he murmured against her lips. "I don't want you to be afraid. I want you to know what it feels like to have someone love you."

She tensed and backed away enough that she could put a finger to his lips. "Please don't say that word. Please, just don't. Don't ruin everything."

His eyes clouded with confusion. "What word?"

"*Love*. Don't ever use that word."

He gave her a searching look and then reached up to brush the hair from her face. "I won't use any words you don't want. I'll simply show you."

She stared back at him and knew he was waiting. Waiting for her to agree. Waiting for her acceptance. It would be so easy to push him away. Far easier than voicing the words that ached to break free.

"Tell me what you want, Lyric. Give me the words."

Her breath escaped in a nearly violent shudder. "I don't want . . . I don't want to be alone tonight."

He came to her again, his mouth brushing over hers in the most tender of kisses. "That's a start."

Slowly he slid his hands up to where her fingers clutched the towel. He paused for a moment and then carefully uncurled her fingers before lowering her hands to her sides.

She shook. Her knees quaked and her breath sped up so fast that she became precariously light-headed. Then he lowered his head and pressed a single kiss to her chest, just above where the towel covered her breasts.

"I won't hurt you, Lyric."

Just the way he said her name with such aching tenderness undid her. On his lips, her name was something different. It wasn't just her name. It was an endearment—something very precious.

He raised his head and met her gaze and she saw herself reflected in his eyes. "Do you trust me?"

Mutely she shook her head, her reaction as automatic as breathing.
He smiled when she thought she might have angered him.

"I think you do," he murmured. "Even if you won't admit it to yourself."

"I feel safe with you," she offered. And it was true. Was that the same as trust? Trust was such a big word.

"I think it's a good place to start."

He reached for the end of the towel that was tucked around her breasts. She stiffened and very nearly raised her hands to stop him, but at the last moment, she lowered them slowly back to her sides.

He didn't simply tear the towel away. Watching her all the while, he carefully unwound it until it was loose and barely covering her flesh. Then with a gentle tug, it drifted to the floor and she stood naked and painfully vulnerable to his gaze.

She lowered her gaze and closed her eyes, unsure of what to do next. Never had sex come with such unsettling emotions. She was in control. She drove the action. She played, she taunted. Everything was by her rules.

But now she found herself at a complete and utter disadvantage, and panic welled from deep within, threatening to overwhelm her.

"Do you know what I see?" he asked in a husky, deep voice that slid over her skin like soul-deep comfort.

He nudged her chin up until she was forced to look back at him. Such honesty was reflected in his gaze. Frank appraisal like he'd judged her and deemed her worthy. What did it matter what he thought? Why was she so torn up over the idea that somehow he'd find her undesirable or lacking and back away? Backing away was what *she* did.

"What?" she asked in barely a whisper, drawn to the earnest blaze in his eyes.

"I see a beautiful woman who's soft in all the right places. Who would be beautiful now or six sizes larger. I see a woman who tries very hard to hide from the world and perhaps herself. But you can't hide from me, Lyric. I'm learning you. I want to learn more."

She inhaled sharply. His words hit her in the gut, driving the air from her lungs. She stared at him, baffled by his assessment. Baffled by the warmth in his eyes and how his gaze stroked over her body as though she were the most beautiful woman he'd ever seen.

It was a silly thought. There were certainly women more beautiful, but in this moment, standing in front of him, she felt like she somehow stood above all the rest.

No one talked to her when they had sex with her. It was just . . . sex. Hot, sweaty and fast. Get it over with; move on; don't dwell on emotion.

But with this man, she had the feeling that it would never be just sex, and that idea unsettled her. It frightened her. Making love was for people who were in love, who used sex as an intimate expression of that love. It wasn't for people like her, to whom love was an ugly, gray thing.

"Nothing to say to that?"

She shook her head again.

He chuckled. "I've never seen you without anything to say. I like it."

Before she could respond, he pressed in close, cupped her shoulders in his strong hands and bent to kiss her.

She loved his kisses. They unraveled her.

Her breasts pushed again his chest. His body cupped around hers, flush, so warm and solid. A restless, itchy sensation prickled over her skin. She wanted to feel his flesh against hers. She wanted no barrier between their bodies.

Before she realized she had, she raised her hands and pushed underneath his T-shirt until her hands slid over his taut belly.

He immediately froze. His tongue stilled over hers and she could feel the huff of his breath over her face.

Thinking she'd jumped the gun, she immediately withdrew and clenched her fists at her sides. She wasn't used to withstanding seduction. She was usually the aggressor. Playing by someone else's rules was alien.

Connor eased back just a step and then he reached for the hem of his shirt. Giving it an impatient yank, he hauled it over his head and dropped it to the floor.

Then he stepped back to her and circled her wrists with his fingers. He raised her hands and placed them against his chest, holding them there against the solid wall of his muscle.

"I love you touching me."

He brought one hand to his mouth and kissed each fingertip before finally sucking her pinkie into his mouth. Hot and moist. It sent a thrill down her spine.

"Take my pants off, Lyric. I want you to touch me. I don't think I'll be able to get enough."

She licked her lips as he lowered her hands to his waist. She shook so bad that she fumbled clumsily with the button of his fly. The sound of the zipper was loud. It broke through the heavy silence and made her flinch as she eased it all the way down.

Slowly she peeled the denim over his hips and down his legs until it gathered around his ankles. He stepped free and stood before her, the burning question at last answered.

She laughed softly and raised her gaze to Connor, a smile twisting her lips.

He arched an eyebrow. "What's so funny? I have to tell you, laughing when you've got a guy down to his underwear is never a good thing."

"I was right," she teased.

"About?"

"You're a boxer brief guy."

He grinned smugly and mischief lit his eyes. "So you *have* been thinking about me."

Damn. "I may have wondered. But that was it."

"Uh-huh. Admit it, Lyric. You've been thinking about me every bit as much as I've been thinking about you."

She hooked her fingers in the elastic waistband of his briefs and pulled him closer to her. "Maybe."

"I got a hard-on for you the very first time we met. You and that sassy mouth of yours had me so hard, and I was desperate for you not to know."

One corner of her mouth went up and she reached gently to caress the very noticeable bulge between his legs. His cock strained against the cotton material, a hard ridge trapped against his body.

What would he expect? Would he want her to take the lead now? He'd seemed to cede control when he'd asked her to undress him. Then she frowned. Or maybe he expected to direct her through it all. Was he in control or was she?

He tipped a finger underneath her chin and nudged it upward until once again his heated gaze bored into her. "Why the frown?"

"Who's in control?" she blurted. "I'm not sure . . . I'm not sure what you want me to do."

"Does it matter?" he asked lazily. "Why do either of us have to control everything? Why can't we just enjoy each other for a while? You tell me what you like, what feels good to you. I'll tell you what I like."

She smiled and sent her hand seeking into his underwear until her fingers wrapped around his rigid erection. His breath caught and he went completely still.

"Does that feel good?" she asked innocently.

"It'll feel a hell of a lot better when you get your mouth wrapped around it," he drawled.

When she would have gone to her knees, he caught her by the elbows and hauled her up against him.

"I don't expect you to service me before I've made you feel good, sweetheart."

Then his mouth closed over hers, so hot and wicked. She melted, let herself go limp against him as he picked her up and walked her to the edge of the bed.

She wrapped her legs around his waist and pulled him down with her when he would have laid her on the mattress.

"You're like a feast and I have no idea where to start," he said in a low voice. "So much to savor. I don't want to miss a single taste of your sweetness."

"You're lethal," she said helplessly. "How can I possibly resist you when you say such pretty words?"

He grinned. "I think the point is that you're not supposed to resist me."

His mouth brushed across her shoulder and he stopped to nibble a path to the column of her neck. Then he retraced back to her shoulder and he sank his teeth into her flesh.

"Mmmm."

"You like that?" he husked against her skin.

"Mmm-hmmm."

He chuckled and then licked the spot where he'd bitten her. As he wandered down her body with his oh-so-delectable mouth, she wondered if she'd have a mark where he'd bitten her. The completely irrational part of her hoped so. She wanted a tangible reminder of his possession.

He dragged his open mouth down her midline, kissing and licking at intervals until he left a wet trail between her breasts to her navel.

Despite his assurances that she was beautiful no matter her size, she tensed when his tongue laved over the soft skin of her belly. She wasn't fat but neither did she have his taut, lean belly that you could bounce a quarter off. Plus she'd gained and lost weight so many times that she sagged in certain areas.

"Relax," he murmured as his tongue dipped into her belly button.

Then he kissed every inch of her abdomen and then lowered his mouth to her pelvis. After pressing a gentle kiss to the flesh just above the juncture of her legs, he raised his head and eased a finger over her bare folds.

"I like this," he murmured.

She didn't raise her head because, really, she'd never had a man do an analysis of her pussy while she was lying beneath him.

"What do you like?"

He stroked the lips of her vagina and then ran his finger over the small triangle of hair just over the hood that shielded her clitoris.

"Your wax job. I hear women talk about them, but I've never seen one exactly. You know, in person."

At that she did raise her head and she arched an eyebrow in his direction. "Never?"

He shrugged. "The women I've been with aren't groomed down there."

She laughed. "You make me sound like a poodle."

His fingers returned to her folds. He seemed to be fascinated with the smoothness because he kept stroking her over and over until she was ready to twitch right off the bed. Didn't he realize he was making her crazy?

"Do you like it?" he asked.

"Yeah, I do. It makes me feel . . . sexy."

At that he grinned and stared up at her with approval in his eyes. "I'm glad, then. You need to be as convinced as I am of just how beautiful you are."

He lowered his head and nuzzled softly through her folds. The tip of his tongue brushed ever so lightly over her clit and she shuddered uncontrollably.

"You taste as sweet as you feel," he murmured.

"You know just how to get to me," she whispered. "Words are my life. How they flow. Their meaning. Twisting and turning them and making them more beautiful. Whenever you talk to me like this, I hear it like it's a song."

"You don't want me to sing," he said in amusement.

She nudged him upward with her knees and then reached for him, wanting him over her body. She wanted him to cover her like a blanket so there wasn't an inch of her skin untouched.

He rose over her and she clutched at his shoulders, reveling in his hard strength.

"You don't have to sing. I hear it in your words. No one has ever said such beautiful things to me."

"Then you're hanging out with the wrong people."

And then he started again. Scorching a path over her body, only this time he stopped at her breasts, lavishing attention on each of them. He coaxed her nipples to rigid peaks and then he sucked them between his teeth, one at a time, alternating until she was making incomprehensible sounds of pleasure.

His movements were like the most beautiful notes. Perfect pitch. So in tune with her body—and her soul. He stroked her like a pianist might stroke the keys of a song he'd composed just for her.

She heard the notes, the raw, exquisite beauty, as they reverberated over her skin.

She no longer even knew what she needed. She needed him. Just him. It was a stupid thought but it was all that echoed in her mind.

"Please, Connor. I need you."

As if realizing just what the admission cost her, he looked down at her tenderly as his hand went to part her thighs. He settled one knee between them and then he reached over her body to pick up a condom she hadn't realized was resting beside her pillow.

He gave a slight groan as he rolled the latex over his cock. "God, I'm so close to coming and I haven't even gotten inside you."

She shifted restlessly, hoping he got the message that she didn't want to wait any longer. Her skin felt too tight. Pressure swelled in her core until she fidgeted. She *burned*.

He eased his fingers farther into her heat and she moaned. His thumb gently circled her clit just as he fitted another finger and delved into her tight passage.

"You're not ready yet, baby," he murmured.

Her eyes flew open. "Please, Connor."

"Not yet. I don't want to hurt you."

She sighed but closed her eyes when he lowered his mouth to her breast while his fingers continued their slow exploration of her most intimate recesses.

He stroked in and out in a perfect demonstration of how his cock would stroke through her insides to the very heart of her. She arched into his touch like a cat seeking petting. A low sound of contentment poured out of her throat and she reached blindly for him as he continued his erotic assault on her senses.

Her fingers curled into his hair, running through the crisp, short hairs as she held him to her breast. She idly stroked down to his nape and followed the thickly corded muscles of his neck and shoulders.

He was a perfect specimen of a man. Long, lean and tight. Clean-cut. Mr. All-American. Which begged the question of why in the hell he was attracted to her—she was decidedly not a fresh-faced girl next door in middle-class America. That was the woman she could see Connor with. Mr. Always Do Right with Miss Sweet Apple Pie.

"You left me," Connor murmured.

She blinked and he came sharply into focus. He was staring down at her, his gaze seeking.

"Am I doing something wrong?"

She softened at his tone. His desire to please her couldn't be more prevalent. Fuck Miss Apple Pie. Lyric hated apple pie anyway. This man was hers at least for the next half hour, and quite frankly, she'd kick some Miss America ass if she came within spitting distance of Connor.

She wrapped her arms around his neck and pulled him down for a long, breathless kiss.

"You're doing everything perfect."

CHAPTER 17

$\mathcal{C}$onnor rotated over Lyric until he came to rest between her thighs, his body held up off her by his hands on either side of her head.

She was ready for him. Satiny smooth and slick with her own arousal. And in her eyes glowed a sweetness that belied her hard edge.

There was something to be said for a soft, willing woman underneath you—who looked at you like you held the answer to all the problems in the world.

Lyric without the bite was sweet indeed. It made him wonder if anyone else ever saw the woman underneath the layers she'd carefully constructed. Did anyone even care?

Wanting to taste her again, he fit his mouth to hers and licked over the seam of her lips just as he positioned himself at her entrance.

"Tell me you're ready now, Lyric," he strained out. "Because I can't wait any longer."

His body screamed at him to take her. To mark her and possess her in every primitive way there was for a man to possess a woman.

"Take me," she whispered.

The fact that her words so perfectly echoed his thoughts made his chest tighten. Desire raged through his veins and he stilled for a moment before the urge to thrust as deeply into her as possible took over.

He eased forward, bathing the head of his cock in her silken flesh. Sweat broke out on his forehead as he fought for control.

"Connor."

His name escaped as a whispered plea and her eyes were glazed with passion. She stared at him through half lids, her vibrant blue eyes looking drugged and unfocused.

He inched forward, pushing farther inside her. God, she was tight.

Her nails raked over his back and came to rest on his ass. She arched and pulled at the same time, trying to force him deeper. With a groan he relented and thrust hard.

It was all he could do to hang on as her sweet heat enveloped his aching erection. He was balls deep and straining to get deeper.

Her shocked gasp startled him from his single-minded goal to bury himself deeper than he'd ever buried himself in a woman.

"Did I hurt you?" he asked urgently even as he began to withdraw.

"No. No!" She pulled at him, almost fighting to get him back, arching her hips to hold on to him.

He smiled and leaned down to fuse his lips with hers. "Well okay, then." He surged back into her and closed his eyes as intense, mind-bending pleasure shattered through his groin.

His balls tightened even as they pounded against her ass. His body wasn't his own. He had no control. And she urged him on. Taking everything he had to give. Demanding more.

Fire coiled low in his balls, clutching the base of his cock with a death grip. It built rapidly, rising like an inevitable tide.

He looked down, wanting her with him. He wouldn't go until she'd found her satisfaction.

"Tell me what you need," he breathed.

She feathered a hand over his cheek, a simple touch he felt all the way to his soul.

"Just you. Just you."

But she wasn't as far as he was and he knew it. He paused though it damn near killed him. He had to grit his teeth and breathe harshly through his nose to prevent his orgasm.

He reached for her hand and gently guided it downward. "Touch yourself. Show me how you like it."

He shifted his body the slightest bit so she could fit her hand between them. At first she hesitated, her expression a little uncertain—and shy—but then she slid her fingers through the damp folds, her knuckles grazing through the hair at his groin.

She gave a restless moan that prompted him to pull out of her and then stroke back, long and liquid. To his surprise her fingers wandered lower and wrapped around the inch of his cock that still remained outside her body.

She caressed his length as he eased out of her. Her fingers danced across the latex, and he cursed the condom that lay between her touch and his flesh. He'd never gone bareback with a woman—not even one he was in a relationship with, because caution was too firmly ingrained. But right now he'd sell his soul to be able to get inside her skin to skin.

Finally he had to pull at her wrist and return her fingers to her own pleasure because he was a nanosecond from exploding all over her hand. At this point he'd likely blow the condom completely off.

"You first," he rasped. "I want to watch you come apart around me. I want to feel it."

His statement seemed to excite her because she fluttered around him. Her flesh rippled across his cock and was so snug that he never wanted to leave its stranglehold.

Seemingly emboldened by his words, she began stroking herself in tight little circles, the backs of her fingers brushing over his sensitive skin.

Wanting her closer, wanting deeper, he reached down to cup her buttocks and marveled at how she filled his hands with such delectable, plump flesh. He squeezed and molded her in his palms and then plunged harder, reveling in the sounds that whispered past her lips.

Her fingers moved faster and her legs circled his waist. They strained and undulated. They gasped. His heart raced. Faster and faster and lightning sparked. His release was like a fast-burning fuse, sizzling through his balls and up his cock.

He cursed under his breath because God, he couldn't last.

She went rigid underneath him and bowed until her back came off the bed. He stroked harder, determined to make it so good for her. The best she'd ever had.

His mouth found her neck, and he sucked at the sensitive spot beneath her ear as her cry split the air. He was instantly bathed in liquid fire. Surrounding him, encasing his cock in the sweetest honey.

He raised his head and stared straight into her eyes. Straight into the heart of her. His hips jerked forward as if he had no control over the beast that arose within him. It was startling. So primitive that he understood why some men were considered little better than cavemen because at the moment, his only consideration was dragging Lyric off to his cave by the hair and keeping her underneath him for as long as he had strength to make love to her.

She withdrew her hand, her body still shivering in the aftermath of her orgasm. When she cupped his face, he turned so he could suck her fingers into his mouth to taste that sweet honey.

"Now you," she whispered.

Her words had the same effect his had on her. A violent shiver overtook him and his balls drew up and his release rushed down his cock and exploded with a force that had him gasping. Pain. Pleasure. It all blended together in a myriad of wicked sensation that he never wanted to end.

His hips were still jerking spasmodically forward when he finally lowered his body to completely blanket hers. He closed his eyes and rested his forehead on hers for a long moment as his cock twitched and shuddered deep inside her. He knew he couldn't stay there long and expect the condom to work, but he was loath to retreat from her snug warmth.

Their breaths worked hot and hard, colliding with each other as they both gasped to catch up. When he finally felt his head stop spinning, he kissed her and, with a reluctant groan, pulled himself away and rolled to the side to dispose of the condom.

When he came back to her, her eyes were glazed—with shock? She seemed at a loss and a little baffled. Vulnerability shone like a beacon, and it riled every one of his protective instincts. She'd hate it if she knew how much he could see right now. The barriers would slam down and the hard edge would return.

He climbed into the bed and pulled her into his arms, but she was already stiff and tension radiated from her in waves. In an effort to ease some of her discomfort, he pressed a gentle kiss to her shoulder but he didn't say a word, knowing that if he did, it would completely shatter what calm remained.

Instead he lay there and turned over the matter in his head. He knew it was stupid to have slept with her but at the time he accepted the inevitability of it. She was like a slow-moving drug that had taken hold of his system, insidious and unrelenting.

He didn't have the strength—or the desire—to deny the intense chemistry between them. Even when he'd thought the worst of her, his body had been achingly aware of every part of her.

But now he had to admit that what he'd done could and probably would cause problems. He'd been contemptuous of her bodyguards for not doing their job because they couldn't take their hands off her, and now he was no better. He was here to protect her—in essence to be that same bodyguard—and he could no more keep his hands off her than give up breathing.

It posed a serious problem—one that he was at a loss as to how to solve.

Lyric hadn't relaxed and now she stirred and rolled away from him. He felt her retreat long before she'd actually done so physically. It pissed him off but there wasn't a damn thing he could do about it.

Still, his perverse side roared to the surface and he caught at her arm. "Where are you going?"

"Bathroom," she murmured as she pulled away.

She got up from the bed and hurried across the room, her arms shielding her nakedness from him. He wanted to growl at her that there wasn't a damn thing she could hide. He'd seen and tasted every inch of her. He'd touched and caressed until she'd responded wildly.

He sighed as she disappeared, and he wasn't at all surprised when she didn't return. He stared up at the ceiling and wondered how much more she'd cut herself off from him now that he'd breached her defenses.

CHAPTER 18

*I*t was a sure sign of just how desperate she was not to be A) alone or B) one-on-one with Connor that she found herself downstairs watching television with men she didn't even like.

Okay, that wasn't entirely accurate or fair. She didn't like Kane, the smug, way-too-sure-of-himself "leader" of her security detail. The other guys were probably just fine, but she found them guilty by association, so the result was that the entire lot of them were assholes.

And yet here she was watching late-night television, trying to work up the courage to go back upstairs and face her empty room and the silence that yawned like a chasm.

She could feel the gazes of her security guys resting on her. One had uttered a greeting when she'd come down an hour earlier, but when she hadn't responded, they took the hint and hadn't spoken since.

To her annoyance, Kane entered the living room and didn't seem inclined to ignore her presence like his men had done. He stood a few feet away openly staring at her.

"Is there something we can do, Ms. Jones?"

"Like you care," she muttered.

"Sulking doesn't become you."

She curled her lip into a snarl. "I'm not sulking. I want to be left alone."

He lifted an eyebrow. "And yet here you are in the room with my men."

"Got a problem with that?" she asked belligerently.

He studied her for a moment. "If I'm to believe Connor when he says you only get more belligerent when you're threatened or unsure, then I'd say you're feeling pretty insecure right now."

She bared her teeth. "Fuck off."

There was a glimmer of a smile. She could swear his lips twitched, but when she looked harder, she saw only his cool blue eyes staring back at her like she was boring him.

"If there's nothing you require, we're going to turn in. Time for the next watch."

"Whatever."

"They won't be coming inside."

"So? What's your point?"

"My point is, in thirty seconds you'll be alone down here."

She flushed and curled her fingers into fists so he wouldn't see her hands shake. How did he know? How could he possibly know?

Without a word, she pushed herself from the couch and bolted toward the stairs. Darkness awaited and she made damn sure she turned on every light between the top of the stairs and her bedroom.

She was simultaneously relieved and disappointed that Connor had evidently gone to his room. The door between her bedroom and his was closed. And silent. No light crept underneath his door.

What was worse? Being one-on-one and vulnerable with him or being alone?

It took everything she had not to get on the phone and call in the troops. Right now she wasn't picky. She could fill her room—hell, she could fill every room in this damn house—with people who'd be only too happy to keep her company and prattle on about everything and nothing.

Connor would have a kitten. Kane would be beyond pissed. And it wouldn't make her feel a damn bit better.

Some memories just haunted you no matter how far or how fast you ran.

She wasn't in denial of her circumstances. She knew how fucked-up she was and made no apologies to herself. Self-preservation was a powerful thing, and she knew that what she did kept what little of her sanity she still possessed.

Being alone freaked her out. She couldn't even think about it without feeling the suffocating darkness close in around her. It brought back the feeling of utter helplessness. Guilt. Despair.

The fact that she'd stood by and watched her mother die and never uttered a word. Too scared to cry out. To say stop. To run for help. To scream for help. She'd known that any movement, any sound, would thrust her back into a madman's attention. And she'd suffered his attentions for far too long.

She closed her eyes and felt the familiar sting of tears. Her head ached from holding so much back, from the constant fight to keep her carefully constructed walls from crumbling.

"Oh, Mama, I'm such a mess," she whispered.

She hadn't spoken to her mother in a long time. There were days she still battled her rage and, with it, the terrible guilt for feeling so angry with a mother she'd adored.

She stood in the middle of her room, surrounded by . . . nothing. Silence. Stillness.

"I'm so tired of this," she whispered.

Panic clawed at her throat at the idea of being here alone. The house. The room. It was all unfamiliar to her. These weren't her things. No matter how much of a badass Kane professed to be, he couldn't keep her safe from her dreams. He couldn't keep her safe from her memories.

Connor.

She stared at their adjoining door and was suddenly filled with such powerful longing that her throat ached and swelled. For several long, wonderful moments she'd found exquisite peace in his arms. He'd made her forget about every bad thing that had ever happened to her.

And she'd taken off like a scared rabbit. He must think she was either crazy as a loon or a first-class bitch. Maybe both.

She took a hesitant step toward his door and then another until she was mere inches away. She laid her palm over the wood and held her breath, listening for any sound from the other side.

It took several minutes to work up the courage to turn the knob. She was half-afraid it would be locked. Part of her hoped that it would be.

The knob turned and she pushed the door open wide enough that she could slide in. Light poured from her room into his and she could see him lying on the bed, the sheet in a tangle around his hips.

For a moment she simply stared, drawn to his chiseled features. His body was beautiful. Lean and muscled. His brow was creased as if he was thinking over an important matter in his sleep. At his side, his fingers were curled into a tight fist.

Now that she was here, she had no idea what to do. She felt like a complete idiot, but the idea of turning around and going back to her empty room filled her with panic.

She closed the door behind her, careful not to make a sound. She waited until her vision adjusted to the darkness of the room and then she tiptoed over to the love seat by the window.

She rarely slept for long periods of time. She could catch a few hours on the couch and be up and out of here before Connor ever woke up. He didn't even have to know she was ever here.

Feeling marginally better about her panic episode, she eased onto the couch and positioned a cushion under her cheek. A blanket would be nice, but she wasn't going to tempt fate by going back for one.

She stared over at Connor as she settled and held back a snort. Some security guy he made. She stifled a yawn and closed her eyes. He hadn't even realized someone had come into his room.

Connor smiled in the darkness as he watched moonlight spill over Lyric's face. She moved once after she closed her eyes and then went still as she slid into sleep.

She'd bolted but now she was back, and from all appearances she had no desire for him to know it.

Patiently he waited, watching as she slept. When he was satisfied that she was down for the count, he slipped from the bed and pulled the comforter with him.

He draped the blanket over her and gently tucked the ends around her shoulders.

"Good night, Lyric," he whispered.

Then he smiled and crawled back into bed.

CHAPTER 19

Lyric's cell phone had rung nonstop since seven that morning. Connor didn't know how the hell it hadn't woken her up yet. Even from the next room, the peal was loud and obnoxious. But she was still curled up on his love seat, covers pulled up to her nose. She hadn't so much as stirred since Connor had risen to shower. For the longest time he'd simply lain in bed watching the soft rise and fall of her chest.

Knowing how little she'd slept in the past days, he was careful not to awaken her. He moved silently around his room, and once he was dressed, he slipped out of the bedroom.

He picked up the annoying cell phone from the nightstand beside her bed—the bed where he'd made love to her just hours before—and pocketed it after seeing there were fourteen missed calls and half as many voice mails.

He'd let her sleep as long as she would. She'd mentioned that she had a lot to do today but he figured she'd manage better with several hours of sleep in her system.

He was halfway down the stairs when his cell phone went off. He sighed when he saw it was Phillip Armstrong.

"Connor Malone," he said when he put the phone to his ear. He continued toward the kitchen, where already he could smell food cooking.

"Where the hell is Lyric?" Phillip demanded. "Is everything okay there?"

"Yeah, fine. She's asleep."

There was a brief hesitation and Connor thought he heard Phillip sigh in relief. "Good. She needs to rest. She's way too high-strung and she goes without sleep for too long at a time. Just make sure she makes her two o'clock at Reliant Stadium. She has to meet with the stage crew and sign off on the details for her performance. I don't like that she's not using her band, but she was determined to give them a break. Hell, I think she's on some weird mission to prove something by taking on so much herself for these two weeks. But who she's trying to prove something to—her or everyone else—I'm not sure."

"There's plenty of time for her to make her two o'clock meeting."

"Be expecting a call from Paul. I gave him your number because he was having a kitten over Lyric not answering her phone."

Connor bit back a curse. Just what he needed. Her asshole manager screaming in his ear. But better his than Lyric's. It pissed him off the way her manager treated her, and Connor had only met the man once.

On cue, the line beeped and Connor pulled the phone away to see unknown caller flash across his screen. "That's probably him now," he said as he put the phone back to his ear. "I'll have Lyric where she needs to be. Don't worry."

He punched the button to switch calls. "Connor Malone."

"Mr. Malone, this is Paul Woodrow. I'll be flying into Houston at noon, and I'll expect to be picked up at the airport so I can meet Lyric at Reliant Stadium at two."

His snappish tone flew all over Connor. It briefly occurred to him that he should probably be conciliatory. Briefly. But he remembered Phillip's advisory that Connor worked for him, not Paul. It was enough for Connor to speak his mind.

"Want in one hand and shit in the other. See which gets fuller faster."

"What? What the hell does that mean? Where is Lyric? Why isn't she answering her phone?"

"She's indisposed and unable to take your call. I'm so sorry. I'll have her return your call later. If I remember."

Paul gave a very unmanly shriek of outrage that made Connor cringe. If he wasn't enjoying himself so much, he'd hang up the phone in mid-scream.

"I'll have your balls," Paul screeched. "You do the job you were hired to do, and you better get Lyric on the damn phone. I'm tired of her flighty, scatterbrained bullshit. She'd better show up on time or it's going to be your ass in the fire. And there had better be a car to pick me up at the airport!"

"Unless you arrange it, I highly doubt there'll be one," Connor said with barely controlled amusement. "Nice talking to you. Have a good day, now."

Connor blew out his breath as he shoved the phone back into his pocket. This was the most half-assed "business" he'd ever witnessed. The guy in charge of Lyric's career was a moron and he didn't give a shit about her. Or what was best for her.

The kitchen was alive with activity. Kane and his men were seated at the table eating a buffet of eggs, bacon, biscuits and bagels. The chef and his two assistants were busy opening and shutting oven doors as the chef barked orders to the woman manning the stove.

"Mr. Malone, what arrangements would you like for Ms. Jones's breakfast?" the chef asked when he caught sight of Connor.

Connor shrugged. "She's still sleeping."

The chef frowned. "Will she be taking breakfast in bed or should I keep her food on the warmer for when she comes down?"

How the hell would he know? He'd never been around such a hyper operation. He was reminded of a bunch of chickens running around with their heads cut off. If this was the way Lyric lived, rushing from one poorly planned event to the next, it was little wonder she looked like she was on the verge of breaking. Hell, he'd already be a permanent resident of the funny farm.

"Fix her a tray. I'll bring it up to her."

The chef nodded and then turned to bark another series of orders. Seriously, did this guy not realize he was just cooking for one woman? You'd think he was making meals for the president and his entire Cabinet.

A few minutes later, Connor was presented a tray that looked like something off of one of those home and garden television shows Faith was forever watching. It was hard to tell what was actual food and what was simply presentation.

He snagged a cupcake and stuck it under one of the silver covers on the tray and headed for the stairs. Lyric had plenty of time to make her appointment and he was determined not to rush her. When did the woman ever get a moment to just be? If he were hounded as mercilessly as she was, he'd be in a permanent bad mood. More and more he was beginning to understand what made her tick, and he'd already come to the conclusion that everything around her sucked balls.

He nudged his door open with his foot to see her still asleep on the couch. Quietly he set the tray down on the coffee table and pulled it over to the sofa.

"Lyric," he said in a low voice. "Wake up. I brought you breakfast."

She stirred and her eyelids fluttered open. Sleepy blue eyes clouded with faint confusion stared back at him. Then she glanced down and around at her surroundings. Consternation creased her brow and her lips pinched together in a bow.

"What time is it?"

He checked his watch. "Almost ten."

She sat straight up, her eyes wide. "Oh shit. Shit!" She started to toss aside the covers and bolt from the couch but he put a gentle hand on her shoulder and pushed her back down.

"You've got plenty of time. Eat first."

She glanced at the tray, then back up at him. "I have so much stuff to do today. My manager is flying in. I should probably be there to meet him. Then we have to go over to the stadium and meet with their sound crew."

Connor shook his head. "No way you're going into a crowded airport. He's a big boy. He can get a car and take himself over to the stadium. You don't have to be there until two, which means we won't need to leave until one fifteen. Which gives you three hours to relax, eat and get your bearings."

She looked momentarily struck dumb, as if it honestly hadn't occurred to her that she didn't have to be running around freaking out every single minute. Then she smiled. Her eyes twinkled and lit up and it struck him how truly beautiful she was.

Behind the façade. Behind all the posing, the bitchy exterior, the hard-ass act. She was a beautiful, sensitive woman and he was in some deep shit.

"You know what? You're right. I pay people to handle details. Let them do their job. My job is to show up at two, right?"

He smiled back and nodded. "Exactly."

She leaned forward to pick up a fork. Before she could take off the covers, he snatched the saucer bearing the cupcake and put it aside. She raised an eyebrow and he grinned. "That one's a surprise."

He took off the remaining covers and she sighed in appreciation at the pancakes, bacon, eggs and grits. There was also fruit, toast and milk and juice.

"I'm never going to eat all this," she said, though she eyed it like she'd love to try. "Have you eaten?"

He shook his head.

She sat up and pulled her feet from the end of the couch. Then she patted the space beside her. "Come eat, then. There's enough to feed the entire security team."

He sat next to her but was careful to keep a little distance between them. Despite her seeming ease, he could sense her uncertainty. She kept glancing over at him. Just little nervous peeks as if expecting him to bring up the fact she'd slept the entire night in his room after she'd bolted out of bed.

He was content to pretend it hadn't happened. For now.

The problem was, she looked so damn cute and snuggly that what he really wanted to do was pull her down to the couch and make love to her all over again.

But he wouldn't stop there. It really made him uncomfortable that beyond making love to her, he had a primitive, chest-thumping, mouth-snarling urge to tie her to his bed and not let her out of his sight for the next year or so.

Yeah, he'd keep that little tidbit to himself. Nothing like making her stalker the more desirable option here.

He was losing his mind—had already lost his mind.

Lyric was wrong for him on every conceivable level, but she just did it for him. Now he couldn't even give Nathan shit about how head over ass he'd fallen for his wife. The man was done from the moment he'd laid eyes on Julie.

In less than two weeks, Lyric Jones would move on, go back on tour, be the fantasy of every boy and man, and Connor would go back to his job and spend his nights reliving the time he'd held her in his arms as she came apart.

Yep, his fascination with her didn't make a whole lot of goddamn sense in that light.

"This is really good," Lyric said around a mouthful. "You should eat."

Connor stared down at the plate she'd fixed for him and realized he'd yet to take a bite. He wasn't hungry for food. He was hungry for the petite blue-haired vixen sitting next to him.

To cover the awkwardness between them, he picked up his fork and plate and began eating, though he'd be hard-pressed to tell what exactly he ate. For the first time in his life, the thought of food didn't appeal. And if that wasn't a huge sign that he was fucked, he didn't know what was.

After a while, Lyric laid her fork down and leaned back into the couch. She hugged the blanket to her chest and sighed as her head plopped against the cushion.

"Full?" he asked as he set aside his own plate.

"Mmmm. Yummy."

"I hope not too full," he said.

She turned, her stare questioning.

He grinned. "I have a surprise. I think you'll like it."

He reached for the saucer and lifted the cover off to reveal the perfectly iced cupcake.

Her eyes lit up and a broad smile curved her lips.

He dipped his finger along the outside edge to capture some of the icing, and then he held it out to Lyric. He smeared just a bit on her soft lips and her tongue immediately came out to lick the sweetness away.

He returned to the cupcake, dipped more of the icing and then smudged a little on her cheek. Her eyes widened in surprise but then half closed to a sleepy, drugged state of awareness when he leaned in to nibble at her frosting-covered skin.

He swept his tongue over the spot and then kissed her cheekbone until all the frosting was gone.

"You're sweeter than the icing," he murmured.

She reached over without breaking their gazes, dipped her finger through the cupcake and then spread the sweetness over his lips. A moment later, she swooped forward and captured his mouth against hers.

The warmth of her tongue rasped over his lips, tasting, licking away the sugary treat. He could taste the frosting on her lips as she nibbled at his.

To his surprise, she rose over him and leaned her weight into his body so that he was forced back against the couch. She straddled his lap and dug her knees into the cushions on either side of him.

"Since you pointed out that there's no reason for me to be in a hurry this morning, I now have plenty of time for dessert," she murmured.

Well, hell. There wasn't a damn thing he could say. He had a hard-on from hell. It wasn't like she wouldn't notice. So saying anything remotely sensitive like *Oh, that's okay* was out of the question. Not to mention he may as well cut his dick off if he ever got that stupid.

He cupped her hips in his hands and let his fingers splay out possessively over her ass. Yeah, he liked that feeling. *Mine.* His woman. He could totally get carried away, and now he could kind of understand Damon being all caveman about Serena. Not that Connor would ever get away with that shit with Lyric. But he definitely had some freaky fantasies going on.

She fit his hands like her ass was fashioned just for him. He cupped and squeezed through the thin material of her pajama bottoms. Then he pulled her forward just enough that the bulge in the crotch of his jeans was straining up against her pussy.

"Take your shirt off," he rasped out. "And give me that damn cupcake."

She laughed and turned, pulling at her shirt with one hand, reaching back for the cupcake with the other.

He ended up helping her, or maybe he was just too impatient. The top came over her head and he tossed it across the room. She held the cupcake up, a mischievous glint in her eyes as she watched him.

He swiped at the frosting, careful to leave plenty still on the cupcake, because damn, his mind was alive with the possibilities. He decorated one puckered nipple with the sweet buttercream icing until the tip was white. His mouth watered but he forced himself to lavish the same attention on her other breast.

She fidgeted and sighed, strained up, but he pulled her back down onto his lap. Her breasts bobbed in front of him like two delectable treats, and he never, ever turned down sugar.

He licked delicately up the curve of her breast, anticipating the point where he reached her straining nipple. She tensed all over and braced her hands on his shoulders. Her fingers dug into his skin as he flicked his tongue over the tip.

His tongue barely brushed across the sensitive peak, and each time he got only a hint of the sweet.

"Connor!" she gasped. "You're killing me here."

One corner of his mouth lifted. "I think that's the point."

She slid one hand up the column of his neck, around to his nape and then into his hair. Her fingers twisted and she pulled impatiently at his head, guiding him back to her breast.

He lapped one more time and then pulled the nipple hard between his teeth, sucking avidly at the frosting. He held her nipple captive and flicked his tongue repeatedly over the point until she twisted and squirmed damn near off his lap.

He loved how demanding she was. Her fingers dug into his head. She wasn't afraid to show him what she wanted or needed.

He pulled away and her nipple gleamed wet and clean of the frosting. It was rigid, so hard and pointed that he couldn't resist swiping his tongue over it again.

She sighed and flexed her fingers over his scalp. His erection pushed upward, cradled by the juncture of her legs. It frustrated him that there were so many barriers between them.

As if sensing his irritation, she rose up on her knees and began sliding her bottoms down. She backed off the couch and stood before him as she let the material fall down her legs.

He smiled at the fact that one nipple was still covered with frosting. He licked his lips and she smiled back just before she palmed her breast, cupping it and pushing it upward. Then she leaned down until her nipple was a breath away from his mouth.

She held it just so, offering it to his mouth. He fastened his lips greedily around it, sucking and nibbling as if he were starved. Her breathing ratcheted up and she trembled from head to toe as he pulled strongly with his mouth.

She pulled abruptly away, her cheeks flushed, her chest rising and falling rapidly. Then she let her gaze drift down his body to the bulge between his legs.

A gleam entered her eyes. One that made him twitchy with anticipation. It was the look of a woman with a plan. A very evil, delicious plan.

He held his breath as she got down on her knees and settled herself between his legs. Then she reached for his fly and pulled at the snaps. The zipper rasped downward and her soft hand gently delved within, finding his cock.

When she reached for the cupcake, he damn near lost his mind.

With exacting precision she trailed a finger through the sticky confection and then proceeded to smooth it over his straining erection.

His breaths came out in tortured huffs. He was sure he was going to hyperventilate.

She took her time, smearing the frosting up and down his length until he was completely coated. Then she wrested his jeans down around his hips and there he sat, his cock jutting upward like a frosted Popsicle.

If he wasn't dying of anticipation, he'd have to laugh at the fact he had a frosted dick.

And then she leaned over and touched the tip of her tongue to the swollen head. His cock twitched in reaction and swung away from her. It was all he could do not to grab it and guide it back because, Lord have mercy, he wanted her mouth around him.

She took care of the matter for him. She followed with her mouth and sucked the head between her lips. She teased him with her tongue, circling and lapping at the tip.

Like she had done, he slid his hand around to the back of her head and his fingers tangled in her hair. Carefully she lowered her mouth, taking more of him as she licked every bit of the frosting from his skin.

She exerted pressure and hollowed her cheeks as she slid up his cock. The head fell free of her lips with a pop and she turned her gaze up to him, her eyes sparkling with amusement.

"You know, more women wouldn't mind giving blow jobs if we could all have buttercream-flavored dicks."

He laughed. What else could he do? She was so damn irreverent.

"Honey, if you'll keep your mouth wrapped around my cock, I'll buy you an entire tub of frosting."

She leaned down and dragged her tongue up the back of his erection, taking more frosting with her. Then she swallowed him up and took him deep until he butted against the back of her throat. She swallowed again, and the softness of her mouth convulsed around his dick. He shuddered uncontrollably and felt semen leak from the tip.

She slowly backed away but held him in her hand, caressing up and down as she licked her lips. "Mmmm, now, there's an interesting flavor," she purred. "I'll admit, the taste of cum has never impressed me. But now? Yum."

His entire body tightened. Her crudeness only turned him on all the more. He reached for the back of her neck again and forced himself back into her mouth. He arched his hips and closed his eyes as her heat surrounded him.

It registered in the back of his mind that he was probably being an ass. He was pretty much assuming that she'd allow him to come in her mouth. Hell, her mouth? He wanted to come down her throat. He wanted to thrust as deep as she'd allow and come like he'd never come.

She never registered a complaint. She allowed him to hold her head, though he was careful to make sure she wouldn't wear his fingerprints afterward. With every thrust, she seemed to open wider and allow him to go as deep as he could.

"Oh Christ, Lyric," he strained out. "If this isn't what you want, tell me now. I'm so damn close."

There. He'd managed to have some semblance of consideration, though he was praying hard she stayed right where she was.

She paused, and for one awful moment he thought she was going to stop. He went completely still as he waited. She merely glided over his hardness, trailing her tongue along the underside of his cock where he was most sensitive.

When the head of his dick rested on her bottom lip, she licked lightly at the seam and glanced up at him with smoky, sultry eyes. She sent him a lazy smile and then she took him hard and deep.

He nearly bolted off the couch. She sucked back and forth, her hand working the base of his cock in perfect rhythm with her mouth.

Lightning gathered in his balls and streaked upward with such force that his vision blurred. His release tore through him, painful and relentless in intensity.

Semen shot from his cock and filled her mouth, bathing him in its sticky warmth. Still, she didn't waver. She sucked and swallowed and all the while kept that silky, sweet mouth closed around his pulsing erection.

On and on, in a seemingly unending orgasm. He was still jerking spasmodically when the last of his release spurted into her mouth.

She released his cock and climbed back on top of him, her body quivering and shaking as she straddled him. His cock butted into her soft belly. She gripped his head and bent to nip at his neck. She was everywhere, twisting restlessly as she sucked and bit at the column of his neck.

She was close to her own orgasm and all from sucking him off. It stunned him and inflated his male ego about ten more pounds. Not willing to let her remain unfulfilled, he slid his fingers between them, down into the softness of her folds.

She was hot and damp, slick with her arousal. As soon as he touched her clit, she arched forward, her back bowing so that her breasts were shoved into his face.

Damn if that didn't make him one happy man.

He latched on to her nipple and suckled as he stroked her. Her heat bathed his fingers. He pressed in with his thumb and rotated in a tight circle as his middle finger slid inside her.

She encased him in liquid velvet. She was so satiny soft and smooth. He added another finger, stretching her as his thumb continued its relentless seduction.

A whimper tore from her throat and she tightened in his arms. So sweet and soft. Curvy and warm. He sighed his own contentment as he moved to her other breast and inhaled her scent.

Her fingers dug into his shoulders. Her cry came out as an ache in the stillness of the room. She trembled so violently as her orgasm crashed around her that she pitched forward against him.

He caught her with his free arm and held her close as he continued to caress her swollen, damp flesh. Her chest pushed against his as she struggled for breath. He buried his face in her neck and kissed softly over her pulse point.

"You undo me," he admitted softly.

She laughed but it came out quivery soft and delicate. "That's my line."

He nuzzled her neck again and pressed kisses below her ear. Gradually he eased his hand from between her legs and pulled her even closer to him so that she straddled him again and her body was pressed as close to him as he could get her.

"Do you doubt how beautiful you are to me?" he asked quietly.

She pushed away just enough that she could stare into his eyes. What he saw in hers knotted his chest and made his throat ache. There was wonder. Amazement and a little confusion. As if she truly couldn't comprehend why he thought her so damn beautiful.

"Not anymore," she said in a whisper. "I don't understand it, but when I look at you, I see it. I don't know what to do about it, but you've made me believe it."

He smiled then and trailed a finger down a strand of her hair to her cheek. Then he pushed it up and over her ear. "You don't have to do anything. I just want you to see you the way I see you."

She leaned forward and pressed her forehead to his. Her hands slid up his neck and her thumbs brushed over his jawline. He shivered at that tiny gesture. It was baffling what something so simple as her touch did to him.

"I wish everyone could see me the way you see me."

There was pain and regret in her statement. It said so much more than just the simple words. There was a wealth of meaning, and, not for the first time, he realized that there was so much more to the woman than what the public saw.

Was it their fault entirely for swallowing what they were spoon-fed by the media and by Lyric herself? No, but right now he could see the vulnerability she tried so hard to hide from the world. She wore indifference like a shield. She needed that protection. She was a complicated, complex woman who had so many pieces that it was nearly impossible to put them all together.

He kissed her, just a simple touch of his lips, more a comforting gesture than one designed to inspire lust. And he simply held her while she regained her bearings and enjoyed the feel of her in his arms.

CHAPTER 20

Lyric took longer than necessary in the shower and lingered
in the bathroom long after she'd dried her hair and done her makeup.
The truth was, she was nervous. She wasn't sure how to act around
Connor now. The last twenty-four hours had seen a 180 in their relationship.

She wasn't used to this uncertainty. She called the shots in all her
sexual relationships. Nothing touched her. Nothing got to her. It was
all casual and meaningless. Everything was on her terms.

With Connor she felt like she was spinning out of control. It was
a helpless, panicky feeling.

A knock sounded at her door. "Lyric, we need to be going."

She hesitated and then opened the door to see Connor standing
there. "I'm ready."

"Kane's waiting downstairs with the car."

"You're riding with me."

He touched her arm. "Of course. You don't go anywhere without me."

She breathed a soft sigh of relief.

He escorted her down the stairs and out front to the circle drive where a limousine was parked. She wrinkled her nose. "Seems a bit conspicuous, don't you think?"

"It's armored," Connor said. "Bulletproof windows. You'll be safe."

Her eyes widened. "Do you really think I'm in that much danger?"

Kane, who was standing by the limo, straightened and opened the passenger door for Lyric. "We always assume the worst. That way we don't get any nasty surprises."

She slid into the roomy interior and scooted around the curved seat to allow Connor to duck in. She held her breath, waiting to see if Kane would slide in as well. To her relief, he shut the door, leaving her and Connor alone.

"He's just doing his job," Connor said with a hint of amusement.

"I don't like him," she muttered. "He makes me nervous."

Connor raised an eyebrow as the car pulled away from the house. "I didn't think anyone made you nervous, Miss Badass."

She pulled a face at him.

"Did you make all the phone calls you needed to make?" he asked.

"Most. Not all," she admitted. "I didn't call Paul. I wasn't in the mood to hear him bitch."

Connor's expression darkened. "You need to tell him to shut the fuck up. You're making him a fuckload of money. He can lighten the hell up."

She shrugged. "Depends on who you ask, I guess. According to him, he's doing me a favor."

Connor snorted. "If he ever thought you were walking, he'd bend over backward to kiss your ass. When I first met you I thought that everyone around you kissed your ass too much. Now I think you're surrounded by a bunch of assholes."

She grinned. "And in the beginning, I thought you were the biggest asshole of them all."

"And now?"

She pretended to consider the matter as she studied him. "Now I think you're a pretty okay guy."

Her phone rang and she checked the display screen. She rolled her eyes and hit the ignore button.

"Does your phone always ring twenty-four/seven?" he asked.

She sighed. "Pretty much. There is no shortage of people always trying to keep me in line. They either want to call me to bitch at me, call me to remind me to be somewhere, or call me to ask me to do something."

"So not very much 'Hi, how are you?' then."

She stopped and considered for a moment and then laughed. "No, I suppose not. I can't remember the last time someone called just to say hi or ask me how I was doing."

Connor shook his head.

Half an hour later, the limo pulled up to the stage entrance of the stadium. Connor got out and scanned the area before reaching back for Lyric's hand. Kane and his men took position around them just as her manager strode out of the back entrance and made a beeline for Lyric.

Connor immediately stepped in front of Lyric and wrapped a protective arm around her, shoving her into his back. Kane stepped in front of Connor while his men pushed in around Lyric.

"Get the hell out of my way," Paul barked. "I'm her manager."

Connor halted him with an icy glare.

"Get her inside," Kane barked. "The reunion will wait until then."

Paul didn't look happy to be ordered about, but he had little choice as the men closed ranks and ushered Lyric inside the building.

"Where the hell have you been?" Paul demanded once they were inside. "I've been waiting here for two hours. There are things to go over and I couldn't very well go over the details of your performance without you."

Lyric sighed and wished he'd just shut up. She had no desire for one of his tantrums in front of everyone else. Connor's face had darkened to a storm cloud and his jaw was set in a rigid line as he glared at Paul.

"I'm fifteen minutes early, Paul. Calm down."

Paul reached for her elbow to pull her down the hallway but Connor cut him off and wrapped a protective arm around Lyric's shoulders. Paul shot Connor a disdainful look but continued to the meeting room where the rodeo execs were waiting.

Paul did most of the talking, and by the time it was over, Lyric had a headache. He made silly demands, argued every point, and finally Lyric told him to shut up. She apologized to the assembled people and then listened as they went over the schedule.

Next they gave her a tour of the rotating stage that was used for all the performers at the rodeo and gave her a preview of the screen graphics for the background. She met with the band since hers wouldn't be making the show and rehearsed the songs she'd be singing for the show.

Three hours later, it was done and she left the building, surrounded by Kane and his men. The car was waiting, but before she could slip into it, Paul caught up to her and grabbed her arm.

She turned in surprise and glanced pointedly at his hand.

"We need to talk, Lyric. What the hell is going on with you? You look like shit. Have you even tried to stay in shape for your tour dates?

You only have a few weeks off and then you go back on the road. You've gained at least ten pounds, if not more. You don't want to look like a slob onstage. This is your career. You could at least act like it's important to you."

Her cheeks burned with humiliation. She wanted to crawl into a hole and die. It shocked her that he would confront her in front of Connor and Kane and the others. But then, he wouldn't consider them important. They were just the hired bodyguards.

Beside her, Connor hissed in anger and took a step toward Paul. Paul was oblivious to just how pissed Connor was, but Lyric could see the fury in Connor's eyes.

"Instead of stuffing your face and lying around, why don't you make it to the gym or, better yet, have some exercise equipment delivered to the house Phillip rented for you? Your fans don't pay big bucks to see your fat ass onstage. They pay to see a lean, sleek performer."

He didn't get another word out before Connor slammed him into the wall.

"What the fuck?" Paul spit out. He looked to Kane. "Get him the hell off me. You're fired. You're all fired."

Kane crossed his arms over his chest. "Get who off you? I don't see anyone. The only thing I see is a loudmouthed, disrespectful asshole who is about to get his ass beat. Deservedly so."

Lyric watched, openmouthed, as Connor gathered Paul's shirt in his hands and got into his face.

"Listen to me, you piece of shit. You shut the fuck up. If I ever hear you talk to Lyric that way again, I'll tear your nuts off and cram them down your throat. Are we clear?"

Paul's eyes bulged out of his head and he gaped at Connor and then at Lyric. "Are you going to let him get away with talking to me that way?"

Connor slammed him against the wall again. "The only words I want to hear out of your mouth are an apology to Lyric. Now."

Connor's hand tightened and pushed into Paul's throat, cutting off his air.

"I'm s-sorry," Paul stammered. "You know I only want the best for you, Lyric."

Lyric recovered her wits and walked forward, her mind still whirling from Connor's reaction. She stopped just a foot away from where Connor's hand was still wrapped around Paul's neck. For a long moment she simply stood there and watched him grow more and more uncomfortable. Sweat beaded on his brow and he glanced between her and Connor nervously.

"Paul?" she finally said. "Fuck off."

She spun around and headed toward the car where Kane had already opened the door. A smile hovered over his lips, and as she climbed in, he murmured, "Well done, Ms. Jones."

Lyric slid over as far as she could and directed her gaze out the opposite window. For the first time, she wanted to be alone. She didn't want to face Connor or have him witness her absolute humiliation. Her face burned, and she was so mortified that she literally wanted to close herself off in her room for a week.

She wasn't so lucky.

Connor climbed into the back of the limo and a few moments later the car pulled away.

She refused to look at him. She didn't want to see sympathy or pity staring back at her. The silence was suffocating and she could feel him watching her.

Connor was furious. He couldn't remember a time he'd been this pissed. He'd wanted to kill that son of a bitch. He still wanted to kill him.

He'd seen Lyric's face when Paul had spewed his venom. He'd seen her pale, seen her draw into herself. Everything that Connor had told her had been erased by a stupid bastard who couldn't see how beautiful Lyric was.

And now she sat so still and rigid, making herself as small as possible, refusing to look at him. She was embarrassed—who could blame her? And that pissed Connor off even more. She had nothing to be ashamed of. Nothing to be embarrassed over.

He couldn't hold silent any longer.

"Lyric. Look at me."

She flinched. Closed her eyes but held her chin firm, her gaze still fixed out the window.

"Lyric."

He waited. He was patient. She had enough assholes in her life only too willing to shit on her. He wasn't going to be one of them.

Finally her shoulders sagged and she turned slowly, her eyes dull. He hated that more than anything. He liked her "fuck you" attitude. He liked that she didn't flinch in a stare-down. That she'd take on anyone and anything. That wasn't the woman he was seeing now, and it infuriated him.

"He's an asshole. You should fire him. You deserve better than that."

She shrugged. "He's good at what he does. He made me. I owe him."

Connor had to call back the snarl. His lips curled and it took a few moments before he could calmly respond.

"Bullshit."

That surprised her. Her eyes narrowed and she cocked her head to the side.

"You don't owe him shit. Lyric, this is business. You ought to know that. If you weren't so upset by what that moron said, you'd realize it. You pay him. If I had to guess, he gets paid way too damn much. That's all you owe him. A paycheck. Until such time as he no longer provides the service you pay him for, and quite frankly, I'd say the only service you need from him is for him to go fuck himself."

The corner of her mouth lifted into a half smile.

"You made yourself. You worked hard. You've got talent. Without those things it wouldn't matter what the hell he did or didn't do for you. You made yourself. Don't forget that."

She smiled fully now and some of the light came back to her eyes.

"No one has the right to talk to you like that," he continued. "Not him. Not Phillip. Your biggest power is the willingness to walk away. The moment they realize you're willing to do that, I think you'll see a dramatic turnaround in their attitudes. I still think you should fire Paul's ass, though. You can't tell me there isn't another manager who can do his job and keep their goddamn mouth shut while doing it."

To his utter shock, she launched herself across the seat and into his arms. She threw her arms around his neck and hugged him so tight that his oxygen was momentarily cut off.

He was happy to tuck her more firmly in his embrace. He curled his arms around her and held her against him, inhaling the sweet scent of her hair. And because he simply couldn't resist, he brushed his lips over her head and kissed and nuzzled, offering her comfort.

"He's wrong, you know."

She went still, waiting. He tightened his hold and laid his cheek over the top of her head.

"You look fantastic. There is nothing about you that isn't drop-dead sexy."

He felt her smile against his neck.

"You probably think I'm talking shit. I'm not. I don't need to kiss your ass. There's no reason for me to lie to you. You can't fire me. You don't have anything I want or need. Except you. Just you. And that drop-dead, sexy-as-sin body of yours."

She laughed softly and her body shook against his. He stroked a hand over her hair, content to let her lie against him, warm, snuggly and relaxed.

"You're good for my ego, Connor. You say things in a way that makes me think you mean them. I don't get that very often. It's become second nature for me to disregard any compliment because I'm always suspicious of the motive behind it. Isn't that sad?"

"Yeah, it is. But hey, at least for now, you have me to keep it real for you."

She pushed away from his chest and smiled down at him, her eyes alight with joy. It made her seem softer. Like a girl instead of a hardened woman. It completely changed her appearance and he was hard-pressed to even put this woman together with the woman he'd first met backstage with the outrageous pink hair and "fuck you" attitude.

It gave him an indescribable thrill that he was likely one of the few people in the world who got to see the woman behind the layers. He may not have earned her complete trust, but on some level she did trust him. Enough to let down the barriers.

He gathered her back in his arms and squeezed. "What's next on the agenda?"

She sighed. "I have that meet and greet after the show. Nothing until then, though. I need to give Kane my schedule. I promised I would. I feel so disorganized right now. I know it sounds bad, but when I'm on the road, I don't have to think about where I have to be or go. I have people to push me here or there, and I've gotten used to that."

He ran his hands over her soft curves and rubbed her back until she was loose and relaxed against him.

"Not bad. I'm sure it's crazy for you. You need people for that, but they need to be people you trust."

"It's hard. I don't trust anyone. I don't expect people to be trustworthy. I never really thought about it before you said something about it, but I suppose it really is a shitty way to live. After a while you just accept that things are the way they are and you just go with it."

"You can change that, Lyric. People will only do what you allow them to do. It's okay to push back. It's okay to expect more from the people around you. That doesn't make you unreasonable. It makes you smart."

"No one's ever accused me of being smart," she said dryly.

"Then they're morons."

She pushed away again so she could look into his eyes. She raised her hand to cup his jaw and she stroked over his face with featherlight fingers. "I hated you when we first met. I could see the disapproval in your eyes and it pissed me off. It made me mad that it mattered to me what you thought."

He grimaced but she shushed him with a finger to his lips.

"I'm glad Phillip hired you. I'm woman enough to admit I was wrong about you. I'm glad you're here," she finished softly.

He kissed her finger, then sucked it into his mouth and nibbled delicately at the tip.

"I'm glad I'm here too."

"Think the chef has any more of those cupcakes?" she asked wistfully.

He grinned as realization hit her. "To eat!" she protested. "I want them to eat!"

"Nobody says you can't eat them," he said silkily. "I don't know about you, but my mama never said anything about not playing with my food."

She laughed, and the sound was vibrant and alive in his ears. It made him want to do all sorts of mushy stuff that he'd give other men shit over. But with her it just felt right.

She shifted and he was afraid at first that she was going to move back to her seat. But she settled down against his chest and he wrapped his arms around her again and cradled her.

She gave a soft little sigh that told him she was as contented as he was. He smiled to himself and nuzzled his face into her hair.

CHAPTER 21

 $\mathscr{L}$ yric was sitting in the kitchen with Connor eating a cupcake when Kane stalked into the kitchen, a grim expression in his face. Her heart sank. What could it be now? She tensed, ready to go on the offensive.

Connor simply placed his hand over hers, a gesture that calmed her considerably.

"Your manager is here and demands to see you," Kane said. "Want me to get rid of him?"

He said it in such a way that sent chills down Lyric's spine. She could envision Kane stuffing him into a trunk and disposing of his body. He looked serious enough to actually be contemplating it.

She sighed. "No. Let him come up. I need to deal with this."

Connor frowned, but this time it was she who put her hand over his.

"I'm coming with you," Connor muttered. "That son of a bitch better be respectful or I'm going to take him apart."

Lyric smiled and stood. "I can take care of myself, though I appreciate the sentiment."

Still, Connor followed her into the living room, where they waited as Kane disappeared outside the house. A few moments later, Kane returned, walking ahead of two of his men.

Paul was held between the two bodyguards and he was steaming mad. His face was red and puffed up with visible anger. When the two men flanking him finally let him go, he shook and then lunged away from them, rubbing his arm as he glared at the offenders.

"Lyric, what the hell is going on here?" he demanded. "This is completely unacceptable! Who are these men to tell me what I can or can't do? They manhandled me! I'm going to sue!"

Lyric rolled her eyes, then crossed her arms over her chest and stared at the man who'd controlled the better part of her life for the past several years.

"You're fired, Paul."

Her calm words had the effect of a gunshot. Paul recoiled and his mouth fell open. It worked up and down but nothing came out for several long seconds. Then he exploded.

"Fired? *Fired?* You can't fire me."

"The hell she can't," Connor shot back.

Again she put a hand on Connor's arm. He quieted and stepped back to allow her to continue.

Maybe it was the calm in her eyes or her demeanor. Paul went from furious to placating and pleading in a nanosecond.

"You can't fire me, Lyric. You owe me. I put you on the map. We're a team, you and me. Look, I'm sorry for the things I said, but you know I was just looking out for you. I want what's best for you."

Lyric glanced at Connor and smiled. He winked, and she drew strength from that small gesture. Connor was right. He was absolutely right and she'd never seen it until he pushed.

She turned back to Paul. "I don't owe you anything. I paid you for services rendered. That's the only compensation I owed you. From this point forward our relationship is severed. You won't be allowed access to me in the future. If you have anything at all to say, you can contact Phillip or my lawyer."

Paul's shock turned to ugly, black fury. He took a step forward and pointed a finger close to her face. "You won't get away with this, Lyric. I know too much about you. I'll bury you."

Connor and Kane both stepped in front of Lyric. The two security men took hold of Paul's arms. Connor waved them off.

"Let me give you a piece of advice," Connor bit out. "Don't threaten Lyric ever. There isn't a place on this earth you can hide from me."

"Or me," Kane interjected.

"If you do anything, if you say anything, with the intent of damaging Lyric's career, her reputation or her personally, I'll hunt you down and I'll take you apart piece by piece."

"You're threatening me!"

"You're damn right, I am. And if you think I'm just blowing smoke up your ass, I invite you to try me. I'm not much on words but I sure as hell will kick your sorry ass if you utter so much as a peep. You got me?"

Paul's face lost color. His eyes darted back and forth between Kane and Connor and he sagged like a deflated balloon.

"Get him out of here," Connor ordered.

Lyric watched as Paul was hauled out of the living room. She felt an odd sense of elation. As if she'd lost the ten pounds that Paul had complained about. She felt ridiculously light and freaking giddy.

She smiled broadly as Connor and Kane both turned their attention back to her.

"I don't suppose either of you know of a good manager, do you?"

Kane actually cracked a smile. She was surprised his face didn't crumble with the effort. Connor slipped an arm around her and hugged her to him.

"I'm proud of you for taking a stand, Lyric. The bastard needed his ass kicked."

"Would you really hunt him down?" she asked curiously.

Connor frowned. "Hell yeah."

"Thank you," she said as her grin got bigger. She turned to include Kane. "Thank you both."

"I can make his life miserable for him if you want," Kane offered.

"You're not even joking, are you," Lyric muttered.

"Nope. I don't have a sense of humor."

At that, Lyric chuckled.

Her cell phone went off and she sighed. "The man works fast. He must have speed-dialed Phillip on his way out the door."

"So don't answer," Connor said.

Lyric stared down at the phone in her hand. Then she looked back up and grinned. "Anyone up for another cupcake?"

"Did he make chocolate?" Kane asked in a hopeful voice.

CHAPTER 22

$\mathcal{T}$hree cupcakes and four missed calls later, Lyric licked the last of the frosting from her fingers and sighed in satisfaction.

Her phone went off again and she lifted an eyebrow at it. "He's persistent, isn't he?"

Connor grunted.

"I'm surprised he hasn't called you."

Connor held up his phone and flashed her the screen that said he had as many missed calls.

"Ha-ha! You turned your ringer off. Smart guy."

"He's probably calling to fire me," Connor said wryly. "He probably thinks I'm a bad influence on you. But if I don't answer the phone, he can't very well fire me, right?"

She snorted. "You, a bad influence on me?"

"Yeah, I know, right? How ridiculous is that? Everyone knows you're the miscreant here. Not me."

He looked so damn innocent saying it that she had to laugh.

"I bet you got away with murder as a child."

He shook his head. "Nope. Pop would have kicked my ass."

"And your mom?"

He grimaced. "She and Pop split up when I was young."

"Oh. Sorry to hear that."

"Shit happens."

"Yeah," she said softly.

"Connor, I need a minute when you get a chance," Kane said. "Just got a report we need to run over."

Lyric's brow creased as she looked between the men. "Report?"

"Yeah. We've been running background checks, criminal histories, stuff like that on all the people who work with you or have access to you."

"And?" she prompted.

Kane shrugged. "Don't know yet. Just got the e-mail on my Black-Berry. I'll need to log on to a computer and print it out. Connor and I can split it up and look over it. This will probably take a while so if you need anything, let one of my men know."

That was it. He wasn't sharing anything further. It frustrated her on one hand, but there was a part of her that didn't want to know if someone close to her was fucking with her. She didn't trust anyone, but that didn't mean she wouldn't be pissed that someone she'd allowed into her circle had betrayed her.

But shouldn't she know these things? Shouldn't she be aware of any potential threat that existed?

Connor stood and then laid a hand on her shoulder and squeezed. "We'll let you know as soon as we've gone through all the information. I won't keep anything from you. You have my word."

She nodded. "I think I'll go for a swim. Is that allowed?" She looked innocently at Kane as she asked.

"You're safe here. My men will be watching. Go take your swim."

Making sure she hid the mischief she knew was brewing in her eyes, she sidestepped Connor and headed for the stairs. "Y'all have fun going through your reports."

As she bopped up the stairs it occurred to her that she actually felt . . . happy. Not in a disgusting "Zip a Dee Doo Dah" way. She wouldn't be busting out the sunshine songs or anything. But she felt relieved, happy and a little excited all at the same time.

She felt strong. Empowered. A little more in control of her own destiny. It shamed her to realize just how much she'd allowed to go on around her. She literally bounced from person to person, always allowing others to control the puppet strings. She performed. She did what she was told. She ate was she was told to eat. She exercised when she was told to exercise. She smiled when someone said smile. She performed like a windup doll.

And she'd been perfectly miserable the whole time. Angry and miserable.

She'd embraced such an existence because she truly felt it was what she deserved. But was it really?

She shook her head, unwilling to mar what was shaping up to be a perfect day with dark memories. She didn't want to go there. She didn't want to think about things she couldn't change.

What she wanted to do was enjoy a swim and maybe tweak Connor in the process. He'd probably be pissed, but the impish demon inside her simply couldn't resist the desire to needle him.

Yep. A simple little swim would be fun. And she hadn't had fun in a damn long time. Not until she'd met Connor and his friends and allowed herself to relax and truly enjoy the company of others. She liked it. Liked it a hell of a lot.

She didn't bother searching her stuff for a suit. She didn't have one. She stripped down until she was bare-assed naked and then threw on a robe and tied the ends for her trip down the stairs.

Connor had told her to enjoy herself. She planned to take him up on it.

"You realize we're going to get totally busted for this," Julie said as Sam rolled to a stop at the gates of the house Lyric was staying in.

Serena waved a dismissive hand as Sam rolled down the window to address the guard. "What are they going to do, shoot us?"

"Maybe," Faith murmured as she surveyed the automatic slung over the guard's shoulder.

"We are here to see Ms. Jones," Sam said in his somber voice.

"Sorry, sir. No one gets onto the premises without direct authorization."

Angelina's eyes widened. *Direct authorization?* she mouthed.

"Let me take care of this. Lyric gave me her cell number," Julie said as she yanked out her cell. She held up a finger through the window to the guard.

She punched in Lyric's number and waited as it rang.

"I could just call Connor," Faith offered.

Julie snorted. "And let him get all pissy with us for coming without his permission? Oh, hi, Lyric, it's Julie Tucker." She held up a finger to silence the other girls. "I'm good. Hey, what are you doing right now? Swimming? Oh that sounds fun. Uh yeah, we're kind of here at your front gates only the dude with the gun won't let us in without proper authorization. Think you could help us out with that?"

Julie's face split into a grin. "Yeah, sure."

She closed the phone and leaned over the front seat to look out at the guard. "Ms. Jones will be calling you shortly."

On cue, the guard reached for his phone and sent a glare into the car.

"Ms. Jones," he greeted. "Yes, there are four women here to see you." There was a pause. "No, I don't think that's a good idea. Perhaps it would be better if I were to speak to Mr. Malone or Mr. Murphy." He winced. "Yes, of course, I understand Mr. Malone and Mr. Murphy are in an important meeting. No, ma'am, I understand. Yes, of course. I'll let them in immediately."

"That's our girl," Serena said with a grin.

The gate swung open and the guard motioned them in, though he looked less than happy to be doing so. Sam drove the car up the drive and parked in front.

"Lyric said for us to come around to the pool," Julie said as they all piled out. "You going to make it, Angelina?"

Angelina shot her a glare as Sam helped her from the car. "I'm not that huge."

"Yet," Julie said with a grin.

"I'm so going to drown you," Angelina muttered.

"I feel it best if I accompany you ladies," Sam said stiffly.

Serena patted his arm. "Of course, Sam. You can keep us safe from all the guys with guns."

He pinched his lips together. "I still don't think this was a good idea. Mr. Roche will be most displeased if I allow any harm to come to you."

"Mr. Roche does not have to know of all my comings and goings," Serena said dryly.

Two guards appeared, both armed, and they glanced warily at the women. Julie couldn't say she entirely blamed them. Women were probably scarier creatures than a whole horde of men with knives and guns.

"Can you direct us to the pool?" Julie asked airily.

"They won't really shoot us, will they?" Faith whispered as they started forward.

"I'll pretend I'm in labor if they do any funny stuff," Angelina said in a low voice. "Pregnant women always scare the shit out of men."

Sam hovered protectively over the women as they traipsed around the side of the house. He shot scowls at the men who flanked them. It was pretty funny because Julie's money was on Sam in a throwdown. He might come across as all starchy and straitlaced, but he was a big son of a bitch and he got growly when it came to "his" women.

As soon as the gate to the pool was opened, they saw Lyric pressed against the side of the pool, staring expectantly in their direction. She lifted an arm to wave, and it was then Julie realized Lyric didn't have a stitch of clothing on.

She started laughing. The others stared at Julie and then back at Lyric, and Faith's mouth formed an O.

"Hey!" Lyric called. "Gosh, I'm so glad to see you guys. How on earth did you manage it? I'm practically kept prisoner here, with no visitation, I might add."

"We're on the lam today," Faith said.

Serena burst out laughing. "Lam? Faith, you crack me up sometimes."

"Well, the men don't know where we are. We're supposed to be 'shopping.' They'd probably have a kitten if they knew we'd come over here. But honestly, what do they think is going to happen? We have Sam, and Lyric has guys hanging from the tree branches with guns."

Lyric chuckled. "I asked Connor if I could have you guys over and he gave me the spiel about how it wasn't safe, blah blah, and he's right, but I'm awfully glad to see you, and you're already here, so there's no reason for you to leave!"

"Are we interrupting?" Angelina asked with a pointed glance in Lyric's direction.

Lyric glanced down and then back up at the women and grinned.

"Oh no. Connor and Kane are mulling over background checks, criminal records and all that fun stuff, so I decided to take a swim. I figure Connor will pop a button when he sees I'm skinny-dipping."

"In more ways than one," Julie muttered.

"Why don't you guys come in? The water's great. I'll have the chef make us something yummy. I'll have drinks made. Whatever you guys want."

Julie glanced at the other women. "We didn't exactly come prepared to swim, and it's cold out today! Aren't you freezing?"

Lyric arched an eyebrow. "So? The pool is heated and you don't need a suit."

"A swim would feel really nice," Angelina said with a sigh.

"We can fire up the hot tub later if you find the water too cold," Lyric offered.

Faith frowned. "But not too hot. It isn't good for Angelina."

"So strip and get in," Lyric said.

Sam cleared his throat. "Perhaps I should relay your wishes to the chef and make myself available inside."

Serena laughed. "Good idea, Sam." She turned to the other women. "Well? Are we up to being totally daring?"

"Or are you *chiiickennn*," Lyric taunted.

"Oh hell no, you did not call me chicken," Julie muttered.

Lyric pushed off from the side of the pool and swam backward to the center of the pool. "Last one in doesn't get the really yummy cupcakes the chef baked."

"Chef? Cupcakes?" Faith shook her head. "I must be doing something wrong."

"I want that cupcake," Angelina said as she started pulling at her pants.

Laughter and shrieks hit the air as the women all started shucking out of their clothes. Shirts and pants flew through the air and soon it looked like an orgy had taken place on the patio as clothes hung from every chair, were strewn on the ground, and panties and bras hung from the bushes lining the walkway.

Soon they were all in the water, and for Lyric, what she'd thought was an absolutely perfect day had just gotten better.

"Did you swear Sam to secrecy?" Angelina asked Serena. "I really don't want the guys to come barging in and ruin our girly day."

"I can have one of the guards shoot them," Lyric said calmly. She swam to the side of the pool and looped her arms along the concrete to hold herself up as she kicked her feet below the surface.

"They won't wonder where we are for a few hours yet," Serena said confidently. "They were all so relieved that he was stuck taking us shopping that they won't even think to look for us."

"Except Damon, who loves to shop for you," Faith said smugly.

Serena shrugged. "What can I say? The man has better taste in clothing than I do."

Lyric eyed the intricate gold band on Serena's upper arm and remembered Damon's possessive caress and the way he touched her there often.

"So how have you been, Lyric?" Angelina asked. "Is Connor still being mean to you?"

Lyric felt heat rush into her cheeks. The other women obviously noticed it too because their eyes sharpened like vultures going after road kill.

"Ohhh," Faith said.

"Okay, spill!" Julie demanded. "Oh my God, Serena and I have been dying to know all about Mr. Stick Up His Ass. I'll admit to him firing more than a few girly fantasies."

Faith clamped her hands over her ears and promptly fell underwater. She came up sputtering and holding her hand out. "Oh please. No. He's my brother, for God's sake. I don't want to hear this!"

Angelina rolled her eyes. "Your brother is hot, Faith. Deal."

"He isn't mean," Lyric defended. "He's been very . . ."

"Uh-huh," Serena said knowingly. "Very good? Very sexy?"

Lyric laughed. "Well, yes and yes."

Julie grinned. "Oh this is great. I love it. Connor Malone has met his match."

"I wouldn't go that far," Lyric said carefully.

"Oh crap, men alert," Faith said as she ducked farther underneath the water.

Lyric looked up to see the chef and one of his assistants carry out a platter of hors d'oeuvres.

"Oh stop it, Faith. You're freaking gorgeous. Let them look and lust over what they'll never have," Julie said cheekily.

"You guys are so never telling Gray about this," Faith squeaked. "He'll kick my ass."

The chef cleared his throat and did his best to avert his gaze, though Lyric could see him totally sneaking glances.

"I would be happy to provide drinks for you ladies. I have a fully stocked liquor cabinet, and one of my assistants is a trained bartender."

"Ohhh, Lyric. You have all the good stuff," Julie sighed.

Lyric grinned. "Well, order up. I've never tried drunk swimming before. Maybe we should see if any of the security team is a trained lifeguard?"

"Not a bad idea," Faith said.

"Ask Sam to come out," Serena said to the chef. "What?" she asked when the other women looked at her. "He's seen me naked before. Hello? Damon keeps me naked pretty much twenty-four/seven when we're at home."

"Do I even want to know?" Lyric asked.

"Oh we'll fill you in on Serena's lifestyle after a few drinks," Angelina said.

Serena turned and lifted an imperious brow in Angelina's direction. "And yours?"

Angelina flushed but laughed good-naturedly. "Okay, maybe not."

"There I go, feeling frighteningly boring again," Lyric said. "You guys are killing me with all these interesting comments."

"I'm the only normal slash sane one in this group," Julie said.

Julie was immediately swamped with waves of water as Faith, Angelina and Serena all drenched her.

"Drinks, ladies?" the chef reminded.

"Oh yeah, forgot," Lyric said. And now that the chef and his wide-eyed assistant had gotten quite the show . . .

"Hmm, why don't you surprise us?" Serena suggested. "Make us some yummy, fruity cocktails with the cute little umbrellas. We can stage our own little beach getaway here at the pool."

The chef nodded, then turned and had to nudge his assistant to get him to snap his attention away from the women.

Angelina grabbed on to one of the floaties and rested her chin atop it as she floated lazily in the deep end. "This is so nice. I feel like a walrus, mind you, but man, this feels wonderful."

"I'm so glad you all came," Lyric said. "This has been such a great day and now it's only better."

"Oh? Do tell," Julie prompted.

Lyric grinned and she reached for one of the floats lying on the side of the pool, then propelled herself along the surface of the water so that she floated close to Angelina.

"I fired my manager."

"Whoa. Really?" Faith asked.

Lyric nodded. "Yep. Thanks to Connor."

"Wow, we obviously need deets here," Julie said.

"I'll tell you all about it. Over drinks," she said smugly.

CHAPTER 23

Connor pinched the bridge of his nose and put down the last report in his stack. He checked his watch. He and Kane had been sequestered for the entire afternoon. They'd crawled through the lives of every single person even remotely attached to Lyric or her tour.

The problem was, there were more than a few who'd raised serious flags. How they ever got hired in the first place would remain a mystery to Connor. Which further cemented his opinion that Lyric's entire operation was half-assed and run by morons.

He laid aside four profiles that required more than a cursory run-through. One guy in particular had riled Connor's what-the-fuck meter. He had priors for assault. There were two restraining orders issued by former girlfriends, and his old man was in jail for domestic violence.

Still, Connor had his money on the two fuck-buddy bodyguards. Maybe he was prejudiced against them, given that they'd slept with the woman he was currently sleeping with, but the evidence was stacked against them. They had opportunity and access. What Connor wasn't sure of, however, was motive.

He picked up the phone to call Gray. He and Nathan could do quite a bit of legwork, which would leave Connor to focus his attention on the most important thing: Keeping Lyric safe.

"Hey, man," he said when Gray answered.

"Hey, stranger. You've survived Lyric, I see."

"She's not so bad," he defended, and then winced. He needed to just shut the hell up.

"Uh-huh. So what's up?"

Connor relayed the information to Gray, who stopped him so he could take notes. "Can you fax me those reports you have?" he asked after a moment.

"I'll e-mail them to you. Kane has them on his computer."

"Kane?"

"He's heading up the security team Armstrong hired."

"Ah okay. He good?"

"Yeah," Connor said. "Seems on top of things."

"What the ever-loving hell?" Kane said from across the room.

"Hang on a second, Gray."

Connor put the phone down to his leg and frowned over at Kane, who was looking out the window. "Something wrong?"

Kane turned around, his lips twitching. "Depends on whether you consider a pool full of naked girls a bad thing."

"*What?*"

Connor got up and strode across the room to look down at the pool below. "Oh Christ!"

He yanked the phone back up. "Gray, mind telling me what the hell your wife is doing over here? And naked, I might add. For God's sake, man, she's my sister! My eyes are burning!"

"What the fuck are you talking about? Faith is out shopping with the girls."

"Uh, no. They're all in Lyric's pool. Butt-ass naked, I might add."

There was dead silence on the other end.

"Look, I got to go. I need to handle this," Connor said. And before Gray could respond, Connor cut the connection.

"Looks like a hell of a party," Kane murmured.

Connor followed Kane's gaze to the clothing draped from one end of the pool area to the other. Hell, there were panties dangling from the shrubbery. He closed his eyes. "Why me?"

"Clearly I don't have your issues," Kane said in amusement. "None of them are related to me."

"You just keep your damn eyes to yourself," Connor growled. "They're all attached. Very attached."

Kane raised an eyebrow. "Oh? I hadn't realized Lyric was taken."

"Fuck you," Connor muttered.

He turned and started down the stairs, trying not to focus on the fact that five very naked, very beautiful women were swimming in the pool. Or how the hell he was going to fish them all out. Preferably before their very pissed-off husbands showed up.

He found the kitchen in turmoil. Every single one of the kitchen assistants was busting his nuts to be the one taking trays out to the pool.

He stopped them with a single glare. They retreated into the kitchen, nearly stumbling in their haste to avoid Connor.

He stalked toward the door leading to the patio and pool area. As soon as he opened the door, the air was filled with chatter and laughter. Music reverberated through the air, and to his horror, the girls had taken up a game of volleyball, using an imaginary net.

Nothing, however, was imaginary about the way they came out of the water to hit the ball back and forth.

He quickly scanned the patio but found only Sam, standing legs apart, arms over chest, his gaze focused on an area much higher than where the girls were swimming.

"Anyone mind telling me what the hell is going on here?" he demanded.

Five women simultaneously slid under the water until only their noses were visible.

"Well hell, don't hide now. Not like everyone in the house hasn't seen you by now."

Lyric scowled. "Sam alerts us when anyone steps out of the door. Or he did anyway. Somehow you got by."

"Uh-huh. And the security team, which is charged with your safety, mind you, are all getting an eyeful as we speak since they can't very well not protect you and watch out for you just because you decided to have a party. Which, I might add, was completely unauthorized, and you were specifically told you couldn't have company. Nor were you to so much as take a piss without mine or Kane's knowledge."

Julie giggled. Then Serena joined in. Angelina snickered and Faith sighed.

"Okay, okay," Faith said in resignation. "So he totally does have a stick up his ass."

The four other women burst into laughter. He glared at every one of them, not that it did a damn bit of good. They laughed and kept laughing until tears ran down their cheeks.

"I'm glad you find this so damn amusing," he growled.

Lyric swam over to the side of the pool where he stood, and before he could react, she pulled herself out and stood before him, naked as the day she was born, and goddamn if he didn't react to the sight of her dripping wet, beads of water running over some very strategic areas. Goose bumps immediately dotted her flesh, causing her nipples to tighten as she shivered in front of him.

"For God's sake," he said hoarsely. "Where are your damn clothes? You're going to freeze to death."

She stuck out her bottom lip in an exaggerated pout. "We're having fun, Connor. The guys are looking out for us, right? What could possibly happen? Are you expecting a team of assassins to swoop in and murder us all in the pool?"

"That's not the point and you know it."

"Look, I didn't know they were coming, but I wasn't going to tell them to go away. I enjoy their company. You and Kane were off doing your thing. I was happy to have them over. I like them."

"We like you too, Lyric," Faith called.

She turned and grinned over her shoulder.

"And you have a very nice ass," Julie said solemnly.

Connor closed his eyes. "For the love of God . . ."

"If I was a lesbian, I'd totally do you," Serena offered.

Connor sighed. He stared at the women suspiciously. "Just how much have you girls had to drink?"

"Uhm, you'll have to talk to the chef. Or the bartender. Yeah, the cute young guy. He makes the most yummy drinks," Faith said.

Connor rubbed a hand through his hair. He glanced over at Angelina, who was tucked behind a float. "You okay, sweetie? You haven't been drinking, have you?"

She rolled her eyes at him. "Oh, for Pete's sake, Connor. I'm fine."

"Can I get back in now or are you shutting us down?" Lyric asked.

"Would you listen if I said no?" he asked dryly.

She smiled cheekily. To his surprise she leaned up on tiptoe and kissed him full on the mouth. He was so shocked he just stood there with a blank look on his face as she pulled away.

"Probably not."

With that she turned and hopped back into the pool amidst cheers from her very inebriated accomplices.

His cell phone rang and with a groan he pulled it out. "Yeah," he said shortly.

"Is my wife over there? And more important, is she naked?" Nathan demanded.

"Hell," Connor muttered.

"Get her some damn clothes. I don't want the whole security team looking at what's mine."

"Too late."

Nathan cursed. "What the hell are they thinking? Are they crazy?"

"You're asking me?" Connor asked in exasperation. "They're demented. But they're not my damn responsibility. Only one woman is. You think I like seeing my sister in the buff? I'm going to have nightmares for a week."

"I heard that!" Faith yelled. "Asshole."

"I'll kick his ass for you," Julie said.

"You tell Julie to stay her ass in the pool," Nathan said, overhearing Julie's exclamation.

"Look, I'm not getting into this," Connor said wearily. "They're having some kind of goddamn party. Sam is here. I assume he'll make sure they all get home okay. I'll drive them myself if I have to."

Before Nathan could argue further, Connor hung up. He surveyed the girls again, glad that dusk was falling and it was more difficult to make out their nudity in the water. But it was also getting cooler and they were just drunk enough not to figure out they risked hypothermia gallivanting around wet and naked.

"Let me guess. No one knows where you are."

Serena snapped her lips shut and slowly shook her head.

"Nice. Throw me under the bus. Now all your husbands will be pissed at me," he grumbled.

"You need to get that stick out of your ass," Faith said darkly.

He stared at her in surprise.

"I've defended you long enough. You need to chill the fuck out."

Connor's eyes widened. "Uhm, Faith? Just how much have *you* had to drink tonight? I'm not sure it's a good idea for you to be in the pool. It's too chilly out here. You're all going to get sick."

"Sam's acting as our lifeguard," Julie pointed out. "Besides, the pool is heated. It's only cold when we get out."

"You need some help, Connor?" Kane asked lazily.

Connor turned and fixed Kane with his stare. "I told you to stay inside."

"Yeah, well, you looked like you needed backup."

Amusement was heavy in Kane's voice.

"Uh-oh," Lyric muttered. "Party's over. Mr. Makes Connor Look Relaxed is here."

Faith giggled. "Is he that bad? I don't know, Lyric. He's cute."

Kane lifted an eyebrow. "Cute? Why do I think I've just been relegated to puppy-dog status?"

"He's mean to me," Lyric said. "Connor isn't."

Angelina frowned in Kane's direction. Serena and Julie both crossed their arms over their breasts—thank God—and glared at Kane.

"Why are you being mean to Lyric?" Serena demanded. "Want us to kick his ass?" she asked Lyric.

Kane laughed softly. "You couldn't fight your way out of a paper bag in your condition, sweetheart. I'm not mean to Ms. Jones. I just expect her to cooperate with my desire to keep her safe."

"Oh," Faith said. "Well, that's different, I guess."

"Now, as much as I'd like to let you ladies continue enjoying yourself in your present state, I'd appreciate it if you could stop giving my men a heart attack and maybe put on some robes if we got you some. We'll be happy to ensure your safety if you'd like to continue eating or drinking. I'd just like you to be dressed and out of the pool when you do it."

"Oh, he's good, Lyric," Serena murmured. "Very smooth."

Kane smiled. "Glad you think so, Mrs. Roche."

At that she frowned. "How do you know who I am?"

"It's my job to know everyone who comes into contact with Ms. Jones."

Faith thrust out her chin. "Just don't be mean to Lyric. We'll kick your ass."

Kane chuckled. "I have no doubt you'd try, Mrs. Montgomery."

"Oh, all right. Get us the robes," Julie grumbled. "But I go on record saying you're even less fun than Connor."

Kane raised his hand and, a few seconds later, one of his men came out carrying several fluffy robes. Connor took them and then motioned for both Kane and his man to leave. He'd be damned if they saw any of the women naked.

He turned back in resignation of the evening ahead. "If I lay these on the table, can I trust you to get out of the pool and into them?"

"You know, if you'd just leave, we could enjoy our nekkid swim party," Lyric grumbled.

"I think I'm being reasonable by allowing it to continue and not tossing everyone off the grounds."

Several sounds of exasperation echoed from the water.

"I'd like to see you try to toss me anywhere, Connor Malone," Julie muttered.

He grinned. "You know I love you all dearly, but you're interfering in my job, not to mention I'll now have to answer to guys I work with as to why I allowed their women to cavort around in the nude."

"Oh, we can handle them," Faith said with a sniff. "It's not like we had an orgy or something."

"Though that could be fun," Lyric added. "I think the only thing I haven't been accused of is a lesbian orgy. Maybe we should call one of the tabloids."

Connor groaned. "For the love of God. Just get out of the pool and into your robes. I'll make sure your bartender and the chef supply you with booze and food. If you really want to be good and get dried off and dressed, you can continue this inside where it's warm."

"Hot chocolate would be nice," Serena mused. "And it is getting cooler. March is such a screwed-up month. Hot, cold, hot, cold."

Connor closed his eyes and sighed. Any other man would be in heaven surrounded by gorgeous, naked women all slicked down with water and all sporting chill bumps from hell. He, on the other hand, was praying for deliverance and for a little cooperation before all hell broke loose.

"Okay, okay, he's getting that look," Lyric said. "Let's get out and get dressed. We'll take over the living room and kick all the guys out. What time are you guys supposed to be home anyway?"

There was a moment of silence and then Faith said, "What time is it?"

Connor checked his watch. "Six thirty."

Serena giggled. "I think we said we'd be home by five. Oops."

"Mr. Roche is aware of your delay," Sam said calmly.

"It would appear that Mr. Montgomery and Mr. Tucker are as well," Faith said on a laugh. "Which only leaves Micah. Angelina? Are you going to call him?"

Angelina shook her head. "Huh-uh. I'm still riding the marriage card. He's so happy I said yes, he can't possibly get pissed at me."

"You know, I'm starting to feel real sorry for the guys," Connor said.

Lyric climbed the steps from the pool and it took all his discipline not to stare. She walked over and snagged one of the robes and wrapped it around her shivering body. Hell, he wanted to wrap himself around her until she was warm and soft against him.

"Trust the guys to stick together," she drawled. "Come on, girls. Let's take this party inside."

Connor whirled around and strode to the door before the other women took their exit from the pool. Their laughter followed him all the way inside.

CHAPTER 24

Connor and Kane got Julie, Angelina, Serena and Faith into the car while Lyric watched from the front door. As they drove away, Lyric waved.

Connor and Kane walked back to the door and Connor looked harassed. His cell phone rang and he jammed his hand into his pocket to silence it.

"Get some damn clothes on," he said under his breath when he walked by her into the house.

She tugged the robe tighter around her and grinned. "I'm perfectly covered!"

"Yeah, but I know your naked underneath that robe and so does everyone else. For God's sake show a little mercy here."

"Okay, okay. I'll go up." She hesitated a moment and then looked at both Connor and Kane. "Are you guys going to be around for a bit?"

Kane looked curiously at her. "If you need us to be."

"I won't be but a minute upstairs. I'd like . . . I'd like to talk to you when I get back down if you have the time."

"Of course I have time."

She glanced at Connor and he nodded, his eyes never leaving her face. She smiled. "Okay, I'll be right back down."

"Want some more hot chocolate?" Connor asked gruffly.

"Yeah. That would be nice. Thanks."

She skipped up the stairs, bobbled a bit, then clung tightly to the railing. She'd sort of forgotten how much she'd had to drink and, as a former nondrinker, she'd discovered she was a lightweight when it came to alcohol.

After steadying herself a moment, she continued up the stairs and into the bedroom. Deciding to take a quick shower to take care of the pool hair, she hopped in and out, threw a towel around her head and quickly dressed.

She combed her hair down and left it wet before heading back down the stairs feeling a good bit more sober than she had fifteen minutes ago.

She found Kane and Connor in the living room sprawled on the couches. Connor looked tired and she almost giggled when he reached into his pocket to silence yet another call. Between her manager, her label and the girls' husbands, Connor was getting it from all corners.

"Feel better?" Kane asked when he looked up and saw her.

"I didn't feel bad before," she said with a grin. "Today has been . . . liberating. Fun."

Connor leaned forward and picked up a steaming mug of hot chocolate. He held it up but didn't make a move to bring it over. He was enticing her to come to him. Once she caught a whiff of the decadent aroma, he didn't have to do much to get her to do his bidding.

She went over, took the cup from him and then sat forward on the couch next to him, cradling the warm mug in her palms. Connor's hand immediately went to her back, stroking up and down.

She drew comfort from that gesture. She loved him touching her. She was so contented right now that she could curl into his arms like a satisfied kitten and purr endlessly.

"What's on your mind?" Kane asked.

She pulled the mug away and held it on her lap. She pursed her lips a moment trying to formulate her thoughts. This was new territory for her. For so long she'd relied on others around her, her management team, her record label, her security, her handlers, to make decisions for her. Her motto was show up, do what she needed to do and then move on to the next show and do it all over again.

Firing Paul had been huge for her. She doubted even Connor knew just what a momentous step it was. It had been a much-needed slap in the face. A wake-up call that her life was out of control because she'd allowed it to be so.

"I'm ready to make some changes." She swallowed. It took all her courage to say the next. "I'm a little afraid. I would like your help."

Connor's hand stilled on her back, then slid up to her nape and squeezed reassuringly.

"Okay," Kane said.

"I don't want my label to hire a new security firm."

Kane frowned. She turned slightly to see the same frown on Connor's face.

"What I mean is that I don't want Phillip to choose. He means well. I have no doubt that he has my best interests and my safety in mind. He'll hire competent people. But I think I should be the one who decides who holds my safety in their hands."

She sucked in another deep breath, gripped the mug a little tighter and then glanced up at Kane. "Would your firm be willing to take over my security while I'm on the road?"

Kane didn't respond right away. He glanced at Connor, then back at Lyric.

"I understand if you're not set up to travel. It's just that I . . ." She wrinkled her nose. "I trust your team more than some random firm that Phillip hires. I don't know them. I know you . . . now."

"I'm sure something could be worked out," Kane said slowly. "But you need to consider whether this is going to cause you trouble with your label."

"I'm going to tell Phillip that from now on I'm going to have a more active part in my career. To be honest, I think he'll be relieved and more than willing for me to take the reins."

Connor's thumb tightened at her neck. He ran his other hand over her arm and squeezed lightly in approval.

Kane's eyes glinted and then he smiled. "I think I may have misjudged you, Ms. Jones."

"Oh please, call me Lyric. Ms. Jones sounds so stuffy."

"All right, Lyric. The problem is that I can't assemble a team as soon as two weeks. Less than two weeks now. I'll need to handpick men for the detail and I'll want to oversee the operation for the first little while until I'm satisfied that everything is progressing well. If you want the best, it'll take time."

"I don't go back on tour right away. I'll be in the studio recording for a bit. I also have a few appearances but they could be cancelled. My tour picks up in six weeks. Runs for two months and then I have a break at which time I'll finish recording the next album. Would that give you enough time?"

"I think you need to decide if you can afford me first," Kane said.

She laughed. "If I want the best, I have to be prepared to pay for it, right?"

"Then the first thing you need to do is ask for a bid. You'll want to know everything I can do for you and you'll want to know how much it'll cost you. I'll want complete control over picking the men for the detail, and each one will be screened personally by me."

She nodded. "How soon can you get that to me?"

Kane smiled. "Now we're talking. You catch on quick."

She turned to Connor and slipped her hand into his. "I know I probably shouldn't ask this. But again, I'm a little nervous. I don't think it will be a problem. But . . ."

"Just ask, baby," he said softly.

"I want to fire R.J. and Trent. Buy them out. Whatever. The problems are that I'm not sure what, if any, out I have in the contract, and they're supposed to come in for the rodeo performance. They aren't going to take it well. I've allowed them far too much latitude in their job. My fault, but there you have it."

He put a finger to her mouth. "I'll take care of it."

She breathed out a sigh of relief.

"Any other earth-shattering changes you're contemplating?"

She pressed her lips together and scrunched her brows. "I want to go whole hog. I've surrounded myself with people I don't trust, who don't care about me, have no investment in me beyond the paycheck I provide them. I know it sounds hypocritical. They don't owe me anything other than to do the job they're paid to do just like I don't owe them anything beyond that paycheck. But I don't want it to be that way. I want . . . I need a change. I don't like my life very much."

"Then do it," Connor said. "If anyone can turn things around, it's you. I don't think there's a person in the world who can run over you unless you let them."

A smile twitched at her lips. "Yeah, I am a good bitch on wheels when given the right motivation."

Kane chuckled and she turned quickly back to glare at him. "You are not to agree with that statement."

He held up his hands in surrender. "For what it's worth, I think you're doing the right thing. It's never too late to regain control over your career. And your life."

"I can't wait to see what the tabloids do with all of this when it gets out," she said wryly. "They'll have a field day. It'll likely be reported that I've checked into the funny farm."

"Fuck 'em," Connor said. "You'll know the truth. The people who care about you will know the truth. That's all that matters."

"And who are the people who care about me?" she asked softly.

He looked straight into her eyes. Then he reached out and touched her cheek, just one gentle brush with his fingertip. "I do."

CHAPTER 25

$\mathcal{C}$onnor returned from taking the cups to the kitchen and saw that Lyric had fallen asleep on the couch. Not that it surprised him. She'd been bobbing and weaving for over an hour as she sat and talked to him and Kane. It was obvious she had no desire to go up to her room. Alone. She'd clung to their company until fatigue had overcome her.

"Want me to get her a blanket?" Kane asked.

Connor shook his head. "I'll take her up. She'll be more comfortable in her bed."

"I'm going to turn in then. See you tomorrow."

Kane walked quietly out of the living room and Connor stared down at Lyric, who was curled against the end of the couch, her head on the arm rest. He reached down and touched a strand of her hair that had fallen over her eyes and gently pushed it back.

"I don't think I've ever met anyone like you," he murmured. "Just when I think I've got you all figured out, you manage to surprise me all over again. I wonder sometimes if you even know who you are."

He leaned down and slid his arms underneath her curled-up body and hoisted her up. She stirred and made a murmur of protest and then promptly cuddled into his chest.

He liked the way she felt in his arms. All soft and snuggly, her head tucked underneath his chin like she was made to go there.

Slowly he navigated the stairs and headed into her bedroom, where he deposited her onto the bed. She yawned and then her eyelids fluttered open and she blinked up at him.

He leaned down and kissed her on the forehead. "You going to be okay?"

As he drew away, uncertainty, and a little fear, flashed in her eyes She was clearly torn between wanting him to go and not wanting to be alone. He wasn't going to push her. She had to make the choice herself, even if he had no desire to go anywhere.

There was something infinitely fragile about Lyric. Behind the badass persona was a fascinating mix of fear and insecurity that he still hadn't been able to discern the reason for.

"Stay," she said. Her gaze traveled over his face and he saw a hint of uncertainty. "I mean, I'd like you to stay. If you want . . ."

He bent down and shushed her with a kiss. He was purposely tender, allowing his mouth to melt over hers. "I want. I want very much. How about we get more comfortable and get into bed."

It hadn't been his plan to make love to her, but he'd gone instantly hard the moment she'd given him that sleepy, seductive look.

She rolled to the side of the bed and rose. He watched in the low light as she began undressing. She pulled her shirt over her head and then peeled down her jeans until she was clad in only her bra and panties.

It was a sight to make a red-blooded man get a raging case of lust. Jet-black and lacy. Ultrafeminine but it also screamed "Bad girl gonna rock your world."

When she turned, he could see the mounds of her breasts pushed up to their best advantage, and the slightest hint of a peach-colored nipple peeked from above the cup.

As if he weren't even there, she stretched lazily and then pushed the frothy lace from her body. As soon as she was naked, she crawled onto the bed and stretched out on her side, her vivid blue eyes trained on him as if telling him it was his turn.

He wondered if she knew what a provocative image she posed. Probably. She was likely grinning like a maniac on the inside because he was standing here with a bulge at his crotch that would make taking his jeans off painful and damn difficult.

When she shifted restlessly and slipped her fingers between her legs to delve into those soft folds, he lost what little patience he thought he was holding.

He yanked his shirt off and then fumbled with his pants. The condoms were where he'd left them—thank God—and he reached for one of the packets on the nightstand while he unzipped his jeans with the other.

She continued to stroke herself and made soft little sounds of pleasure that drove him insane. He itched from the inside out, like he'd been invaded by a thousand bugs.

He finally managed to get his pants and underwear off and he had to work at getting the condom on. He was so hard, the latex stretched tight over his aching erection until he worried he'd split the damn thing.

He strode to the bed and she gave him an innocent little smile that told him she knew precisely how naughty she was being. He reached for her ankles, yanked her around and then pulled her to the end of the bed. He spread her thighs, held them wide apart and then stroked inside her with one forceful thrust.

Her pussy rippled over his flesh, hugging, fighting, sucking him deeper. His entire body went so taut he was going to get a frigging cramp. But damn, she felt good. So good.

He closed his eyes and clenched his jaw, determined not to come. He was close. After one thrust he was fighting off his release with everything he had.

He leaned down and kissed the valley between her breasts as he pulsed inside her, dying to move, dying to thrust hard and long until she begged him to stop.

Drawn to the plump swells of her breasts, he slid his tongue over the underside and then up over her nipple. A spasm rolled through her body and her pussy contracted around him in little, fluttery pulses that damn near made his eyes roll back in his head.

He nipped at the taut peak and then sucked it strongly between his teeth. She flinched and moved restlessly beneath him and then finally dug her fingers into his shoulders and lifted her hips.

"Please, Connor," she gasped. "Move. Fuck me. Do something."

"Christ," he muttered. "I'm going to come, baby. Give me just a minute to calm down. I want to make this good for you, not get inside you and be done within two minutes."

She laughed softly and stroked her hands over his back, up the column of his neck and then into his hair. She was everywhere, touching, caressing. She curled her legs around his waist and arched into him, trying to get him deeper. As if that were possible. He was already balls deep, pressed so tight against her ass that it would take a crowbar to separate them.

"Relax," he whispered. "I'll make it good for you. Let me love you. Let me show you how good it can be with someone who cares for you."

She went so still that he worried he'd crossed some invisible line. She looked—for lack of a better word—lost.

Worried he'd lose her, he kissed a line to her jaw and then nibbled over to her lips before sealing his mouth over hers. He was consumed by her. He had to be careful or he'd devour her. He had to pace himself and measure his kisses. She just tasted so good that he lacked control.

Raising his hands to frame her face, he pulled back just an inch or so and then thrust again as he claimed her mouth once more.

Their tongues slipped over each other, exploring and tasting. He began moving, withdrawing and thrusting, slowly at first and then harder and faster as he finally managed to leash the raging caveman inside who just wanted to claim his woman, mark her and slake his lust endlessly.

Oh yeah, he could do this all night.

Touching her. Tasting her. Getting so deep inside her that she couldn't shake him. He wanted her to believe in him. He wanted her to trust him. He wanted a lot of damn things.

He wanted to wrap himself around her so tight that nothing or no one could ever get to her or hurt her. He wanted to be her refuge.

His mouth slipped from hers and glanced over her cheek to her ear and then down her neck, kissing and sucking. He hadn't given her any sort of foreplay but he couldn't even muster the regret he should. She'd been sleek and ready for him. Hot and damp. So fucking tight that he thought he'd die getting inside her.

"Connor," she whispered. "I'm close. I can't hold back."

He closed his eyes. Damn, but he didn't deserve this. He hadn't done anything to ensure her pleasure. He'd gone after her like a rutting pig. Pinned her to the mattress and held her down while he got inside her.

It took everything he had, but he pulled out of her. His cock screamed hell no. She let out a whimper of protest. He kissed her belly and then dropped to his knees between her thighs. He was determined to make her feel every bit as good as he did.

Her pussy was swollen from his invasion. The soft pink lips were spread and her opening was red and distended from his size. Damn, but she was sexy.

He pressed his mouth to the opening. She flinched and let out a sharp cry of pleasure. Then he swept his tongue over and then pushed in until he tasted the very heart of her.

She went satiny sweet in his mouth. Like liquid silk.

Her legs came up and looped over his shoulders, squeezing his head and holding it in place. She pulsed against his mouth. Shudder after shudder rolled through her body. She lifted her hips but he grasped them and held them in place for his seeking mouth.

He tongued her clit, rolling the tip in a tight circle and then sucking softly at the quivering peak. She was as tight as a bow at full draw, her thighs rigid on his shoulders.

"Connor," she said softly. So sweetly it was like music over his ears. "Connor," she said again on a sigh.

He rose and stared down at her half-lidded eyes, glazed with passion and yearning. She was sprawled out like a feast before him and he ate her with his eyes.

Then he reached and flipped her over until she was facedown on the mattress. She turned her head so that her cheek rested against the mattress and she closed her eyes as if anticipating where he'd take her next.

He cupped her plump behind and kneaded the soft flesh, pushing and spreading so that her pussy was bared. He pulled until she was bent over the edge and then he pushed into her from behind, his abdomen pressing into her as he stroked deep.

Man, he loved her like this. His hands left her ass and smoothed up her delicate spine to her shoulders, and then he gripped her neck and thrust again, pulling her to meet his forceful thrusts.

He leaned down until his body was completely covering hers. Protecting. Sheltering. Completely blanketing her. Then he began fucking in and out, the sounds of his hips slapping against her ass rising in the silent room.

She moaned and stretched her arms out above her head as if surrendering completely to his dominance. He nipped at her shoulder, lightly at first and then harder.

He wanted to own her. He wanted to put his mark on her, to let her know she belonged to him. No one else. No other man would touch her. No other man would possess what he considered his.

She may not know it yet, but he was it for her. It was going to require patience. He was a patient guy when the reward was high.

She was going to be the biggest challenge of his life, but he was up to it. He wasn't going to fail.

She was his.

He lowered his body until his chest was flush with her back. She was cupped perfectly to him and he moved both their bodies as he stroked in and out in long, lazy thrusts.

Over and over he made his point, driving her so close to orgasm and then stilling as she moved restlessly beneath him, trying to make him take her over the edge. He waited and then began all over again, pushing into her, feeling the exquisite sensation of her pussy clutching at him.

"You're mine, Lyric," he whispered next to her ear. And then he thrust hard and deep and began pumping against her with renewed urgency.

He planted his palms on either side of her and levered himself up so that he could power more forcefully into her.

She cried out and went slick around him so that he glided with ease so deep, into the very heart of her. Faster. Harder.

Mindlessly he kept thrusting, even when her entire body went rigid and his name spilled from her lips over and over.

He chased one orgasm from her and went after another. Relentless. Wanting her to know who she belonged to. Who commanded her body and her pleasure.

She begged and pleaded. *More. Stop. Don't stop. Oh God. Again.* "Connor!"

Her fingers curled into fists above her, and she raised her head and pushed back against him as another orgasm raced through her body, igniting fire within him.

"Oh God, I'm coming. Baby. You feel so good. Come with me, Lyric."

He swelled within her, so tight he could barely move even after she'd come twice and her moisture bathed him. He withdrew and rolled her over roughly, spreading her legs and mounting her again, this time face-to-face. He wanted to see her. He wanted to drown in her eyes while he finally came.

He plunged deep. Withdrew and then plunged one last time. She wrapped herself around him. Arms, legs. She raised her head and buried it in his neck.

He came apart. It was the most gut-wrenching orgasm of his life. He couldn't be still. He kept thrusting and thrusting, like he was about to come out of his skin. He came and came, and he worried about the condom but he couldn't stop.

She held him, stroking her hands over his back, clutching at him with her legs, pulling him deeper until there was no separation between them.

He slumped down over her, embedded deeply in her pussy as the last of his release tore from his body. He sucked in deep breaths. His entire body shook. He couldn't catch up. Couldn't process the magnitude of what he'd just felt. It was earth-shattering. Weren't women supposed to be the ones who came undone during sex? He'd never felt so damn vulnerable in his life.

Knowing he couldn't stay inside her after coming so violently, he groaned and rolled to the side, still holding her tightly against him.

He eased out of her, hoping like hell the condom wasn't already leaking. Then he reached down and pulled it off. He leaned back and aimed for the garbage can but he didn't give a shit if it made it or not. He'd clean it up later. Right now he didn't want to separate himself from Lyric even for the two seconds it would take to dispose of the rubber.

She trembled against him and was so quiet, it worried him. What was he supposed to say after something like this? What was there to say?

He'd scare the shit out of her if he spouted what he was thinking or feeling. Hell, any woman would waste no time getting the hell away if he told her that he wanted to tie her to him for the next year and never let her out of bed.

Sex made a man crazy. There was no other explanation for it.

No, it wasn't sex. And maybe that was the problem. He knew it went far deeper than that. It hadn't been sex even that first time. He knew it. He accepted it. He just didn't know what the hell he was supposed to do about it.

Worse, he had no idea how to handle Lyric. He couldn't afford to fuck this up. One wrong word and the walls would go up and he'd be frozen out.

How the hell was a man ever supposed to know the right thing to say or do at precisely the right time? It was a wonder relationships ever worked.

Relationship. Hell. He was getting way too far ahead of himself. He was thinking too much. You weren't supposed to think after mind-blowing sex. That was his problem. He was getting all analytical—and, God help him, all touchy-feely—when he needed to just enjoy the moment and take things as they came.

Weren't women supposed to be the emotional creatures who couldn't separate sex from love?

He was fucked. So fucked.

He glanced down to see her eyes closed and her chest rising and falling as she cuddled against him. With a resigned sigh, he made the mental effort to shut his brain off. One should never make life-altering decisions when holding a naked woman in his arms.

For a long moment they lay there, silent and unmoving. He was about to drift into sleep himself, content that she hadn't hauled ass, when she stirred against him and started to push away.

The alarm went off in his brain as she started to roll. He reached for her but she slipped from his grasp.

"I need to go to the bathroom," she whispered, just as she'd done the first night they'd made love.

And he knew, just as he'd known then, that she wouldn't be back.

Chapter 26

*I*t was somehow fitting that during the night a cold front moved through and brought with it raw, rainy temperatures. In a lot of ways, it suited Lyric's mood.

Fear was cold. Fear had icy fingers that gripped your heart and spread its chill through your soul.

Connor scared her. Not him, but what he represented. No matter what she did, she couldn't rid herself of the panicky, tight feeling in her chest.

How could she face him after what she'd done? He'd been . . . perfect. Just perfect. More than perfect. She didn't even have words to describe it simply because she'd never had a man look at her, touch her . . . love her as Connor had done.

And her response? Run like hell.

She rubbed tiredly at her forehead as she stood shivering in the rain. She hadn't slept. She'd spent the entire night secluded in the small library off the living room. Now she stood staring over the front lawn, taking in nothing and everything all at once as the rain fell softly around her.

A warm hand slid over her bare shoulder and squeezed. She knew instantly it was Connor, and she went still, dreading what he'd say or do. He surprised her.

"Come inside, Lyric," he said gently. "It's cold and you have a performance tonight. Have you slept at all?"

She shook her head mutely as he pulled her into his side and shielded her from the rain with his big body.

She wanted to say she was sorry but the words hung painfully in her throat. She wanted to tell him that she'd never felt this way about another man and that she was scared shitless. She wanted to turn into him and hold on for dear life. Take what he offered and never let go.

But the fear wouldn't thaw. She was cold and frozen. Unable to move. Unable to reach out. And so she went quietly back inside and stood in front of the fireplace while he rubbed a towel through her hair.

Would he say something now? Would he ask her for explanations she couldn't provide? Ask her to reveal things long hidden?

But all he did was wrap a robe around her and pull the ends snug so she'd be warm. He rubbed his hands up and down her shoulders several times and then said, "You have a few hours yet. You should try to sleep. I'll wake you in time to get to the arena."

She nodded and stood there a moment longer. She couldn't meet his gaze because she knew he'd see too much. Then he leaned down and pressed his lips to her forehead. She closed her eyes and tilted into his embrace, but he didn't touch her. Didn't hold her. Just one simple kiss and then he was gone.

She didn't want to go back up to her bedroom. The fire crackled and sparked behind her and she turned to warm her hands. Warmth seeped into her bones and made her heavy with lethargy. She glanced over her shoulder to the couch. It was as good a place as any and she knew the security guys would be in and out, as would Connor and Kane, so she wouldn't be alone.

With a sigh she stepped over and then crawled onto the couch. She turned to face the back and pulled her knees to her chest until she felt safe, warm and secure.

On the ride to Reliant Stadium, Lyric was tense and jittery. Connor rode in the back of the car while Kane remained up front. A car carrying the rest of her detail followed and another team had already gone ahead to set up for the show.

"Can you make sure that the girls got the tickets I arranged for them?" she asked anxiously.

Connor slid a hand over hers. "They got them. Don't worry. They're going to have a blast."

She fell silent again and watched out the window as they approached the stadium. She wasn't sure why she was so nervous. It was like any other show. She'd done it a million times. She wasn't the type to suffer stage fright. Singing was what she loved. It brought her peace. It was the one thing she did for herself. That others liked it and paid for the privilege of hearing it was just added bonus.

The car rolled to a stop outside the entrance to the myriad of rooms on the lower level of the stadium. The area was roped off and security was heavy, but there was still a crowd of fans who screamed the moment Lyric stepped from the vehicle.

Despite Connor urging her forward, she paused and turned to wave. She smiled broadly, blew kisses and then allowed Connor to pull her inside the building.

Almost immediately her shoulders relaxed as she stepped back into her world. The hustle and bustle backstage was something she was familiar with and embraced. She was back in her element.

Connor stopped at her dressing room. Kane and four of his men stood to the side. She started to open her door but Connor put his hand on her wrist.

"Stay here while I check it out."

She stepped back and Connor opened the door. To her surprise, R.J. and Trent were both sprawled on couches in the room. They both bolted up when Connor stepped into the room, but when she tried to follow, Kane stepped in front of her and blocked her entrance.

"You asked him for help," Kane said in a low voice. "He'll handle it."

The sounds of R.J. and Trent arguing had her taking a step back. Kane moved with her, shielding her, careful to keep his body between her and the men at all times. Two of his men flanked her. One of them pulled out a handgun and stood alert while two others went into the room to give Connor help.

"Send her a bill," she heard Connor say. "Or don't. Either way your employment has been terminated. You'll be escorted from the premises, and if you step foot on or around her tour again, I'll have you arrested."

Her eyes widened when a thump sounded. And then a crash. Then she heard what sounded like something or someone hitting the wall.

She took a step forward but Kane pressed in close and maneuvered her farther away until she was against the far wall in the hall. She was surrounded by male bodies, and it drove her crazy that she couldn't see what was going on.

A few moments later, Kane stepped back just in time for her to see R.J. and Trent being manhandled down the hall by Kane's men. Blood smeared Trent's nose and R.J. was sporting a swollen eye.

"Oh my God, Connor!" she exclaimed as she rushed into the room.

He turned and she saw he was fine. In fact, he looked cool and calm, like he hadn't just taken on men larger than himself. Her only sign that he had in fact mixed it up with them was the curling and uncurling of his hand. The knuckles looked bruised and there was a smear of blood over the top of his hand.

"Are you okay?" she asked anxiously as she reached for his hand.

He cracked a smile. "I think your boyfriends fared the worst."

She scowled. "They aren't my boyfriends."

"You don't have to worry about them anymore. I told them if they had anything to say to you at all, to contact your label and they'd provide the name of your new manager whenever you get around to hiring one."

"Thank you," she murmured. "I suppose that was cowardly of me but I didn't want to have a confrontation with them."

"Lyric?"

She turned to see Kane holding a piece of paper in his hand. His face was dark with a frown as he concentrated on the note. Then he turned and stared at Connor.

"I think you need to go after those two and bring them back. This was hanging on her mirror."

He held out the note and Connor yanked it from him before Lyric could reach for it.

"Son of a bitch," Connor muttered. "I *knew* it was them. Those bastards."

"Connor, what does it say?"

He held it out to her. She took it and glanced down at the colored cutout letters in varying fonts and sizes.

You won't be safe.

Her brows came together and unease skittered down her spine.

"Run them down," Connor ordered Kane. "Detain them and I'll call the cops. We'll turn the matter over to them. Our priority is Lyric's safety."

Kane nodded, then motioned to his men. They disappeared from the room a few moments later, leaving Connor and Lyric alone.

"I'll leave you to dress. Your people should be here any moment now to help you get ready."

"Don't go," she said, reaching for his arm. "I mean, it'll be boring. They'll do my hair and makeup and arrange my clothing, but it won't take long. There aren't any wardrobe changes for tonight's show. It's really like a miniconcert. Just eight songs total."

A knock sounded at the door, interrupting them. "I'll get that," he said as he turned to open it.

Moments later, the room was filled with people. Chatter rose. Lyric was poked, prodded and made up until she barely recognized the woman staring back at her. For several days she'd lived a normal existence. No makeup. No outrageous clothes. Would Connor be repelled by the role Lyric played?

She glanced into the mirror to see him leaning against the back of the couch, hands shoved into his pockets as he watched her stylist put the finishing touches on her makeup.

Lyric couldn't make out the expression on his face. She had no idea what he was thinking.

"You look great, Lyric," the stylist said with a bright smile.

"Thank you, Stacy. You did a great job."

Another knock sounded and Kane stuck his head in. "Five minutes, Lyric. They need you outside."

Lyric rose, smoothed her tight jeans down her body and checked her appearance. It was a good costume choice for the rodeo. Though she didn't sing country music, her outfit would appeal to the more conservative types, and what was the saying? When in Rome?

She pulled on her boots, slapped the sassy straw cowboy hat over her hair and grinned at Connor. "Showtime."

Connor saw the light reenter Lyric's eyes. Her confidence was back in spades and he was so relieved he nearly keeled over. She strutted into the hallway where he and Kane's men surrounded her. Kane led the way and they stopped at a black Ford jacked-up pickup that bore the performers to the stage in the middle of the dirt-packed rodeo arena.

The lights were dimmed and the crowd buzzed with excitement.

Connor helped Lyric inside, then crawled in behind her. Kane's men started ahead of the truck, even though the arena had security positioned at intervals around the stage.

Kane's men positioned themselves between the area where the fans who had chute seats were allowed from the stands close to the stage and the stage itself.

It seemed the entire stadium was electrically charged and waiting for Lyric to arrive.

With a roar, the truck lurched forward and drove toward the stage just as it lit up and the stadium came alive with laser lights. The huge LCD screen that wrapped the back of the stage flashed Lyric's sassy face and smile. The crowd went wild as she stepped from the truck and ran up the ramp to the stage.

Lyric yelled a greeting to the Houston fans and immediately launched into one of her upbeat songs.

The stands thumped and rocked along with her. Cameras flashed a repeating staccato of light, peppered throughout the thousands of people gathered for the rodeo.

Connor gained a new appreciation of what it took to get out and perform the way she did. She threw herself into it. She held nothing back. It was loud. It was raucous, and the fans loved every second of it.

She was sassy, cute, seductive and endearing. Her fans loved her and she clearly loved them.

At one point during the show, a mechanical bull rose from underneath the stage through an opening in the floor and Lyric climbed on and proceeded to ride like a champ. She waved and rotated and threw her hat into the crowd of fans assembled near the stage.

The bull sped up and she was tossed several feet into the air. His heart pumped into his throat and he was about to leap onto the stage to see about her when she popped up, laughing uproariously.

Then she slowed things down and sang the ballad that Connor had liked so much. "Going Home." The crowd sang and swayed with her, and when she finished, the lights dimmed for a moment and then blazed back on as she led into her last song choice of the evening.

The show had lasted only a little more than an hour, but sweat gleamed on her face. Her hair was damp and her shirt clung to her like a second skin.

But she wore a smile and waved enthusiastically as she headed down the ramp toward the truck. Connor and Kane met her at the bottom, ushered her into the back, and she stood, holding on to the roll bars as they drove across the dirt. They circled once while she waved to the cheering crowd and then they disappeared behind the gate to the backstage area once more.

As soon as they stopped, Connor hopped off and then reached up to lift Lyric down. She was buzzing with energy. Her muscles jumped and jittered and she beamed from ear to ear.

He took her hand in his and led her back to her dressing room. He was gratified to see that food and drink were waiting for her. A few people with security passes milled about. Lyric ignored them, latched on to a bottle of water and chugged it down without taking a breath. She tossed the plastic and then reached for another as she slumped onto the couch.

"I have it on good authority you're going to be having company in a very few minutes," Connor said dryly. "You want to shower and change and I'll hold them off for you?"

She sent him a puzzled look.

"The girls. They have passes with their tickets. I thought you knew."

Lyric's face lit up. "Oh that's great. I asked Phillip to make sure they were taken care of but I wasn't sure what arrangements he'd made for them."

"The blue-haired brigade will descend."

She chuckled. "You make us sound like a horde of little old ladies."

"Hey, it wasn't my idea to dye your hair blue."

"Okay, let me shower and get into some nonsweaty clothes. You can let them in. They can wait in here so they won't be pushed and shoved around by the crew outside."

Connor nodded and checked his watch. He needed to call and get a report from the police on whether charges would be pressed against Frick and Frack.

CHAPTER 27

As soon as the hot water hit Lyric, she wilted like a flower in a hundred-degree weather. All the adrenaline left her and she sagged against the wall as water beat down over her. All those sleepless nights were catching up and all she really wanted to do was go to sleep for about a week.

It took considerable effort but she washed her hair and rinsed off and then stepped out to dry. She combed through her hair but left it wet and then pulled on jeans and a T-shirt. It was nice not have to be meeting with regular fans. She could relax, kick back with the girls and not have to worry about a façade.

And Lord, but she was starving.

She trudged back into the dressing room to see Faith, Serena, Julie and Angelina sprawled on the couches while their guys stood to the side talking to Connor.

It was evident Connor had been watching for her, though, and it sent a giddy little thrill coursing through her veins. He looked up, and when he saw her, he broke from the group of men and came directly to her.

"You okay?"

She smiled. "Yeah. It was a good show."

He leaned in to kiss her, shocking her into silence. Everyone was watching them but he didn't seem to give a shit.

"You were fantastic. Now come sit down and rest. I'll get you something to eat."

A warm buzz, not unlike an alcohol-induced haze settled over her as she went over to the couch. She was smiling. Not just smiling but smiling ridiculously, and it had nothing to do with the show.

"You were awesome, Lyric!" Faith exclaimed when Lyric plopped onto the couch next to her.

"Terrific show," Serena said in agreement. "You looked kick-ass out there."

"Thanks, guys. I'm so glad you're here."

Angelina shifted position and Micah came to stand behind her. He slid his hand over her shoulder and offered a gentle squeeze. He leaned down and whispered something in her ear, and Angelina smiled and shook her head.

"Very well done, Lyric," Damon Roche said as the guys gathered around the girls. "I think Serena mentioned that we'd caught one of your shows in Vegas. We enjoyed it and tonight very much."

"The chute seats were awesome," Julie said with a grin. "All those cowboys so close I could almost touch them."

Nathan scowled. "I swear I can't take you anywhere."

"Thank you all so much," Lyric said sincerely. "It was a fun show. I admit I had reservations about bringing my act here. Wasn't sure it would be appreciated given the venue."

Gray settled on the other side of Faith and shot Lyric a sly grin. "I think you may have converted Mr. Tight Ass, who only listens to country music."

Lyric's eyes widened innocently. "I can't imagine who you're talking about."

Connor snorted as he set a plate of food on the coffee table in front of Lyric. "I admit to a few musical prejudices." He glanced up at Lyric. "Eat," he said softly.

She didn't need any encouragement. She sat forward and began to eat the yummy assortment of sandwiches and finger foods.

"We all need a picture together," Julie said. "The Smurfettes and all, you know."

The men groaned.

"At least it's just the tips," Damon said with a grin. "They can be trimmed."

"You're not touching my hair!" Serena gasped. "I think we look awesome."

"Well, there's no denying you ladies look fantastic," Micah said with an easy smile. "I was worried we'd need some of Lyric's security detail just to escort you girls back here. There were a lot of good ole boys sizing up our muscle."

Angelina laughed. "You're so full of shit, but we love you for it."

Lyric leaned back with her plate and sighed. A few weeks ago, she would have never guessed that she'd meet such great people or make actual friends. Real friends. People who didn't want anything from her. Who liked the real Lyric.

Now that her show was over, she had a few days to do nothing and then she'd have to move on. Things to do. Albums to record. More concerts. For the first time she felt regret over her nomadic existence and the fact she didn't have a home base.

How great it would be to get to come home after days on the road and have friends like this group where she could relax and not worry about what face she was presenting to the world.

The yearning was so keen that it made her chest ache.

"I hate to break this up, but Lyric's tired and I really need to get her home so she can rest," Connor said.

She blinked in surprise and realized she'd zoned out on the couch while conversation went on around her.

"I'm okay," she said. "They don't have to go."

"You look exhausted," he said bluntly.

"Of course you need to go rest," Serena said as she stood gracefully from the couch. "I can't imagine how you're holding your head up after such an energetic show. We'll see you again before you leave Houston."

Lyric managed to get up and hug all the girls. "Thank you all so much for coming. It really meant a lot."

"Thank you for the great seats!" Faith exclaimed. "Even the guys had fun."

"More like we didn't trust you out on your own again," Gray muttered.

The women rolled their eyes.

Angelina smirked. "Think of how boring your lives would be without us."

"Dear God, did you say a mouthful," Nathan said. "I can safely say that's one word that will never apply to our lives ever again."

Julie wrapped her arms around the big guy and grinned cheekily up at him. "Admit it. You led pitiful existences before we swooped in and saved you."

He lowered his mouth to kiss her, smiling all the while. "I don't dispute that either, honey."

Lyric walked them all to the door as the men herded the women, and then she was left alone with Connor and Kane and her security detail.

She closed the door and turned. "Any word on R.J. and Trent?"

Connor shook his head. "I have a call into the lieutenant handling their questioning. He's supposed to call me when he knows something."

She sighed. "Call me naïve but I just can't imagine them doing this. What could they possibly have to gain? It doesn't even make sense."

"I'm inclined to agree with you," Kane said. "But the evidence does support their involvement. We'll let the police do their job and see what they come up with."

"The important part is that you don't have to worry about them anymore," Connor said.

She didn't miss his face darkening at the mention of them. He looked . . . jealous. Her lips twitched but she didn't smile. Maybe later she'd tell him that she hadn't slept with either man for the last several shows. For now, she liked the idea that he was possessive of her.

"You ready?" Connor asked. "You really do need to get some rest. You're going to fall over soon."

"Yeah, let's go. I could use a cupcake and maybe a cup of hot chocolate. An evening in front of the fire sounds really nice right now."

He pulled her into his side and they walked out to the waiting car.

Lyric lay against Connor on the couch, her feet stretched to the end, watching the flickering flames from the hearth while Connor absently ran his fingers through her hair.

An empty cupcake wrapper lay on the coffee table beside the half-finished cup of hot chocolate. She was warm, sated and drifting closer and closer to the veil of sleep.

"This is nice," she murmured sleepily.

He didn't answer but pressed a kiss to her hair in response.

"If I fall asleep, will you carry me up to bed again?"

She smiled as she awaited his response.

"You don't have to be asleep for me to carry you up to bed."

"Mmm." She snuggled deeper into his chest and rubbed her cheek against the solid wall of muscle. "I kind of like you carrying me around. Makes me feel small and dainty."

Connor snorted. "You are small and dainty. You don't even come to my chin. I could probably stick you in my pocket and carry you around."

"So what do we do now?"

He tipped her chin up so she looked at him. "What do you mean?"

She shrugged. "I mean now that the show is over. There never was a real threat to me. Whatever reason R.J. and Trent had for leaving those notes, I don't believe for a minute they were going to hurt me. So that's resolved."

"Well, if I remember correctly, the point of this whole venture was for you to do your show, take some down time and lay low. So I guess the answer to your question is, you can do whatever you want."

"And you?" she asked hesitantly.

He cocked his head. "Lyric, if there's something you want to say, say it. I'm not a mind reader."

"I just wondered if you'd want to do stuff with me. I mean just us. Not job related."

His eyes gleamed in the low light. His thumb ran over her jaw and then to her lips, rubbing softly over her mouth.

"I'd like nothing more than to spend some time with you."

He followed his hand with his mouth, turning her face up to meet his lips. Warm and melting, his heat invaded her, moving sluggishly through her veins like a narcotic.

He was dangerous to her. He did things to her heart and mind she couldn't explain. He made her want things she'd always been afraid of. But now she wanted to try. She wanted a normal relationship, but how was such a thing ever possible for her?

"In fact, what I'd really like to do right now is take you upstairs and make love to you and for you to sleep in my arms afterward."

She swallowed and nodded. She'd try. God, for him she'd try.

He pushed himself from the couch and then reached down to curl her into his arms. He lifted her effortlessly from the couch and carried her up the stairs to her bedroom.

She curled her arms around his neck and tucked her head under his chin. If she could stop time, she'd live in this moment forever. The entire past week had been nothing short of . . . life changing. It sounded corny and melodramatic, but it was absolutely true.

Maybe she'd finally found purpose. Or maybe she was finally growing and stretching beyond the past. She'd simply existed for so long but now she wanted to live. She wanted to grab on and enjoy every moment and take nothing for granted.

He laid her gently on the bed and tonight she didn't play coy. She wanted him. Wanted him skin to skin, his body on hers. She got up on her knees and circled his neck, pulling him into her kiss.

He tasted like chocolate and he smelled of wood and smoke from the fire. It was a heady, intoxicating blend that she savored.

Her hands drifted over his shoulders and then to his chest, rubbing and caressing his tight body. Lean and hard and so damn delicious.

"Take your shirt off," she said huskily. "Take it all off. Right there while I'm watching, and then come back to me."

His gaze never leaving hers, he shucked his shirt and pants, and his underwear quickly followed. She sucked in all her breath as he stood naked, a thing of beauty, all hers to do with what she wanted. Oh damn. It would take a week to do everything she wanted with him.

"If you don't stop looking at me like that, it's going to be all over before it begins," he growled.

"What am I looking at you like?" she asked innocently.

"Like I'm dessert and you're about to eat me."

"Mmm, but that's exactly what I'm going to do," she purred.

She leaned over and pressed her lips to his shoulder and then bared her teeth and nipped. He flinched and let out a low groan. She let her tongue slide sensuously up to the column of his neck and then she took another nip, right below his ear.

His big body shuddered and his hands curled into tight fists at his side.

She leaned back and placed her palms to his chest and ran her fingers through the light smattering of hair at the hollow, then followed the line down to his belly and lower to the crisp, light brown hairs at his groin.

His cock stiffened and jutted upward, directly into her hands. She wrapped her fingers around his length and traced his erection downward until she cupped his sac in one hand and fondled while she stroked up and down with her other hand.

"May I say you have very impressive equipment, Connor Malone."

He made a sound of frustration and leaned closer to her.

"More impressive that you know precisely what to do with it."

"You're killing me," he rasped.

She blinked up at him with pretended dismay. "I find I have no idea what to do with such a wealth of manhood. Do you have any suggestions?"

"Get down on your knees and wrap that pretty mouth around it."

"Mmmm, kneeling has such a submissive overtone, don't you agree?"

"Honey, there is nothing submissive about you. Hell, I don't care if you stand on your head. I just want to get inside that sweet, lush mouth and drown."

She grinned. "Well, since you asked so prettily."

She quickly undressed and then lay down on the bed, positioning herself so that her head hung over the edge, directly in line with his cock.

She stared up at him and then reached to caress his length. "Fuck me, Connor. Just like that. Fuck me hard."

His hands trembled on her face. His fingers stroked over her mouth and her cheekbones and then one hand left her to grasp his cock and guide it toward her waiting mouth.

"Open up, baby. Take me. Take all of me."

She licked her lips and then parted them just as the broad head of his penis bumped against her mouth. Her tongue flicked over the crown and he flinched and then pushed in, sliding over her tongue.

His taste burst through her senses. Musky and exotic. Warm and spicy with a hint of soap. He slid deeper, checking himself at intervals, but when she offered no protest he sank to the back of her throat.

His balls brushed across her nose and then pressed inward as he strained forward. His hands tightened on the sides of her head and then he began thrusting back and forth.

He delved his fingers into her hair, separating and brushing through the strands. His movements were slow and measured. He never overwhelmed her. He seemed to know just how far to push and when to pull back.

She wanted to give him something back. She wanted to give him all the pleasure he'd given to her.

She reached behind and slid her hands over his hips to his taut buttocks. They flexed and rippled with each thrust, hard beneath her touch. She dug her fingers into his flesh and pulled him to her even as she swallowed him deeper.

Connor moved his hands from her face and then leaned over her to kiss her belly. She shivered and danced beneath his mouth and then his hands glided down her hips to part her legs.

He pulled them back until they were double and her pussy was exposed to his touch. His hips continued to pump against her mouth as his fingers dipped between her folds to the damp, sensitive flesh underneath.

She moaned around his cock and twisted restlessly as his fingers slipped inside her, stroking gently as his thumb toyed with her clit.

Then he withdrew and pulled back and knelt behind her. Gently he stroked his hands through her hair and closed his mouth over hers, smooching softly, her mouth, her cheeks, her eyes and then her forehead.

"I want inside you, Lyric," he whispered. "I love your mouth, but I want you in my arms, your body wrapped around mine while I dive so deep that we lose ourselves in each other."

Tears pricked her lids and they burned as she blinked to keep the moisture at bay. Didn't he know she got lost in him every time he touched her?

He kissed her again, so exquisitely loving and gentle that she let out a sigh. He stroked her cheekbones and ran his fingers through her hair, and then he carefully raised her up so she was sitting on the bed.

She turned and got on her knees and wrapped her arms around his neck so she could kiss him. Everything she had, everything she was, she put into her kiss. She let go of all the things she'd been holding back and so dear.

She couldn't get enough of him. She ran her hands up and down his back, up to his hair and then down again, hugging him to her, pressing her body into his as she devoured his mouth.

He wrapped his arms around her and hauled her up, holding her so tight she could barely breathe. He maneuvered them around and then fell forward onto the bed, his body over hers, her back pressed to the mattress.

"If I live to be a hundred years old, I don't think I'd ever get enough of you," he said between kisses. "You're an addiction I can't wait to feed. When you aren't with me, I can't wait to see you again. When you walk into the room, something inside me lights up. No one makes me feel like you do."

"Oh, Connor," she breathed. Whatever else she wanted to say got trapped behind the knot in her throat. Her nose swelled and stung as emotion clouded in and overwhelmed her.

"Make love to me," she whispered. "Please. I need you."

He went still above her and stared down as if he couldn't believe she'd said the words. There was triumph—and relief—blazing in his eyes. He looked gobsmacked. Joy exploded onto his face and the lines around his forehead eased. It was as if she'd handed him the world, but in fact it was he who gave her so much. Every time. Himself.

"I'd give you the world if you asked," he said as he nudged her thighs apart.

He reached for a condom and rolled it on, his gaze never leaving her.

His cock slid between her legs and he rubbed his length along her folds, teasing her with his rigid heat. She opened for him, wet and wanting.

He paused at her entrance, the head tucked barely inside. He nudged, opening her a little more, and then he stopped.

Again he kissed her, his tongue tangling hotly with hers. Then he propped himself on his forearms and flexed his hips forward, sliding smoothly, rippling through her pussy like a dive through deep water.

He was bowed over her, his much larger body covering hers protectively. But he moved like a dream, with grace that belied his size. There wasn't a clumsy bone in his body. He made love like some people danced.

He nuzzled her neck and she turned, arching so that he had easier access. He tongued her ear and danced a circle around the shell until a thousand chill bumps skittered across her flesh.

Her heart was beating so hard that she could barely catch her breath. Her pulse raced and her body was alive as though a thousand ants crawled under skin. Every touch of his mouth, every thrust into her body, brought a shattering wave of pleasure so keen that it was nearly painful.

He withdrew until the head of his cock barely rimmed her entrance, and then he shoved back in, rippling through her slick flesh, sending aftershock upon aftershock coursing through her abdomen.

Her nipples tightened and dug into his chest like diamond points. Each movement abraded the ultrasensitive peaks until she was sure she was going to come apart.

"I want you there," he murmured next to her ear. "You with me, Lyric. I won't come until you're there."

"Oh God," she panted. "I'm almost there, Connor. I can't take it anymore. I feel like I'm going to break into a million pieces. Please. Don't hold back. Harder."

Her words seemed to unleash the beast he held in tight rein. A sound of near pain, harsh in the silence, ripped from his throat. He gathered her tightly to him, wrapping his arms around her, pulling up as he plunged deep and hard.

His thighs slapped against hers and their bodies made wet sucking sounds as he pounded into her over and over.

The world went blurry around her. She closed her eyes, dizzy as she splintered and seemed to sail in a dozen different directions.

Her body was so tight, painfully so, that she cried out, begging for release.

And then she was catapulted up and over, free-falling at a hundred miles an hour. Her orgasm went on and on, never ending, wave upon wave crashing through her body.

He was coming too, his body commanding hers, owning her, possessing her. His.

She went limp beneath him, no longer able to even keep her legs or arms around him. He was in the last throes of his orgasm as he twitched and continued to thrust, easier and slower now as he slid in and out of her.

"Lyric," he whispered and gathered her close to him, holding her as he breathed harshly in her ear.

He turned, rolling them to their sides, and pressed her face into his neck as he stroked her hair, her back, over her buttocks and back up again.

"I love you. God, I love you."

Her heart stuttered, took a painful leap in her chest that stole her breath. She went still as his words drifted over her ears, quiet and sincere.

Her throat tightened, so tight it sent a wave of panic through her body.

Afraid that she'd completely lose her composure, she tried to push away from him and roll from the bed. But he caught her and held her, refusing to let her up.

It set off another wave of panic and she twisted and tried to sit up.

Connor rolled until she was underneath him once more. His body covered hers and he stared down at her with glittering eyes. She expected anger, but what she saw was grim determination.

"Goddamn it, Lyric, I just told you I loved you and you act like you can't get away fast enough."

She swallowed and shook her head helplessly as tears filled her eyes.

"I've been patient. I've let you run. But I'm not letting you run any longer. I want to know what the hell is going on and why you bolt every time we have sex."

Chapter 28

$\mathscr{C}$onnor stared down at the panic in her eyes. Her entire body was tense and there was a wildness that reminded him of a spooked animal about to take flight.

He knew he was taking a huge risk by forcing the issue. He could lose her. She could shut down and freeze him out, but he had to try. Damn it, he had to try. He couldn't just give up and let her walk away. Not when this was the most important moment of his entire life.

"Stay with me, Lyric," he said in a low voice. "Stay with me and explain why me telling you I love you has you in such a panic."

"It doesn't mean anything," she whispered. "It's not real."

"Doesn't mean anything? Do you think I said that to get into your pants? Do you think I go around telling every woman I've slept with that I love her? I've got news for you, baby. I've already been in as deep inside you as a man can get. I didn't need the words to make love to you. I didn't have to say them now. But goddamn it, I love you. That's real. It doesn't get any more real."

An endless stream of tears leaked from her eyes and rolled down her cheeks. His chest ached so bad he wanted to cry with her. Whatever had hurt her, whatever had destroyed her faith in love, was killing him as well.

"Talk to me," he pleaded. "I'm begging you not to walk away from this. I think you feel something for me too. Am I wrong? Did I get you all wrong?"

Slowly she shook her head as more silver trails slid from her eyes.

A tiny twinge of relief loosened the knot in his throat. It was an admission. A reluctant admission, but at least she hadn't denied feeling something for him. He could work with that.

He shifted his weight to the side so he could discard the condom, and he hoped she wouldn't use the opportunity to bolt. But she lay there on her back, staring up at the ceiling as tears etched a crooked path on her face.

She looked tired. Fragile. And scared.

He reached a tentative hand to brush away the moisture on her cheek. "Will you talk to me? Do you trust me enough to tell me what's hurt you so badly?"

For a long moment she lay there, unmoving, quiet, as if gathering herself. To run? Or to confide in him? He couldn't say with any authority which of the two she was leaning toward. Maybe she didn't know herself.

When she finally did stir, he tensed, and then she rolled slightly until she faced him with haunted eyes. He wanted to do a fist pump. She'd made her decision and she was still with him. Still next to him. But he remained still, waiting for the revelation that was buried deep.

"My real name is Carly Winters. And you were right. I was born and raised in the South. Covington County, Mississippi."

She waited a moment as if grappling with whether to go on. He willed himself not to stir, not to react. He didn't want to do anything to change her mind.

"My father—my real father—left my mother when I was a baby. For a long time it was just me and her. We were dirt-poor but I was happy. She loved me and did her best. I adored her. She encouraged me to sing. In the evenings, I'd sing to her while she did dishes. She said she never got tired of hearing her baby's voice. She always swore I'd be a star."

She drew in a deep breath. "When I was nine, she met Danny Higgins. At first it was nice. She was so happy. So alive. I hadn't realized how hard it had been on her until then. Suddenly she had help. She wasn't alone. We moved in with him after they got married. He insisted my mother didn't work. She'd worked two jobs until then. She worked in a local factory during the week and she waitressed in a café on the weekends.

"I can remember thinking that it was the start of a great new life for us. Suddenly we didn't have to worry about where our next meal would come from. She no longer had to bring home leftovers from the café, and for the first time ever, she bought me new clothes from the rack in a store instead of getting them from Goodwill or neighbors who gave us their kids' castoffs.

"But it didn't last," she said faintly. "Danny had a quick temper. It got even nastier when he'd drink. It was the whole cliché, stereotypical abusive husband. He'd drink. Hit my mom. Get sober. Apologize. I still think to this day she only stayed because I had a better life. Or at least she thought I did."

Dread curled in Connor's stomach. He had a very good idea of where this was headed and it made him ill.

"Danny lost his well-paying job and he yelled at my mom that it was time for her to start carrying her weight. She went back to work at the factory. Waitressed on weekends. It seemed all she did was work. She'd come home tired and have to contend with Danny's nasty moods. I did everything I could to make things easier for her. I cooked. I cleaned."

"Jesus," Connor muttered. "You were only a baby yourself."

Lyric went on as if he hadn't spoken. Her eyes were glassy and had a distant look, as if she were unaware that he was even here anymore. She was lost in her past. Reliving each and every moment.

"Danny started paying a lot more attention to me. Got all lovey and affectionate. Wanted me to sit on his lap. Freaked me out but I was afraid of him. I'm sure you know where this is going. The whole thing could come straight out of some made-for-TV movie. Evil stepfather. Messing around with the stepdaughter."

Connor had to bite his lip to call back the savage curse that threatened to boil out. She was so casual. So flip. As if because it happened to so many, it didn't matter that it had happened to her.

"He'd come into my bedroom at night while my mom was working, and he'd rape me. And the entire time he'd whisper how much he loved me and how beautiful I was and what a good girl I was."

Connor closed his eyes against the sting of tears. God. No wonder she hated to hear those words. Especially during sex.

"If you're wondering why I didn't tell my mom, I did. It took me a while to work up the courage. I waited until he had gone out and then I told her and I begged her for us to leave before he got back. She was devastated. I'd never seen her cry. Not through us being poor and hungry. Not when he hit her. She never cried until I told her what he'd done."

Unable to keep from touching her and offering comfort, Connor stroked his hand over her cheek, smoothing away the tears that still crept over her cheekbone. He let his fingers trail into her hair and then he rubbed up and down her arm.

To his surprise, she scooted closer, as if seeking the comfort of his body. She curled into his arm and laid her head against his shoulder.

Maybe she could no longer face him and it was easier to let loose the poison of her past when they weren't staring eye to eye.

He wrapped his arms around her and entwined their legs, wanting no separation between them. Never once would he want her to feel like she was somehow less for what was done to her. He'd hold her forever if that was what it took.

"I thought we'd just go. But I underestimated my mom's anger. She confronted Danny when he got home. For the first time, she stood up to him. She told him she was going to have him arrested and that she hoped he rotted in hell."

"Good for her," he said softly.

Lyric shook her head. "No. It was the wrong thing to do. We should have just gone. Left and never looked back. She wanted justice. I just wanted us safe. He flew into a rage. I think he forgot I was even there. I hid in the cabinet under the sink while he beat her to death."

She made a sound like a wounded animal. The moan tore from her throat and her fingers dug into his skin. "There was blood. So much blood. I remember peering through the crack in the cabinet door, so terrified I could do nothing. I *did* nothing. I hid like a coward while my mother died. I let him kill her because I was afraid he'd turn on me. Or worse, he'd keep me and abuse me. So I sat there and listened to her screams."

Connor pressed his mouth to her hair as nausea rolled through his stomach. He trembled against her even as he held her so close it was a wonder she could breathe.

"Worse than the screams and the sounds of him hitting my mother was the silence afterward. So silent you could have heard a whisper. I stayed under the sink for three days. When they finally found me, my mom had been dead for over seventy-two hours, and I hid there and never did anything to help her."

"Sweet mother of God," Connor swore. "Lyric, you were just a child. A terrified little girl who'd already been horribly abused by the son of a bitch. Do you think your mother would have wanted you to die with her? Do you think she wouldn't have wanted you to hide?"

"I just know that I did nothing and I traded my life for hers. I could have run. I could have gone to a neighbor's. I could have done something," she finished with a sob. "Those three days were the worst of my life. I was alone in that house while she lay dead just feet away. Even after I knew he was gone, I couldn't make myself leave my hiding place. I've never liked being alone since. It terrifies me."

Connor gathered her close and turned her face up so he could kiss her forehead. He smoothed his hand over her hair and simply stroked as he willed some of the burning rage he felt on her behalf to calm.

"My testimony put him in prison for life. Because I was a minor and was so traumatized by the event, they sealed the records and I was born again, so to speak. New name. New life. No one knew of my past. Not even my string of foster parents. They only knew I had been sexually abused and my mother had died. I chose Lyric to honor my mother's vision of my future. I was determined to become a singer for her."

"And you did," he said softly. "You became the best."

She let out a pitiful laugh that sounded more like a sob. "No, not the best. I've lived my life afraid that someone would find out about my past."

"Baby, you have nothing to be ashamed of. You were a victim."

She shook her head adamantly. "I don't want anyone to know. I've never told anyone. Except you . . . I couldn't bear it to be splashed across all the papers and magazines."

"Is that why you give them so much else to talk about?"

For a long moment she remained silent. "Maybe. I don't know.

That sounds like an excuse. I don't always like the things I do, and yet I still make stupid choices. It's sort of a self-fulfilling prophecy, I guess. I've tried so hard to project this give-a-shit attitude. Maybe I'm preparing for the day when someone does find out about my past. I don't want anyone to ever see me that vulnerable."

Did she have any idea how very vulnerable she sounded right now? Something inside him came loose and the ache in his chest intensified. He hurt for the child who'd suffered so much. He hurt for the young woman who still hurt, for whom those horrible days were relived on a daily basis.

"I didn't want anyone to judge me. If I thought so badly of myself, how much worse would others feel about what I'd done?"

"Honey, you didn't do anything," he said gently. "You survived a horrible experience. How is that bad?"

When she didn't answer, he once again tilted up her chin so she could see his eyes. "Lyric, I'm not judging you. I don't think badly of you. I hurt for you. I'm angry as hell at the son of a bitch who terrorized you and took your mother from you. But I love you. Your past doesn't change that. Love doesn't come with conditions. It just . . . is."

"No one but my mother has ever loved me," she said quietly. "I don't know how to react, Connor. I'm worried I'll piss you off. Or maybe you'll get tired of my stupidity. I'm worried I can't give you what you need. What you deserve."

He smiled and rubbed his cheek over her forehead. "Why don't you let me worry about what I can handle?"

"How can you love me? You didn't even like me at first."

"If you're asking me to explain how or why people fall in love, you're barking up the wrong tree. I watched all my friends fall hard for the women in their lives. I secretly thought they were all morons. They completely lost their shit. I never understood it. Until now. Now

I can see exactly what they were thinking and feeling. Because I've completely lost my shit over you."

She laughed softly and buried her face in his neck. He could still feel the dampness on her cheeks and he cupped the back of her head, stroking and soothing away her grief.

"I want to be right for you, Connor. I want it so bad I ache."

He kissed her again, compelled to keep touching her, to keep the link between them. "You are right for me, Lyric. Just as you are."

She shifted a bit and snuggled deeper into his body as if seeking refuge. He wanted to be that refuge. Her safe place where she was protected from the world.

"You know what I'd like?" he asked softly.

"What?" she whispered back.

"I'd like for you to sleep with me. Just like this. You in my arms where I can hold you all night. And I'd like to wake up in the morning and have you be the first thing I see."

She nodded sleepily. "I think I'd like that too."

He smiled and reached behind him to turn off the lamp. Then he turned back to her and settled her against him once more. When he was satisfied that she was snuggled as tight as possible into his arms, he laid his cheek on the top of her head and processed everything she'd told him.

Lyric slipped into an exhausted sleep within moments of him turning off the light. But Connor stayed awake long into the night.

CHAPTER 29

Connor awoke to the sound of his cell vibrating on the night-stand. He blew a strand of Lyric's hair from his mouth and smiled at the fact she was draped across him like a blanket.

Her body was soft and warm and her cheek was pressed to his chest. Her upper body was covering him entirely and one leg was slung over his.

He could wake this way every morning and die a happy man in sixty years or so.

The phone quieted and then immediately started again. Connor cursed under his breath and eased his arm over so he could reach the phone.

"What?" he demanded in a quiet voice.

"Connor Malone? This is Lieutenant Donnelly. We spoke yesterday regarding R. J. Miller and Trent Carnes."

Connor grimaced. It was awfully damn early in the morning to be calling with case updates. "Give me a second," he murmured.

He disentangled himself from Lyric, who woke and stared up at him with sleep-clouded eyes. He leaned down to kiss her. "It's nothing. Go back to sleep. I'll be right back, okay?"

"Okay," she mumbled.

He moved from the bed and walked across the room toward the bathroom so he wouldn't disturb her.

"What do you have for me?" he asked the lieutenant.

"Your guys confessed. It was pretty pathetic really."

"What the fuck were they trying to do?" Connor demanded.

"They saw the writing on the wall. They weren't happy that Ms. Jones had started pulling away from them. Their words, not mine. They hatched this ridiculous plan to make it appear that there was a threat against her. Their hope was that they'd provide support and protection, thus making themselves invaluable to Ms. Jones."

"What a bunch of dipshits," Connor muttered. "What will happen to them?"

"We can't hold them on much. The best option will be for Ms. Jones to take out a restraining order on them. We can arrest them for harassment, but they'll likely be out on bail in less than a day, and no way is the DA going to pursue this beyond probation and maybe a little community service. They'll plead out and be on their way before the ink is dry on the paperwork."

"Figures. Thanks, Lieutenant. I appreciate your taking care of the matter."

"Not a problem. Let me know if there's anything else I can do to help."

Connor hung up and then noticed he had a missed call from his dad. He winced. It had been several days since he'd talked to Pop, a fact that wouldn't make the old man very happy.

"I hear there's some serious bodyguarding going on over there and that you've taken a personal interest in a certain pop star's body," Pop rumbled as soon as he picked up the phone.

Connor shook his head. Trust gossip to have already reached his ears. "She's the one, Pop."

He could practically hear his dad grinning through the phone.

"Well, I'll be damned. That's great, son. You two got things worked out?"

Connor frowned and looked back toward the bed where Lyric was curled into a ball, her arm thrown over his pillow. "Not yet, but we'll get there."

"Good things shouldn't be easy. You'll work hard at it, and it'll be all the sweeter for it."

Connor shook his head. Pop was so full of shit. Good as gold, but he had something to say for every occasion.

"Bring her home for Sunday dinner. She should see what she's getting into."

Connor laughed. "We'll get to that eventually. Right now we have more important fish to fry."

Pop made a disgruntled sound. "What's more important than my Sunday lasagna?"

"Faith and Gray have spoiled you by catering to your neuroses."

"At least they eat with me every weekend. Well, when they can."

"And I don't?"

"Well, sure you do. But you're single, and no single guy turns down free food. The test is when you have a beautiful woman at home as to whether you'll give your old man the time of day anymore."

Connor rolled his eyes. "Like I'll ever get rid of you, old fart."

Pop's raspy chuckle filled Connor's ear. "Damn straight. I plan for you and Faith to visit me in the old folks' home when I'm old and toothless."

"You already are old and toothless."

"Don't make come over there and kick your ass."

Connor laughed. "Okay, Pop. Let me go. Take care of yourself."

"Will do. Give my love to Lyric and tell her welcome to the family."

With a smile, Connor disconnected the call. He'd love nothing more than to welcome Lyric to his family, but he wasn't going to get ahead of himself. Right now he was just happy Lyric hadn't run the other direction when he'd expressed a desire for them to be together.

With a look at the bed where Lyric was sleeping, he pulled on a robe and crept out of the bedroom and down to fill Kane in on the latest developments. Kane promised to do some investigating on his own. Connor intended to devote his time and energy solely to Lyric.

When he returned a few minutes later, he shed the robe and crawled back into bed with Lyric. She stirred and snuggled up close to him, breathing a soft sigh of contentment.

"Sleep well?" he murmured.

"The best night's sleep I've had in longer than I can remember," she admitted.

"Good. You needed to catch up."

"Who was on the phone? Is everything okay?"

"It was the lieutenant who handled R.J. and Trent's arrests. They confessed to leaving the notes."

Her lips twisted into a perplexed frown. "But why? I don't understand."

Connor related what the lieutenant had told him and she shook her head. "That's pretty pathetic, but what's even more pathetic is that I was involved with those clowns. That I trusted them."

He leaned down and kissed her forehead. "Quit beating yourself up. It's all in the past. You won't let it happen again."

"Damn right," she said with a grin. Then she reached up to touch his face. "What should we do today? We have hours yet until I have to be at the music store."

"Anything you like or nothing at all. It's solely up to you," he said in a solemn voice. "You tell me what your pleasure is, and I'll make sure you get it."

She kissed his chest and pleasure melted through his body at the affectionate gesture.

"If I weren't here and your job wasn't to keep me safe, what would you be doing today?"

"Hmmm. I'd probably eat at Cattleman's. Hang out with Micah, Nathan, and Gray. Nothing earth-shattering. Throw back a few beers."

"I want to do something ordinary."

He lifted a brow. "Define *ordinary*."

"Something everyday. Average. What someone who leads a perfectly normal life would do."

"You up for a jog?"

She pushed herself up and looked at him in horror. "You mean like exercising. Running?"

He chuckled. "Yeah. I like to keep in shape. I usually run in the mornings but I've missed a few days lately. We could go for a run. Take a shower together. Go eat breakfast at a little café I know of. Dad wants us to come for dinner tonight. He cooks lasagna every Sunday. It's a family tradition. Maybe we can swing by after your signing."

Shadows lurked in her eyes. Her gaze filled with uncertainty and she bit at her bottom lip. "Do they know? I mean, I guess they know, but do they know—know about us?"

He smiled at the way she sputtered around the subject. "Yeah. They know. Or at least Pop does. And now that he knows for sure, he'll waste no time telling Faith, who'll waste no time telling the other girls, who will waste no time telling their husbands. I should start receiving phone calls giving me shit within the hour."

Her eyes lightened and she smiled back at him. "Sounds like a veritable gossip train."

He shrugged. "We're close. I guess that's what friends do. Hard to keep anything from anyone in that group."

"Yeah," she said wistfully. "You're lucky."

"Hey, they love you."

"I like them a lot too. I'm so glad I met them. And you."

"Yeah, me too," he said huskily as he leaned in to kiss her. "Now, how 'bout that run?"

"Oh my God, I'm dying," Lyric wheezed when they walked—or, rather, she dragged—back up the drive to the house.

"You did great," he said cheerfully. "Let's hit the shower. I don't know about you, but I'm starving."

"Of course you are," she muttered. "You'll eat like a pig and not gain an ounce. I'll look at a cupcake and swell up like a blowfish."

He jogged in place and then swatted her on the ass. She shot him a glare but followed him into the house and up the stairs.

They played in the shower and Lyric couldn't remember the last time she'd laughed so much. She soaped him. He soaped her. They got fresh and frisky and groped each other shamelessly, and by the time they stumbled out to get towels, they were both breathing heavily.

He advanced on her menacingly, his cock rigid and standing straight up. She held up her hands to halt his advance. "Hey, none of that. You're starving, remember?"

"Uh-huh. I'm starving. But not for food."

She rolled her eyes. "When are you ever not hungry for food?"

"Now," he growled.

She clutched the ends of the towel around her but he pried her fingers away, letting the towel fall to the floor, leaving her naked and still damp in front of him.

Her nipples beaded and her belly clenched in anticipation as he reached for her.

"There better be a goddamn condom in here."

She sucked in her breath, knowing that if they were going to actually be in a serious relationship, they'd need to discuss things like sexual history, condoms, all the icky stuff that she was used to shoving under the table.

"You don't have to use one," she said in a quiet voice. "I mean, if you didn't want to."

He regarded her curiously for a moment and then picked her up so she sat on the edge of the counter, her legs wrapped around his waist. He kissed the corner of her mouth and then nibbled a path to her neck that had her arching and sighing in contentment.

"How about I go find that condom, and we'll have this discussion after I've fucked you six ways to Sunday."

Arousal rose sharp, like a bite. She shivered under the intensity of his gaze. In response, she looped her arms around his neck and he hoisted her up until she straddled his midsection. Then he turned and carried her into the bedroom.

When he got to the bed, he tumbled forward on the mattress, taking her down underneath him. With one hand, he groped toward the nightstand and snagged one of the packets.

"I'd apologize about how quick this is going to be, but I wouldn't be sincere," he said as he rolled the condom on. "I've got to have you or I'm going to explode."

She smoothed her hands over his muscled shoulders and then down his sides to grasp his hips. "Sometimes foreplay is overrated."

With a groan, he spread her thighs and then slid his thumb over her clit and below to her opening. Then he eased his fingers inside her and she smiled. Despite his urgency, he was still making sure she was ready for him.

She arched into his touch and sighed as fluttery sensations danced through her groin as he stroked through her dampness.

He pushed so her legs were splayed open and then he guided his cock to her entrance. But still he didn't thrust. He rubbed the head up and down, bathing it in her wetness, and then finally he plunged deep. In one long stroke he was all the way in, and the shock of his entry made her gasp. So hard and full. She was stretched tight around him, and already the buzz of an orgasm had begun.

What followed could hardly be called making love. There was no sense of sweet and gentle wooing. It was an animalistic fucking that had her begging and pleading. It was like nothing she'd ever experienced.

Hard and furious, he stroked rapidly, his hips pumping against hers and the slap of his flesh against hers rising sharp in the air.

His entire body moved over hers, and his muscles strained tight underneath her fingertips. Suddenly he rolled, holding her tight against him, so that she was sprawled on top, her legs straddling him.

For a moment she lay there, her breaths coming harsh as she sought the strength to do what he wanted.

But all he did was reach down and hold her hips while he did the work, arching into her, thrusting upward, his hands holding her pinned tight against him.

Finally she managed to push herself up, her palms braced against his chest. The movement sent him deeper, and they both groaned as she repositioned herself, his cock tucked so deep and snug within her that she could barely breathe.

His hands left her hips and slid up her body to cup both breasts.

He gently squeezed and ran his thumbs over the puckered crests. Each brush sent an electric bolt straight to her pussy that had her squirming.

"Ride me, Lyric," he said. "Ride me as hard as I rode you. Let me watch you come all undone. I want to watch your face when you come."

She closed her eyes and threw back her head and began sliding up and down his cock. Her knees pressed into the mattress on either side of his hips as she undulated her body in a comfortable rhythm.

She felt like a wild thing. Free and beautiful. She glanced down at Connor through half-lidded eyes and saw that his gaze was fastened on her, his eyes burning with approval. Desire. *Love.*

It was completely her undoing. Her orgasm flashed like a streak of lightning in the summer air. Beautiful and electric. Her entire body trembled with the shock.

His hands closed around her waist, holding her, supporting her. He closed his eyes and his face creased as though he were experiencing agony. His entire body went rigid and she continued to move through her own orgasm, determined to bring him the ultimate pleasure.

She was still moving when he leaned up and gathered her in his arms. "Come here, baby," he said softly as he pulled her back down to sprawl over him.

They lay there breathing hard, their chests colliding as they sought to pump more air into oxygen-starved lungs. He kissed the top of her head and smoothed a hand over her hair as she wilted like a wet noodle atop him.

Her breasts were smushed flat by his chest and her flesh was stuck to him like a second skin, but she lacked the strength or the desire to move. She fit him. He fit her.

He was sturdy and rock hard. Her refuge. Her oasis from everything in the real world.

She loved him too.

She closed her eyes, wondering why she couldn't simply give him the words he'd given to her. Why were they so hard to say?

He continued to play with her hair, separating the strands and pulling his fingers through them as they lay there in the quiet. He seemed as content as she was for her to blanket him.

"Now, was there something you wanted to talk about regarding condoms, past lovers or anything similar?" he asked.

She raised her head. "You really think now is a good time to discuss it?"

He smiled. "It's the best time. I didn't want to get into who you've slept with before we had sex. Definite mood killer. But now I couldn't get it up again to save my life, so I'd say the timing's perfect."

She laughed and slid to his side. He wrapped an arm around her and hugged her close until her head rested atop his shoulder.

"I was just going to say that we could not use condoms if you preferred not to. I know some guys don't like them."

He danced his fingertips over her arms as he considered what she'd said.

"I suppose there are guys who don't use them. I've never been one of them. Sex is great but it doesn't seem worth the risk, especially in the beginning of a relationship, where you may not know a lot about your partner's past."

She swallowed as she measured how to bring up her past. "I'm no saint. I'm sure you've gathered that much. I was determined that Danny wouldn't control my sexuality for the rest of my life, but maybe I've been fooling myself. It seems everything I do is a direct result of his impact, so in fact, maybe he still has far more control than I'd ever admit to."

"Makes sense."

"I haven't slept with anyone in a while," she admitted. "I did sleep with R.J. and Trent. At the same time. I've slept with others. Being alone—truly intimate—with a man always freaked me out. But I could do meaningless sex."

"You don't have to justify yourself or explain yourself to me, Lyric," Connor said gently. "I've slept with my share of women. Not at the same time, mind you. I leave that sort of thing to my friends. What's past is past. It's the future I'm more concerned about."

"I know. But I wanted you to know that I'm on birth control and that I'm safe. I mean, I always insisted on condoms. That doesn't make me miraculously safe, but I've always been careful and I have regular checkups and tests. I even made R.J. and Trent both have thorough checkups before I'd allow them in my bed."

He squeezed her to him. "I'm glad. I'll be even happier if I'm the only man in your bed from now on."

She stopped breathing for a moment as his words settled over her. He couldn't mean what she thought he meant. Or did he? It sounded so . . . permanent. Permanent was for women like Faith. Wholesome. Girl next door. Women like her screamed commitment and happily ever after. She was the kind of woman a man brought home to his family.

Oh God, Connor was bringing her home to his family today.

"Tell you what," Connor said casually. "Why don't we go have checkups together? We'll get everything out in the open so there aren't any surprises. We'll find out together that we're perfectly healthy and able to start something new and lasting. Then we'll burn the box of condoms and have hot, sweaty sex and I'll get you all sticky and then you'll complain about the fact we aren't using condoms anymore."

Her body shook with laughter and she swatted playfully at his chest. "You're a nut. But yeah. That sounds great. Let's make an appointment."

He raised his head and she turned to meet his kiss.

"It'll be one of the many things I plan for us to be doing together from now on," he murmured.

CHAPTER 30

"*H*oly hell in a bucket," Connor muttered when they turned down the street where the music store was located. "Is this normal?"

Lyric surveyed the cordoned-off street, the throng of people outside the store, at least three police cars and a slew of people carrying cameras. With a puzzled look she shook her head. "No. I mean, I draw a crowd, but it's never like this. Are you sure nothing else is going on?"

"You're it, babe. I'm damn glad Kane went ahead of us to set up his team. This is going to be a fucking nightmare."

She clasped her hands nervously in her lap as they glided to a stop. They were immediately besieged by people shoving their way to the car, cameras flashing, microphones shoved forward. She blinked in bewilderment and Connor swore.

"Drive," he barked at the driver. "Make the block, circle. Do something. We'll have to come in a different way. No way I'm letting her out in this."

Connor snatched up his cell phone as the driver pulled away. "Kane, what the hell is going on out there? Where are you? I can't let Lyric out in that."

Lyric only half paid attention as she stared back at the mass of people.

"Okay, we'll wait fifteen minutes, then circle around to the back. Be waiting and make damn sure the scene is secure. I don't like this, Kane. I don't like it at all."

Connor hung up and reached for Lyric's hand. "Don't worry, baby, okay? I'll cancel the damn thing before I let you go into an unsafe situation."

She smiled. "I'll be fine, Connor. It's a part of the job."

He scowled but didn't comment further.

Several long minutes later, they traveled down the alley. Two police cars had blocked off the street and had secured an entryway for Lyric into the store.

"When we stop I want you out and into the store, no delays. Don't stop for anything, okay?" Connor said. "I'll be with you the whole way."

She nodded as the car pulled to a stop. As he'd directed, she bolted from the car, he right behind her. Kane was at the door holding it open for her as he spoke into a receiver close to his mouth.

Once inside the store, she breathed a sigh of relief until she remembered the horde of people out front waiting to come in. She hoped to hell the store was prepared for the onslaught. A tall, blond woman strode briskly toward Lyric, her hand outstretched. Lyric recognized her. Sort of. She just couldn't remember where she'd seen her before.

"Ms. Jones. Leslie Burke from Cosmic Records. I'll be here to make sure things go smoothly for you today. I've already spoken with the store management and everything looks great. You've got quite a crowd out front but we have plenty of security."

"We're working in cooperation with the police officers here," Kane interjected. "We're only allowing so many in the store at one time and the press won't be allowed in at any time. It's solely your choice whether you want to go out and address them or answer questions, but only fans will be allowed inside for the meet and greet."

Lyric pondered for a moment and then glanced at Leslie whose expression said she was willing to let Lyric make the call. "That sounds reasonable. Maybe it will keep the reporters from doing anything stupid if you tell them I'll make a brief appearance after I've met with fans."

Kane nodded. "I'll let them know."

Connor brushed a kiss across her temple. "I'll be standing right beside you. If at any time you need me or you want to stop, just let me know."

She smiled. He really was too sweet. She was touched by his caring and concern. It sent a pang of longing through her. How wonderful it would be to have him with her all the time.

Kane held up a hand from the door to signal five minutes. Since many of the fans would want photos, a tall signing table had been arranged that allowed Lyric to stand so she wouldn't have to continually sit and get up.

Leslie did a quick check of the promotional material, spoke quickly to two of the store employees and then moved to stand a few feet away from Lyric while they waited for the signing to start.

A few minutes later, the doors opened and people began to surge inside. Here at least, Lyric was in her element. She fielded questions. Took photos. Signed shirts, CDs, iPods, pants and even a few body parts. Although you could have broken a stone on Connor's face when one particularly beefed-up guy stripped off his shirt and asked Lyric to sign low—very low—on his abdomen.

She complied laughingly and grinned when Connor glared holes in his back.

After an hour, Connor forced water into her hand and waited as she drained it. For a second she leaned against his side, grateful to have a moment's rest.

"Okay?" he murmured.

"Yeah, thanks."

She greeted the next fan in line and began all over again. After three hours, she was dead exhausted as the last of the line filtered through.

Kane walked over and stood until the last person finished with Lyric, and then he leaned over. "We're shutting down the line. The signing is officially done. Police are herding people away. The reporters are still out front. Want to just slip out the back?"

She shook her head. "No, they kept their part of the bargain. I need to keep mine or next time they might not be willing to wait. I can't imagine what I've done lately to merit such attention from the press, but I'm sure it's juicy whatever it is. Maybe they're still buzzing over my supposed arrest."

Connor scowled. "They can kiss my ass."

She grinned and slipped her hand through his. "Okay, give me fifteen and I'll be done."

Leslie caught Lyric's eye and then nodded toward the entrance. She walked ahead of Lyric so that she could make a brief statement before Lyric spoke.

Kane and Connor flanked her protectively as she stepped to the door. Kane paused when he saw the police barricade and the fact that there were several police officers doing a good job of keeping the crowd under control.

"I'll go back and get the car," Kane said as he turned to Lyric.

"We'll be in back. I want to make sure you have a clear avenue to the vehicle from the back entrance."

She touched his arm. "Thanks, Kane. I appreciate it."

He smiled. "I know you do. Good luck. Fifteen minutes. Don't go over."

She turned back, took a deep breath and braced for the onslaught.

As soon as she stepped from the building, the frenzy began. Even Leslie looked bewildered. She tried valiantly to direct the media attention back to herself, but once they saw Lyric, they were having none of that. She was pushed aside as the reporters surged past the barricades and surrounded Lyric.

At first she had no idea what was being shouted at her. She flinched at the immediate barrage of shouted questions, and as she tentatively moved forward, her hand up to try to calm the volley, some of the questions sank in.

"Lyric, is it true your real name is Carly Winters?"

"Ms. Jones! Tell us about your mother!"

"Lyric, over here! Can you tell us about your stepfather, Danny Higgins?"

She swayed and her knees buckled. Shock rolled through her body, leaving her so shaken she thought she'd faint. Connor swore violently and grabbed at her arm.

"Lyric, can you confirm your stepfather is in prison for your mother's murder?"

"Can you give us a statement? Is it true you had a sexual relationship with your stepfather and that your mother tried to kill you?"

Lyric gasped and felt the world tilt around her. She stared at Connor in utter disbelief. She stared at the man she'd trusted with everything she was, her past, her present, things she'd never shared with another person. Hurt tore through her with crippling intensity.

As the reporters hurled all the details of her past, like little poison darts, she stood, her gaze locked onto Connor as her world crumbled around her.

"That's enough, goddamn it!" Connor bit out. He grasped her arm to pull her back into the building.

She yanked her arm from Connor's grasp and turned on him as the world went to hell around them. They were jostled and pushed. She nearly went down under the onslaught. One of the police officers shoved her toward the building.

Pain splintered through her head. She realized one of the cameras hit her in the cheek. An elbow caught her temple and then something hard hit her nose.

She tasted the bitter metallic of blood, but she was numb. From head to toe. She stumbled forward as two officers and Connor lifted and carried her into the music store.

As soon as she broke the entrance, she yanked away from all of them. Connor stood, his eyes glittering, and she flew at him, her fists clenched. She hit him but he didn't so much as flinch.

"How could you?" she cried hoarsely. She tried to scream it but she honestly couldn't speak past the knot in her throat. "My God, did you roll immediately out of bed with me after I bared my soul? Was that the phone call this morning? Did you waste any time at all before selling me out?"

Tears streamed down her cheeks. Each word was agony. Oh God, her chest was going to explode.

Nothing, *nothing* in her life had ever hurt as much as his betrayal. Not Danny Higgins. Not the death of her mother. Never before had she trusted a living soul with any part of herself. Not until now. Not until Connor.

"How could you?"

"Goddamn it, Lyric!" he exploded. "You can't think I did this. What the fuck?"

He advanced toward her and she stumbled back so fast to get away from him that she tripped over a chair and went down hard.

"Get him away from me!" she spit out. "Oh God, get him away."

The last ended in a moan and she huddled into a ball, so devastated, so numb from shock, that she wanted to die. The entire world knew. They knew everything. No more secrets. No more lies. Her shame, her pain, was laid bare for the world to see.

There was a scuffle. Connor's curses split the air. She scrambled to her feet and then lunged for the back entrance. Connor shouted at her but she ran as hard and as fast as she could. Away from him. Away from her past. Away from the awful reality that awaited her.

She ran straight into Kane. He caught her and she swung violently, connecting with his jaw.

"What the fuck?" he demanded. "Lyric, what the hell?"

She twisted away, intent only on running as far and as fast as she could. Kane hit her with a flying tackle and rolled them to the ground. He wrapped both arms around her and held her immobile as she kicked and raged against him.

When she realized her efforts were futile, she collapsed against him, sobbing great, gasping sobs.

"Shhh," he said. "Lyric, what the hell is going on? What's the matter?"

"Get me out of here," she choked out. "Please, Kane. Just take me away."

"Where the hell is Connor?"

She went rigid. "He sold me out. Please, please, Kane."

The last of her fight left her and she simply shattered. Her chest hurt so badly she wondered if something wasn't broken. She felt broken. So damaged that she'd never recover.

She leaned her head on Kane's shoulder as sob after sob welled from her throat.

"Son of a bitch," Kane murmured. He got to his feet and hauled her up into his arms, then made a run for the car. He shoved her inside, climbed in behind her and then ordered the driver to take off.

"Where are we going, Lyric?" he asked. "What do you want to do?"

"Away," she said brokenly. "Just away from here. Somewhere safe."

He put a tentative hand on her arm as she lay huddled on the seat. "What the hell happened back there, Lyric?"

She shook her head and closed her eyes as more tears slipped down her cheeks. How could she explain to him that she'd just been destroyed by the only man she'd ever trusted? The only *person* she'd ever trusted?

She felt like the worst sort of fool. Why had he done it? Did he hate her so much? None of it made sense. Surely he didn't need the money. Phillip was likely paying him a fortune for his babysitting job. Had his supposed infatuation with her been some sort of twisted game?

Her throat was raw but she couldn't stop the sobs. Grief welled out of her heart. Grief for her mom. Grief for herself. Grief for everything she'd believed of Connor and the dead hope for someone who loved and cherished her.

She was dimly aware of the car stopping and then the door opening.

"Lyric," Kane said softly. "Can you make it out? We're at the house."

It took her a moment for his words to sink in. She stirred slowly and looked at him through dull eyes.

"I don't want anyone here," she said in a voice that cracked and was painful from the crying. "Do you understand? No one."

Kane nodded shortly. "If that's what you want."

She tried to sit up but found she lacked the strength. She felt dead on the inside. She was in complete and utter shutdown. Was this what it felt like when you finally broke from reality? Maybe it had been a long time coming for her. There was only so long you could live in denial.

Kane gently helped her from the car and wrapped an arm around her as he walked her toward the house. She trudged like an old woman, stumbling once when her feet dragged like lead.

Wordlessly, Kane led her up the stairs and into her bedroom. She halted as soon as they got through the doorway, and she went rigid.

"Not here," she burst out. "I won't stay in here." She stared at the bed she and Connor had made love in. The same bed where she'd told him all her secrets. Had shared the pain of her past. The bed where she'd trusted him implicitly.

"Okay," Kane said softly. "There are other rooms."

"I don't care where. Just not here."

He guided her toward one of the other bedrooms and she crawled onto the bed, curling into a ball and shutting herself off from him.

She felt him sit on the bed, but she kept her eyes squeezed shut as she turned further into herself where it didn't hurt quite so bad. The next thing she knew, a cool cloth was dabbed carefully at her face. The cut at her lips stung. The spot under her eye ached.

"You going to tell me what the hell happened back there?" Kane asked in a quiet voice as he touched the cloth to her mouth again.

"You'll know soon enough," she said bitterly. "It'll be all over the news and the tabloids. You can thank Connor. He's the only person I've ever told."

Kane swore. "Lyric, I don't think . . ."

"If you're going to defend him, get out. Just leave me alone. Please."

She hated the pleading tone of her voice, but she was begging. She just wanted to be alone.

Kane sighed and she felt him leave the bed. "If you need anything, let me know. I'll check in on you later."

She didn't respond. She listened to his retreating footsteps and then shoved her fist into her mouth as more tears began to fall.

CHAPTER 31

"You going to tell me how you wound up in jail?" Micah asked as he and Connor walked from the police station.

"They tried to keep me from Lyric. I resisted," he said shortly. "Thanks for coming so quickly. Pop didn't answer the phone, but to tell the truth, I'd rather not get into it with him right now."

"No problem," Micah said with a shrug. "What the hell happened?"

Connor ignored Micah as they climbed into his truck and opened his cell phone. It had been three goddamn hours since things had gone to hell at the music store. He had no idea where Lyric was, if she was safe, or just how upset she was.

Well, that wasn't true. It was pretty damn obvious she was destroyed by what she thought was his betrayal of her. It pissed him the fuck off. How could she think he'd ever do that to her?

There was only one missed call and it sure as hell wasn't from Lyric. It was from Kane.

He hit the button for his voice mail and listened to the short message.

"Connor, I have no idea what the hell happened back there. Lyric's a mess. She's here at the house and she doesn't want anyone allowed on the premises. You included. Give me a call when you get this so you can fill me in. I'm working without a net here."

"Son of a bitch," Connor swore.

"Is there anything I can do?" Micah asked quietly.

Connor pinched the bridge of his nose between his fingers and closed his eyes. "This is a goddamn mess, Micah. I don't know what the hell to do. I'm going to lose her and I'm not sure there's a damn thing I can do about it."

Micah winced in sympathy. "Been there, done that. Don't ever have the desire to do it again. Tell me what happened. Maybe an objective opinion will help."

"I can't," Connor said helplessly. "She already thinks I betrayed her trust. The shit's going to hit the fan any minute now. Maybe it already has. She thinks I sold her out to the media. She trusted me. Only me. It looks bad, but goddamn, I told her I loved her. How can she believe I'd do that to her?"

"Sounds like you've both had a shitty day," Micah murmured.

"Yeah," Connor said bleakly. "You could say that."

"So where am I taking you?"

"Home."

Micah lifted a brow as he stared over at Connor. "Giving up that easily?"

"I have to give her some time. She's devastated. She's told her security not to allow anyone on the premises. I can't pile on her right now. It's going to goddamn kill me, but I've got to give her time to cool off and get over the initial shock."

Connor curled his fingers into tight balls. He wanted to put his fist through the window. He should be with her right now. He should be holding her. He should be her shield against the world. But she was desperately alone and she was hurting and he couldn't get within ten feet of her.

"Look, why don't you come home with me and have a few beers? It beats going home and driving yourself insane."

Connor sighed. "Thanks, man. You know I'd love to see Angelina, but the truth is I'm really shitty company right now."

"Okay. Offer stands, though."

Twenty minutes later, Micah pulled into the apartment complex he shared with Connor. Connor got out, waved his thanks to Micah again, then headed for his apartment while Micah walked back to his.

He unlocked his door and went inside, home for the first time since the day he'd gone to Lyric's hotel room after their meeting at the office.

Boy, had his life changed dramatically since then. That day had started something he'd never dreamed would happen. It seemed a life-time ago.

His apartment had always been comfortable. Lived in. Slightly cluttered. His comfort place. A place he always enjoyed coming back to.

Tonight it was barren and sterile. The silence was suffocating and the walls seemed to close in on him from every direction.

He flopped onto the couch and reached for his phone to call Kane. He hadn't wanted to go into the details in front of Micah. No matter that she already thought he'd betrayed her. He'd never tell anyone the things she'd shared with him.

"How is she?" Connor demanded when Kane answered the phone.

Kane sighed. "Not good. What the fuck happened?"

"It's a clusterfuck, Kane. I can't get into the details. They'll be public soon enough. She thinks I sold her out. It's bullshit."

"Yeah, I figured."

"You sit on her, Kane. Keep her safe. Don't let her do anything stupid. I'm going to give her until tomorrow and then I'm coming over and I don't give a fuck how many guys you throw at me. All I'll say is that you better be up on your workman's comp, because if anyone tries to stop me, they'll wind up in the hospital."

Her head ached. Her jaw ached. Her heart ached. Her eyes were swollen and her nose felt like it had run off her face. She looked and sounded horrible. She had no voice, which was pretty stupid considering it was how she made her living.

Her throat was so swollen it was hard to swallow but no matter how much she tried to turn it off, tears still leaked endlessly down her cheeks.

She'd lain in bed for hours. Kane had come and gone with an ice pack for her face. He'd hesitated and she could tell he had no liking for leaving her, but she shut him out and curled in on herself even more until he'd left with a sigh.

Grief was a living, breathing entity inside her. It swelled so much that she feared she would break. Maybe she was already broken. Maybe she'd always been broken and had slapped enough Band-Aids on to muddle through.

She tried hard to conjure her mother's face, to remember her smile, but every time she thought of her she saw only blood, heard the sounds of her being beaten and heard her cries of pain.

She hadn't even attended her mother's funeral. Had there even been a service? Lyric doubted it. There had been no money and no one to care. Lyric had been hospitalized for days and afterward she'd been released into the care of the state.

They'd tried their best. Lyric had lived in a poor county without many resources. No one had been willing to foster the silent, grieving child. She'd been too steeped in violence. Many were afraid that Danny Higgins would come after her. After the trial she'd been shipped off to Jackson and shuffled around there.

She'd been awarded a new life. New name. New birth certificate. The kind judge had told her that this was her opportunity to rise above her circumstances. It was the only thing that had managed to break through the thick wall of defense she'd erected.

She'd taken him at his word. She's chosen her name to honor her mother's love for her singing. And she'd made a vow that one day she'd get the hell out of Mississippi and she'd never look back.

She'd spent every day after that running. Always running from her past. Burying everything under a don't-give-a-shit, abrasive exterior so that no one ever dug deep. Until Connor.

A fresh surge of pain nearly paralyzed her. She'd believed him. Or maybe she'd been so desperate for someone to love her that she'd been blinded. But she had believed in him and his love for her. She'd wanted it so bad even when it baffled her.

She sat up in bed and wrapped her cold arms around herself and hugged as she rocked back and forth. A glance at the clock told her it was nearly two a.m. She laid her cheek on her knees and stared sightlessly toward the window.

She didn't even know where her mother was buried.

The thought hit her like a thunderclap and she flinched from the realization. She'd been so focused on her own survival that she'd never gone back to see her mother's grave. Didn't even know if her life had been marked by a cold slab of concrete.

Had she been forgotten? Brushed aside as a county expense? Had anyone ever brought flowers to acknowledge the life, however short it had been?

Lyric struggled out of bed. Her clothes were wrinkled. She hadn't changed. Blood stained her shirt. Her pants sported a new tear. She thrust her feet into a pair of flip-flops by the bed and went in search of Kane.

He wasn't asleep. It shouldn't have surprised her. The man was more machine than human. He was awake in the living room, a book propped on his knee.

He looked up when she entered and got to his feet with a frown. "You look like hell, Lyric."

She blinked at the personal assessment. It was very unlike Kane to offer more than a professional opinion. But it was clear that concern burned in his eyes.

"I need to go to Mississippi," she said in a stark voice.

Kane's brows drew together in a frown. "I don't think that's a good idea."

"I have to go. Now. I'd like you to go. I may be crazy but I'm not completely without a sense of self-preservation. I'll pay you. Of course. Your travel expenses. Whatever."

Kane rubbed a hand through his hair. "Look, Lyric, you're clearly distraught. No decision should ever be made under this kind of emotional duress. Get some sleep. If you still feel like you need to go tomorrow, I'll take you."

She turned, her back ramrod stiff. "I'll go alone, then."

A curse exploded from Kane and he crossed the room to grasp her arm. "What the hell is in Mississippi?"

She glanced dully up at him. "My mother."

Connor's phone rang at six a.m. He hadn't slept a wink the entire night. He'd been too pissed and too worried. He reached for the phone he'd tossed on the couch and put it to his ear.

"Malone," he said shortly.

"We're coming over," Gray said in his ear.

"Don't bother," Connor muttered.

"Fuck you."

The line went dead and Connor slouched back on the couch. He rubbed his forehead tiredly. He should have slept. He had to be at his best to confront Lyric. She was going to listen to him, damn it.

He checked his watch. Two more hours. He'd give her two hours and then he was going to take no prisoners.

His doorbell rang and he cursed. Damn interfering friends. He dragged himself to his feet and went to open the door.

"Don't look so happy to see us," Micah said dryly as he shoved his way in.

"What the hell do y'all want?" he asked irritably.

"Our women heard of the hoopla. They're all pretty pissed," Gray said as he and Nathan came in behind Micah. "That was quite a scene yesterday."

Connor sighed in resignation and slammed the door before turning to follow the guys into his living room.

"Is everything out?" Connor asked wearily.

Nathan's mouth twisted. "Yeah, I'd say so. Or at least all the sordid details of her past. Julie's ready to go kick some serious ass even though she has no idea whose ass she wants to kick."

"Lyric thinks I sold her out," Connor said bleakly. "She confided in me the night before. And then at the music store, it all came out."

"That's rough," Micah said. "That had to be a huge shock for her."

"I told her I loved her," Connor bit out. "I laid it all out. How could she think I'd betray her like that?"

"I understand why you're pissed," Gray said carefully. "But Lyric doesn't strike me as someone who has a lot of trust. In anyone. Can't say I blame her if all that shit is true. You have to admit, the timing of it would cause a knee-jerk reaction."

Connor dropped into a chair and rubbed the back of his neck. "Yeah, I get it. I do. I can see how it looks. It looks pretty damn bad."

"The question is, who spilled her story to the media?" Nathan asked.

Connor scowled. "My money is on her fuck-head of an ex-manager. When she fired him, he threatened her. Told her he could bury her and that he knew things. If not him, then her ex-bodyguards are likely suspects, provided they knew of her past."

"Want us to find out?" Micah asked a little too eagerly.

Connor surveyed the anger in his friends' eyes and was grateful to have their support. "Yeah. Whatever you can do would be great. I'm going to be a little busy."

Gray lifted an eyebrow and a smile glimmered on his lips.

Connor stared over at his friends, his expression resolute. "I'm going to make Lyric listen to me. I get why she thought what she did. I don't even blame her. It pissed me off, but she was totally unprepared for that to come at her and she reacted. But I'm not letting her go."

His friends' faces broadened into grins. Gray chuckled. "I always knew that, of any of us, when you fell, you'd fall the hardest."

Connor held up his middle finger and they burst into laughter.

CHAPTER 32

*L*yric stood over the small, plain grave marker that was smudged with dirt and mildew. Weeds had grown over the plot so much that she'd had to shove them aside to even read the inscription.

It was short and to the point. No inspirational quote or little tag like loving mother, beloved sister or friend. Just her mother's name and the dates of her life. Like she hadn't mattered or she wasn't important enough to rate something nicer.

The flowers shook in her hands. So much so that a few of the petals floated to the ground, marking a stark contrast between the dead, brown grass and the vibrant purple of the violets.

They were her mom's favorite. She'd loved anything purple, but violets were her favorite and they'd grown wild in their yard. Lyric remembered picking them in the spring and her mother's bright smile when she'd taken the limp flowers from Lyric's two-fisted grip.

Lyric knelt and carefully arranged the violets in a decorative pattern. In the distance she could hear the sounds of cameras and shouted questions. Kane had done a wonderful job positioning his men to keep back the small crowd of reporters who'd flocked to the small town of Collins, Mississippi, the instant the details of her past had been made public.

Kane stood a short distance away, keeping to the side to afford her as much privacy as possible. Three of his men formed a wide perimeter around the grave and kept diligent watch on the crowd that the rest of the security team controlled.

"I'm making you a promise, Mama. As soon as I settle somewhere and have a home, I'll make sure you're moved. There's nothing for you and me here. You should be somewhere happier. I'll make sure you have a respectable headstone that celebrates the mother you were and that you died trying to protect me from a monster."

Tears slid down her cheeks and made a pattern in the dust surrounding the grave. Her sobs caught painfully in her chest and her throat swelled with unbearable grief.

"I'll bring you flowers. Violets and maybe some purple irises. I know it's been a long time since we spoke. I spent so many years angry at you for leaving me. I was wrong. So terribly wrong. I wanted you to know that I did it. I became a singer. Just like you always wanted. I got to choose my new name when everything changed after the trial. I chose Lyric for you. As a promise that I'd fulfill your dream for me. I hope you're proud of me. I haven't done a lot to make you proud but I'm going to change that. You deserve more from the daughter you died protecting."

She wiped at her face with the back of her hand and rose to her feet. Kane was there to steady her and he tucked her against him as they walked slowly back to the convoy of SUVs they'd driven from Texas.

She'd given Kane the address of her old house. She didn't even know if it would still be there. She was torn on whether or not she even wanted to face the place where her mother had died, but some force inside her propelled her. Maybe it was her need for closure, or maybe it was finally time to face her demons.

She knew only that she couldn't move forward until she'd come to grips with the terrible hurt inside her.

"Are you sure you want to do this?" Kane asked as they pulled away from the cemetery.

She nodded, not trusting her voice not to crack if she spoke.

The scenery was a blur as they rolled out of town and turned down a series of dirt roads that led farther into the country.

When they came to a stop, she sat still in her seat, looking out the window at the run-down, overgrown wooden house where her life had irrevocably changed.

It seemed smaller now. Not nearly as menacing as it had when she was a child. She would have sworn it was huge, so large that it swallowed her whole. In reality it was barely larger than a shack. Windows were broken out. Shutters were either missing or barely still hanging. Most of the white paint had long since peeled and chipped away. Boards were missing from the front porch and the lawn obviously hadn't been maintained since her mother had been murdered.

It was a sad, frail house where ghosts of the past still lingered.

Carefully she opened her car door and slipped out into the sun. She shivered slightly as the breeze nipped at her skin. It wasn't a cold day. In fact, it was a glorious day. South on the cusp of spring. The violets she'd remembered growing wild were scattered among the growth of weeds, little bursts of color against the grass still dead from winter.

But she felt as though she were encased in ice, as though the spring sun hadn't quite reached her soul.

She stood staring at the shell of a place she'd once lived. Where her most painful memories sprang to life. And she knew she couldn't go in. That there was no purpose in going in. It was just a house. Just a bunch of wood and nails barely held together. It didn't have any power over her.

The sound of another engine registered in her consciousness. She dragged her gaze from the house, expecting to have Kane shove her back into the car. It was probably more reporters. They'd been pursued ever since they'd arrived in town.

To her shock, Connor got out of his truck and strode in her direction, his expression one of great fatigue, hurt and concern.

"What the hell are you doing, Lyric?" he demanded as he drew closer. "You shouldn't go in there alone. You shouldn't go in there at all."

She stared numbly at him, alternately so glad to see him and so furious that he was here. She was too tired to summon any sort of reaction and so she just stood there, trying to gather the strength to tell him to go.

"My God, you look like I feel," he muttered just as he yanked her into his arms.

It didn't occur to her to push him away. His heat surrounded her, bathing her in a blanket of comfort so sweet that she melted against his chest. She closed her eyes and inhaled his scent and savored the feeling of warmth she'd been denied for so long.

He held her so tight it was hard to drag breaths into her lungs. He trembled against her. Shook so hard that she shook too.

Finally he pulled her gently away and he stared down at her with haunted eyes.

"Why are you here?" she managed to croak out. "How did you know?"

"I drove all day to get to you. I went to the house but you had already gone. I'm probably wanted in two states for breaking so many speed laws. I couldn't stop until I was here with you. I didn't want you to have to do this alone."

Tears glittered in her vision, blurring him and the world around her. "I don't understand."

He swore softly and touched her cheek. "Lyric, I didn't betray you. I know how it looks. I understand why you were so upset. But it wasn't me. I *love* you. I'd never do anything to intentionally hurt you."

His explanation muddled her brain. Could she have been so wrong? Who else could possibly have known? She took a tentative step back, a protective measure because, when he touched her, she forgot how to be angry. "Who, then?"

Connor glanced around and then rubbed his hands up and down her arms. He leaned back against the SUV she'd gotten out of and pulled her with him so that he looked down at her.

"Paul sold you out. He was pissed that you fired him. His threats weren't empty. He went to the media and spilled his guts."

Her eyes widened in shock—and hurt. "But how . . . ? Why? How did he know? How do you know? I don't understand any of this."

His chest ached at the pain in her gaze. "Gray, Nathan and Micah paid Paul a little visit. I'm sure they scared the shit out of him. The thing is, he's known for a long time about your past. Back when you signed with him, he launched an extensive investigation into your background. According to him, it took a year, but he was able to uncover the truth. He kept it to himself—as insurance—and when you fired him, he sold his story for a hell of a lot of money."

She frowned and sighed. "I guess I'm wrong about everybody. Clearly I have poor judgment when it comes to people."

He touched her cheek. A light caress as his fingers stroked over her face. "You weren't wrong to trust me, Lyric."

Her eyes clouded and she blinked furiously, determined not to shed more tears. "But I didn't trust you. How can you even stand to look at me after the awful things I said to you?"

He pulled her into his arms and pressed his lips to her forehead. "Trust is something you have to work at, baby. We'll get there. I plan on being around to make it happen. You suffered a horrible shock, and in your mind the only person it could have been was me. That hurt you and I'm so damn sorry. I would have done anything in the world to keep you from being hurt."

She wrapped her arms around his waist and held on for dear life. She trembled against him and he held her close, his hands rubbing up and down her back.

"I love you, Lyric. I love you so damn much my teeth ache. I want us to be together."

"I love you too," she whispered.

He went still against her. His heart thudded wildly against her cheek. He gently pulled her away, cupped her chin and tilted her head until their gazes met. "Say that again," he said huskily.

"I love you. I love you so much it scares me."

He lowered his head and kissed her, his lips melting so sweet over hers. Just a warm brush, so gentle and loving that it made her ache.

When he drew away, his eyes were aglow with warmth and contentment, as if she'd given him what he most wanted in the world. It unsettled her that she had.

"We've got a lot to work on, baby. You've got a lot to deal with. I'm going to be with you all the way but you need to get help to deal with everything that's happened to you. I want you to be healthy and happy for *you* first."

She swallowed and nodded. He smiled and touched her nose.

"I want you to marry me eventually. I want it all, Lyric. You, me, together. But I'm willing to wait as long as it takes for you to come to me happy and whole. Healed. That won't happen overnight, but I'll be here when it does."

Her pulse sped up. Adrenaline hummed through her veins, leaving her unsettled and excited. She wrinkled her nose and stared up at him. "I suppose this is where we talk about me quitting my job, marrying, settling down, popping out babies, getting a house with the picket fence and the whole shebang." She took a deep breath. "I love my career. I know it doesn't seem like it. I haven't always had my head screwed on straight. I'm my own worst enemy. But I love singing. I don't want to stop it."

He gathered her close and stared down at her, his eyes so earnest, so focused on her.

"No, this is where we talk about the fact that I'm going to quit *my* job and follow you around on tour making sure you're safe and that you take care of yourself the way you should. Babies and the picket fence are purely optional."

"Oh, my," she breathed. "You aren't real. You can't be real."

"I'm real. I'm the man who loves you more than anyone else will ever love you. I'm the man who wants to be with you and will do everything I can to keep you from ever being hurt again."

A tear trickled down her cheek and she sniffled. "Damn it. You're going to make me cry again."

He held out his hands and she slid her palms over his, lacing their fingers together.

"Why don't we get out of here," he suggested. "Let's go on down the road. Find a hotel where we can sleep for about twenty-four hours. Right after I make love you to for about six."

She squeezed his hands and leaned up on tiptoes to kiss him. "I love you, Connor Malone. I never thought I'd love someone the way I love you. I never dreamed someone would love *me* the way you do."

He smiled and pressed his forehead to hers. "The funny thing about dreams is that every now and then they come true."

CHAPTER 33

"*I* can't wait to see everyone," Lyric said as Connor bundled her into the waiting limo.

Connor smiled as he slid in beside her. He reached over, wrapped his arm around her shoulders and squeezed. "Have I told you how gorgeous you look?"

She flushed and ducked her head. No matter how often he told her how beautiful she was, she never got used to hearing it spoken with such conviction. He truly meant it.

The thing was, she was still a size twelve. Closer to a fourteen now. And Connor didn't give a shit. He couldn't keep his eyes or hands off her, a fact she delighted in.

"I haven't seen Nia since she was born. I bet she's half-grown by now," Lyric said with an unhappy frown. "I miss everyone. We need to get home to see them more often."

Connor chuckled. "If you weren't wildly successful and so in demand that tour dates keep being added, you'd have more time to go home."

She burrowed into his chest and sighed her contentment as the limo left the Houston airport. Home. It was kind of weird to consider a place home, but Houston had become that for her.

It was where Connor's family and friends lived. Family and friends that had become hers. Connor didn't know it yet, but she planned to surprise him with the house she'd bought not far from where his dad and sister and brother-in-law lived.

Though they weren't married yet, she and Connor were insepa- rable. At first she'd worried that he'd been so willing to quit his job and travel with her—working with Kane and his team for her. What if he got bored, tired or regretted his decision to leave his life and career? For her.

It was humbling and awe inspiring. Never before had anyone been willing to sacrifice so much for her.

She loved him like she'd never imagined being able to love an- other person.

Her cell rang, and she reached into her purse, grinning when she saw that it was Faith.

"Where are you?" Faith asked when Lyric said hello.

She smiled over at Connor. "We're in the car now. Should be there in twenty minutes."

Faith's squeal of delight made Lyric warm all over. In excited tones, Faith relayed the news to the other girls and a chorus of cheers greeted Lyric through the phone.

"Hurry!" Faith said. "We'll see you when you get here."

Lyric slowly closed her phone and battled the knot of emotion in her throat.

"They love you," Connor said. "Just like I do."

She smiled and leaned up to kiss him. "I'm just so . . . happy. Ridiculously happy. Like so happy I get paranoid that the world's going to go to shit tomorrow."

He laughed and squeezed her again. "So tell me. How drunk are you girls planning to get?"

Lyric grinned. "Who knows with those four. They're bad influences. I never touched alcohol before them."

A few minutes later, they pulled into the parking lot of Cattleman's. The parking lot was empty. Tonight was a private function. The entire restaurant had been shut down so the girls could get together. Of course the guys would inevitably show up, but no one minded.

Life was pretty damn good.

Good family. Good friends. A man she loved with everything she had.

As soon as the limo came to a stop, the entrance of Cattleman's flew open and Faith, Julie, Serena and Angelina—a very slim, gorgeous Angelina—flew out to the car.

Connor, laughing, opened the door and climbed out, holding his hands up. "Since I know y'all aren't that excited to see me, let me get Lyric out so y'all can attack her."

Julie rolled her eyes. "Pouty, isn't he?"

Faith hugged Connor as Lyric got out and then Angelina gave him an affectionate squeeze and a kiss on the cheek.

"It looks like you've taken very good care of her, Connor," Serena said in a pleased voice. "You both look wonderful."

"Amazing how love does that," Faith said smugly.

The girls gathered around Lyric, all hugging her and smothering her as they laughed and babbled all at once.

Connor stood indulgently to the side until they quieted enough for him to get a word in edgewise. Lyric smiled up at him, so happy she could burst.

"Okay, time for you to shoo, Connor. The guys aren't supposed to show up for two hours yet," Julie said.

Connor raised an eyebrow. "What? We're being allowed entrance into the goddess domain? I thought we were forbidden to be seen on girls' night out."

"We're making an exception this time," Lyric said with a grin. "We get a two-hour head start and then you guys can come join the fun. By then we'll be too shit-faced to care."

He chuckled and then climbed back into the car. "I'm going over to Gray's. I'll send the car back in case you all need it. No taking a cab," he said sternly.

"Oh, we're staying put," Serena said airily. "We have our gorgeous bartender who spoils us rotten and I have it on good authority that Carl had some yummy food made for us."

"I'm starving," Lyric said mournfully. "Food on the plane sucked."

"Well of course it did," Faith said as she tucked her arm through Lyric's. "Bye, Connor! We'll see you in a few hours."

Connor laughed. "I know when I've been dismissed."

He leaned down and kissed Lyric before pulling away. "Have a good time, baby."

Lyric waved as he got into the car and then allowed Faith to drag her into the restaurant.

As they headed into the quiet and empty place, Lyric grinned in sudden remembrance.

"What's the shit-eating grin for?" Julie asked suspiciously.

"Do you guys know that this is where Connor and I first kissed? Well, I can't really say he kissed me. I kissed him. Right there at the bar."

The girls laughed and Lyric turned her attention to Angelina, who'd been mostly quiet to now.

"You look fantastic, Angelina. I'm so jealous. You lost all the baby weight."

Angelina grimaced. "Not all. But I'm getting there."

"How is Nia?"

At the mention of her daughter, Angelina positively lit up. "Oh she's gorgeous. Such a wonderful baby. And Micah is so in love with her. It's really disgusting how she has him so wrapped around her finger already."

Julie rolled her eyes. "Like mother, like daughter."

Serena and Faith laughed at Angelina's startled expression.

"Well they do have you there," Lyric pointed out. "That man is an idiot over you."

Angelina's soft smile glowed.

"Hey, ladies. I am here to serve. Just tell me what your pleasure is."

Lyric turned to see a young—and hot—bartender grinning at them.

"That's Drew," Serena murmured. "Isn't he yummy? He's seen us drunk before so you don't have to worry that he's going to take photos and sell them to tabloids. Damon has already threatened him with bodily injury if he so much as breathes a word about us being here."

Lyric laughed. "I do love your husband, Serena. He looks and acts so civilized, but underneath he's a complete barbarian."

Serena beamed. "I know. Isn't it great?"

"Let's quit talking and start drinking," Julie said. "We have a lot of catching up to do!"

For the next two hours, the drinks flowed freely, as did the laughter and the conversation. Though Lyric had never enjoyed being alone and surrounded herself with people, she'd never surrounded herself with really *great* people. People she could trust. People who loved her and she loved in return.

Being with those people? She didn't even have the words to describe the feeling.

Drew was the dream that the girls had reported him to be. He kept their glasses full, cleaned up their spills and never blinked an eye when their conversations detoured into the way-too-much-information department.

"Soooo, Lyric," Faith began. "Tell us when you're going to put Connor out of his misery and make an honest man out of him."

Julie, Serena and Angelina all eagerly sat forward, their attention focused solidly on Lyric now. Lyric blushed, but she couldn't help the wide smile that attacked her face.

"Soon," she said serenely. "I want it to be perfect. Connor's been . . . He's been so patient and understanding. He's been just perfect."

"Of course he has. He's in love," Julie said. "Men are pretty stupid when they're in love."

Angelina snorted. "You love that Nathan is stupid over you."

Julie grinned. "Yes. I have to admit. I do."

"So how soon?" Serena asked Lyric.

"I have another month of touring and then I have a surprise for him. You guys can't breathe a word!"

They all solemnly crossed their hearts and swore never to tell.

"I've bought a house here in Houston."

The squeals were deafening. It took several minutes to get everyone quiet again and Lyric beamed at them all, thrilled with their excitement.

"I'm going to surprise him with the house and then I'm going to ask him to marry me."

"Ohhh, I like it," Serena said.

"You would," Faith said with a laugh. "She popped the question to Damon after she finally decided to marry him," she explained to Lyric.

"I'm so excited for you, Lyric," Angelina said. "I'm so glad you're happy and ready to make the commitment. Connor loves you so much. I want you both to be happy."

"He makes me happy," Lyric said with a catch in her throat.

"I have something I want to tell you guys," Serena said when things got quiet again. "I wanted to wait until we were all together."

Lyric and the others exchanged worried glances, but the look on Serena's face was one of utter contentment. She all but glowed.

"Damon and I are going to start trying for a baby."

"Oh my God!" Faith shrieked.

Julie and Lyric looked at each other with something akin to horror and Angelina promptly laughed when she caught the exchange.

"Are you sure, Serena?" Julie asked. "I mean have you worked things out to the point you feel comfortable bringing a baby into the picture?"

Serena smiled. "It means that some things will change for us, but not for a while. We're comfortable with the change. We want . . . we want to start a family."

"That's awesome," Lyric said softly. "I'm so happy for you. You look . . . delirious."

"I am. This time last year I wouldn't have been able to imagine having a baby. I wasn't ready. But now? It's time."

"I'm still not ready," Faith muttered. "That pregnancy scare I had awhile back was enough to convince me I won't be ready for a bit yet."

"Me either," Julie seconded.

Lyric nodded her fervent agreement. "We'll leave the procreating to the earth mothers over here," she said, jabbing her thumb in Angelina and Serena's direction.

Angelina snorted. "Earth mother. Yeah. That's me all right. It's a wonder I didn't kill my poor child her first week home. I couldn't even figure out how to change a diaper. Micah had to help me. Isn't that pathetic? I swear he has more maternal instinct than I do."

Faith giggled and then the rest joined. It was hard to imagine a dominant badass like Micah being all maternal.

"Are you all still conscious?" Nathan called from across the room.

The women whipped around on their barstools to see the men trailing into the bar. Lord but they looked good. Although as soon as Connor appeared, Lyric lost all interest in everyone else.

Then Micah appeared and Lyric's eyes narrowed. She cocked her head to the side before she realized what it was she saw attached to Micah.

The room went dead silent as all the girls focused their attention on Micah. And then Julie shrieked with laughter. She damn near fell off her barstool as she pointed at Micah and laughed her ass off.

"Oh my God!" Julie wheezed. "I win. I win!"

"What the hell do you win?" Faith asked with a frown.

Tears streamed down Julie's face as Micah fixed her with a ferocious scowl.

"He once bet me that I'd be tamed before he ever would be. We made a bet. Oh my God, I totally win. Look at him. He's wearing the baby!"

There Micah stood, a rueful, somewhat abashed look on his face, Nia securely attached to his chest in a Snuggie.

The women died laughing and then the rest of the men joined in. Micah rolled his eyes heavenward and then slung an arm around Angelina.

"They're all just jealous they don't have my fashion sense," he muttered. "Nia would make any man look good."

Damon shot Serena a queasy look. "You aren't going to make me wear our baby, are you?"

Serena grinned mischievously while the rest of the room roared with laughter. "I don't know, Damon. You might look cute with a baby strapped to your chest."

Connor came to stand beside Lyric and wrapped his arm loosely around her shoulders as they laughed with the rest of the group. He stared down into her eyes and what she saw reflected in his warmed her to the bone.

"I'm so glad we're home," she whispered close to his ear so he could hear over the din.

He kissed her lingeringly, ignoring the rest of the group. "Don't you know, Lyric? I'm home whenever I'm with you."

Love and so much joy flooded her soul. Tears glistened in her eyes as she stared around at the friends—family—who meant so much to her.

"Don't you dare cry," Julie threatened. "If you make me cry in front of everyone, I'll kick your ass, Lyric."

Lyric sniffed. "I love you guys."

And then the girls all crowded around her, shoving Connor out of the way as they wrapped their arms tightly around Lyric.

"We love you too," Faith said in her sweet voice.

"Hey, Serena. So who gets to be the baby's godmother?" Julie asked innocently.

Serena rolled her eyes. "Oh, I'll wimp out like Angelina and have to name you all. Poor kid. He or she won't have a chance."

Lyric gathered them to her again, or as well as she could. Her eyes were all goopy and she probably had mascara everywhere, but she didn't give a damn. She was with . . . family.